THE LINK is the second book in a trilogy: the first, PREMONITIONS OF AN INHERITED MIND, is already available in *Star Books*. The third, THE EMBRYO, will shortly be published,

THE LINK

Andrew Laurance

A STAR BOOK

published by
the Paperback Division of
W. H. ALLEN & Co. Ltd.

A Star Book
Published in 1980
by the Paperback Division of
W. H. Allen & Co. Ltd
A Howard and Wyndham Company
44 Hill Street, London W1X 8LB

Printed in Great Britain by
Hunt Barnard Printing Ltd., Aylesbury, Bucks.

ISBN 0 352 305312

Paul first saw the two children on his nineteenth birthday.

They appeared in the far corner of his room as he was undressing to go to bed.

They were both naked, their hair was white, their eyes a strangely penetrating grey and their skin translucent, an opacity which hinted at ashen bones within.

They made no sound, but stared at him. The boy, maybe six, clutched the older sister's hand.

A repugnant smell of burning flesh had filled the room, then they had suddenly turned to face each other and, embracing like midget lovers, had started to writhe and twitch violently, their skin palpitating, the rhythm of the spasms increasing rapidly till they had reached a climax, become transparent skeletal shapes, and faded altogether.

Now, three years later, taller, older, more threatening, they were standing over the charred remains of his mother's body.

He had known she would die, had foreseen the accident, but he had not expected these fearful children to be there.

Until then he had never connected their presence with the other unexplainable manifestations he had experienced.

But now he knew there was a link.

An undeniable, hideous link.

CHAPTER ONE

It was three o'clock in the morning and everybody seemed to have their television sets switched on.

He lay, stark naked, on his mother's king-size bed, all the windows and doors open, the curtains drawn back, but still there was no air, still he couldn't sleep.

The sounds that came in at him from all sides were hardly relaxing. Male voices threatening, women screaming, guns firing, sirens wailing. New York in the throes of its usual night hysteria.

There was laughter from somewhere, the clink of glasses, a party. He hadn't been invited.

'You don't go to many parties, do you Paul?' His mother had said again only yesterday. 'Why's that? Why haven't you got any friends?'

'I don't need any.'

'Everybody needs friends.'

She disliked him because he preferred his own company to anyone else's, because he didn't know how to enjoy himself like others, because he didn't know how to join in.

'Go back to your books,' was her greatest rebuke, always said with contempt.

Well, she wouldn't annoy him for a week at least. For a week he'd be able to read without interruption, be able to sit and think without being asked what he was doing.

The problem right now, however, was that he couldn't sleep even though he'd moved to the coolest room. But then he didn't really mind. He preferred to be hot than cold. He could always get the binoculars and look out the back at how other people were coping with the heat, watch the rainbow couple screwing the night away on their multi-coloured divan in their duplex, though by now they would probably have fallen asleep with exhaustion.

It would have been nice to have Patty with him, feel her body next to his, but he had bummed out on that relationship.

His choice.

'The trouble with you, Paul, is that you are dull,' she had said.

And he hadn't answered because he hadn't found it necessary to defend himself. If she had found him dull that was her problem, not his, besides he had already known that within a month she would leave him.

Intuition, a premonition, whatever it was called, he had known.

'You're going to have an affair with your sister's husband. She'll find out and leave him. You'll then move in,' he'd told her.

She had looked at him amazed.

'How do you know? How do you even know anything about my sister or her husband. I've never mentioned them.'

'I get these messages,' he'd said, because it was true. He didn't know how or why, but thoughts just came to him, ideas rather, an awareness about a situation often before it happened, which he took seriously. Everyone had them, but few ever believed them or even considered that they might have a use.

It was not so much a question of concentrating, but of taking notice of the obvious. For some reason everyone was taught to look for subtleties, read between the lines, search out alternative meanings. When an idea, a thought, an image came to mind, it ought to be examined immediately for what it was.

Like right now, even while thinking, he was getting this very clear image of his own bedroom, not as it was, but very brightly lit, with a spotlight, up in the corner above the door, shining directly on to his bookshelf. He had never thought of spotlighting his bookshelf before, but there it was, a very clear picture of his own room, bed unmade, curtains drawn, varnished pine floor shining, the Indian carpet in the middle, and all his books.

He coud go from the top shelf to the bottom shelf, from left to right and name all his books, title, author, publisher. Some time back he had arranged them by colours, the whites, the blues, the greens together, and by height. But now he had them arranged like in the bookshop, geography, history, philosophy, occult, psychology, fiction and the authors in alphabetical order.

His mind was now on the third shelf down with the drama books; the plays – Becket, Chekov, Fry's *The Lady's Not For Burning*. The image came to him, the thin black volume with gold lettering, such an apt title for the playwright's name. It was sticking out, about two inches from the rest of his books. It meant something. He accepted that, worked on such signs. They were clues, he didn't know where they came from or why, but they were clues that demanded investigation.

Was it the word 'burning' again?

He had tried to ignore the feeling that anything to do with burning led straight to the memory of those children, but it was obvious there was a connection. That sickly smell had been too overpowering and the vision too nightmarish for him to forget.

So something was going to burn?

Or someone?

And in his mind he saw his mother light a cigarette. Heard the match strike, saw her stubby fingers with short fingernails and their overcoat of nail polish covering the dirt, her hand trembling shakily trying to keep the cigarette steady, the flame dominating the image in his mind.

He turned over and lay flat on his stomach, buried his head under the pillow to keep out the noise of the outside world.

Follow the thought through. Don't hesitate, don't think it foolish, be totally uninhibited about it.

The trembling match drops, the flame for a moment seems about to go out, it has fallen on a bright green carpet next to a bottle of brandy. His mother is now looking at it, she is watching this flame die out curious to know whether it will burn the carpet or not. It flickers with life and her finger dips into a brandy glass and draws a ring round the flame. She is bored, she is drunk, lying on a bed drunk, her head and arms hanging over the edge above the flame which now catches on to the brandy, a weak blue flame, fascinating.

He is above her, behind her, watching over her shoulder. Her finger dips into the brandy glass again, draws another circle. The flame goes out. Inexplicably she picks up the bottle and pours some of the brandy on the carpet and now lights a match and sets it really alight.

He pulls his vision back. The room is unfamiliar. He has

never been there, it is a guest room, a hotel room, a room in a large house. She lies there on her stomach in her white turtle neck sweater and jeans watching the blue flame dance.

Then it flares up and catches her hair.

He sat up and pummelled the pillow against the wall and backed himself up on it.

Daydreams, nightmares, imaginings.

The bed smelt of her tobacco and scent.

She used plenty of that, it saved her from washing.

Deodorants and scents, tobacco and alcohol, that was what she was all about.

And now she no longer wore anything under her jeans. When other women had burnt their bras she had discarded all underwear.

Then the fearful image came to him again. The cheap hairspray ablaze, the bedspread catching alight. He shook his head violently ridding himself of the image, then a chill gripped him behind the neck and ran down the small of his back, his throat tightened, his mouth went dry. He was going to see the children again. They were in his room, they would be in that corner where he had seen them before, three years ago, they would be there staring at him and holding each other's hands.

The feeling was so strong, so compulsive, that he slipped off the bed, ran out of his mother's room and down the corridor before the fear could build up. He put his hand quickly into the darkness of his room and switched the light as he kicked the door open.

The centre bulb in its Japanese paper globe eliminated shadows, so did the white light above his bed. Since seeing them he had avoided shadows. He looked around, there was nothing unusual. They were not there.

No smells.

Nothing.

He looked up at the ceiling corner where he had imagined the spotlight. It would be a good idea. Then he went to the third bookshelf to Fry's plays. *Venus Observed, A Boy With a Cart, A Sleep of Prisoners*. He'd never had a copy of *The Lady's Not For Burning*. That was in the bookshop, the thin volume with the black spine. He'd never bought it.

He went to the bathroom to take a shower which would help him get cool. He stepped into the tub, pulled the plastic curtain across and turned the cold water full on.

For a moment the anticipation of the shock followed by the cold water itself brought him out in goose-pimples, which was marvellous. He stood there under the rain, his face turned to the shower hose, his mouth open, drinking in the freshness.

After a few minutes he turned the shower off, shook himself, pressed his curly black hair down, squeezing out the water, and stepped out of the bath.

It started when he bent down to dry his feet, the feeling that his skin no longer belonged to him.

As he drew the towel up his legs, round his thighs, over his chest, he felt it was peeling, a strange sensation that did not hurt but was revolting to the touch. He dropped the towel and ran his fingers over his body. There was a crispness about the skin's surface, as though it had blistered, and then pieces of it came away. It was like running his hand through a pile of dead, rotting autumn leaves, and he was black, his body was charred. The sensation lasted seconds, maybe less, but it was hideous and, when he put his hand up to his face, he felt no skin at all, no flesh, but immediate hard sticky bone.

Closing his eyes tight he crossed the bathroom to the wash-basin to stand in front of the mirror. Terrified he then opened them to find himself staring at a quite horrific reflection of a burnt skull with its jaw moving, its sockets staring accusingly at him, its grey bones showing through the paper-thin brown parchment of burnt skin.

He closed his eyes and opened them again. The reflection was of himself, drawn, white, but normal.

He breathed out and smiled.

It was his mother's smile.

A premonition of her death, then?

But when? And should he tell?

And who would heed a warning from him?

Not her.

Least of all her.

He switched off the lights and made his way to the kitchen, opened the icebox and took out a tin of Coca-Cola.

Did he really want to be psychic? Did he really want to

experience such traumas, live in the perpetual fear of being faced with repellent visions?

'It's not a question of choice,' he said out loud, and immediately wondered why he had said it.

Who had said it? Was he talking to himself? Was it him talking? Or was it someone else, some *thing* else talking through him?

'The trouble with you, Paul, is that you are dull.'

He wasn't dull. His world was just not that of other people's. It had another dimension which no one else seemed to understand, which he could not share.

'Tell me my fortune, Paulie,' twelve-year-old Mary-Jane had asked at her birthday party when they all lived in Syracuse and had neighbours.

The palm of her left hand was placed in his and he had made up a future. 'You're going to be given a puppy, a little black and white puppy, but it'll get run over.'

Everyone had thought him horrible. He had not known why he had said it, but of course it had happened. A few months had gone by and Mary-Jane had turned up at his house holding a black and white puppy. A week later it had been caught between the back wheels of a truck.

Intuition, premonition, he had no idea. Such visions had not happened that often. Four times to be precise. Mary-Jane's puppy dog, Mrs Kleinman's death in the hospital – which anyone could have foreseen – but somehow he had known the exact day and time. The disaster at the chemical plant, the acrid smell of which had permeated his clothes for days before. The Gipsons' car crash, which again could have been guessed considering how much Mr Gipson drank.

Four premonitions in eight years, one every two years.

Was he due for another?

He switched off all the lights and went back to his mother's room to lean out of the window.

It hadn't been a premonition tonight, it had been a simple train of thought. It had started with his mother because she was away and because he was in her bed which reeked of her scent, her reproaches about him reading leading to his books, the unexpected idea of lighting them with a spot, then a direct focus on a book which he did not have that happened to mention burning. After that it was pure fantasy, maybe based on a subconscious fear that his mother might injure herself if she went on drinking the way she did, and a pang of jealousy too because she was with yet another man he didn't know.

Did she love these men, or did she just use them? Whored herself to a better position, to an extra week's vacation?

'Tis a pity she's a whore!

Well he didn't have that book either, but he knew where it was in the bookshop. Top shelf on the left where they had the few English classics. And if he didn't get any sleep he would not be too good in the morning to serve the customers, and Mrs Lidman would not like that!

He put the empty Coca-Cola tin on the window ledge and padded to the bed. The tin might slip, fall down to join the debris of New York rubbish below, maybe hit someone on the head.

He was about as psychic as a lamppost.

As he was walking along West 4th Street from the subway to go to the Greenwich Bookcase he saw Mrs Lidman coming towards him.

She was attractive, there was no doubt about that, five men had turned round to look at her legs since he'd spotted her. It was the ash blonde hair, the smart slick Scandinavian look, and her sincere blue eyes that killed them after that. He enjoyed working for her, watching her flirt in order to sell one paperback.

'Paul! There's been a call from Lake Champlain, some kind of accident involving your mother. A man named Warren asked could you ring him immediately, I have his number.'

The burning image came to mind, the flames flashing up the side of her face, the crisp hair crackling, the red hot ends like fine straw catching alight. He rushed through the shop between the book counters to the telephone at the back.

He dialled, sat down on the swivel chair, tried to control his breathing, to relax, smile at a customer who wanted to pay for a book. He indicated Mrs Lidman.

The call went through.

'Could I speak with Warren . . . ?'

'Warren speaking.'

'This is Paul Saralyn.'

'Hi, Paul.' A quiet, calm, deep apologetic voice. 'You're mother's had an accident. Best if you could get up here soonest.'

'What sort of accident?'

'I'll explain everything when you get here.'

'My imagination can get pretty rough. It would ease things in my mind if you could just tell me now.'

'A fire, Paul. The house she was in caught fire.'

'When?'

'During the night.'

'Is she dead?'

'We don't know. The whole place was gutted and she's missing. Can you hire a car, got enough cash?'

'I'll manage. Let me just check the address.' He had it somewhere in his notebook in the top right hand pocket of his denim shirt. He read it out, Warren added directions, told him he would wait for him at the West Burlington gasoline station.

Mrs Lidman drove.

She shut up the shop and bundled him into her new hatchback and drove. It was the first time that she had ever shown any regard for him, she had always imposed an employer-employee relationship though at times they had been alone in the shop for hours, sometimes working late during stock taking. She was much older than him, of course, and married, and wealthy.

He'd never made an approach, always kept his place preferring to be respected for his mind than being reprimanded for an abortive attempt at a pass. But she had style, with her Christian Dior sunglasses, the gold bracelet watch, the art jeans, the chequered blouse.

His mother hated her.

The car had all the equipment of efficient professional ladies, cassette deck, radio, everything electronically controlled and she drove well, knew exactly where to go, the right exit, no problems.

He said nothing, just sat next to her, biting his thumb nail, gritting his teeth,

'Who is this Warren?' she asked, once they were clear of the heavy traffic and heading for Route 90.

'I don't know. Some guy she started shacking up with a week or so ago.'

'Is that a pretty normal occurrence?'

'Yes.'

'I'm sorry,' Mrs Lidman said.

Nobody had ever sympathised with him over his mother. Now that she might be dead he'd get sympathy from everyone. She *was* dead, of course. They both knew that. But when would he believe it?

'Were you close?'

She had slipped into the past tense already.

'Not very.'

He didn't want to talk, but he felt he should, impolite not to. She was being really nice.

'Thanks for helping me out like this,' he said.

'It's the least I can do. I don't like the idea of people driving long distances when preoccupied.'

He stared at the road ahead, his mind a complete blank. He didn't want to think out anything.

'Did she have a car?'

'No. Couldn't afford it, and in New York . . .'

'How much of your salary went towards helping her out?'

'Oh, not that much. She worked as a secretary at East Coast Trust, been there years. Fifteen I think. That's why she drank and had all those men. A dull job, did it to relieve the monotony. And she was lonely.'

'What about your father?'

'He died when I was seven.'

'Grandparents?'

'All dead a long time ago. It's always been just mother and me.' He made it sound pretty awful. 'Mother, me and books.'

'What about your writing?'

Mrs Lidman had taken an interest in him when he had first started working at the bookshop. He'd shown her one of his diaries and she'd said there was talent.

'I haven't got the confidence or the patience, and I've nothing to write about. Events like this tend to make you think a diary might interest others, but I can't just write for myself.'

'I'm thirsty,' she said. 'Mind if we stop for a rest.'

She pulled in at a roadhouse. He got out, watched her lock all the doors. He walked a little bit behind her, the pencil slim skirt and high heels accentuating the sensuous way she moved. And she knew it.

Inside they sat down opposite each other.

'What will you have?' she asked.

'I'd like you to be *my* guest, Mrs Lidman,' he said.

'Paul, I'm your employer. I'm also older than you and richer, so I will allow myself to say this just the once. Relax, let me take the burden of the little things, let me organise because that's what I'm good at and stop being a pain. I'm not only doing this for you, I'm doing it for myself. I'm getting something out of it.'

'What?' he asked.

The waitress brought them each a menu card.

'Choose what you want to eat and we'll talk about it.'

He chose a hamburger, french fries, thousand island dressing and a milkshake. She chose a tuna fish salad and a Coca-Cola.

Behind the counter a couple of chefs were flash frying steaks. A sheet of flame shot up the ventilator, a perfectly normal occurrence, but it unsettled him. Mrs Lidman noticed and turned to look at what had caused his reaction.

'What's up?'

'Nothing. Just the fire. I have a fairly vivid imagination.'

'Yes. I do know that. How long have you been working for me?'

'About a year?'

'You're a real dreamer. You started at the shop Christmas '77. That's well over two years now.'

He'd lost track.

'Doesn't time matter to you?'

'Not much.'

'Do you still have dreams?'

'Dreams?'

'When you first came you used to talk about your dreams.'

He'd stopped that. He'd stopped telling her about his dreams as he had stopped telling his mother, Patty, other girl friends. He'd stopped after telling her about the children. It had been like divulging a terrible secret, instinctively he had felt it wrong to talk to anyone about them, and after telling Mrs Lidman about them he had never mentioned them to anyone again.

'You were going to tell me what you were getting out of being kind to me,' he said, changing the subject.

'It's not being *kind* to you . . . I'm getting the pleasure of helping you out when you need help. And I'm the sort of woman that likes taking care of people.'

She was looking him straight in the eyes.

He felt himself blush. The flush came up his neck, up round his ears, flooded his face.

'I also like to get away from my husband once in a while. This is a perfect excuse. We could be away for days.'

The waitress came with their order just as his silence was getting embarrassing.

He had no idea what to say, what to do.

He looked at the plate in front of him. He wasn't hungry. He was aware that his emotions were dormant but that soon they would be awakened, and he was afraid of that.

He looked at the french fries, the salad, put some dressing on the hamburger, then realised he had helped himself before Mrs Lidman and quickly gave her the dressing with an apologetic smile.

'Sorry, I was just miles away, then.'

'I don't think I really want any on this salad,' she said, then: 'How much did you depend on your mother?'

She was doing it on purpose, reminding him of his new situation. Maybe it was a good thing.

'I'm not sure.'

'In everyday things, like the laundry, food, medicine?'

'Not much.'

'What was your daily routine? What time did you get up, go to bed, what did you do on Sundays?'

'Ma always got up first, then woke me up when she finished in the bathroom, then made us both coffee. After that she left and maybe we'd see each other briefly when she got back, maybe not.'

'What about Sundays?'

'If she was there she'd make an attempt at a meal. But she

usually stayed with friends, she always seemed to go to a party Saturday night.'

'And your own friends?'

'Not many.'

He toyed with the dressing, spread it over the hamburger with the flat of his knife. He wasn't hungry at all.

'None, in fact,' he added.

'Girl friends?'

'One or two a few months back.'

He cut a piece of crisp lettuce and put it in his mouth, then looked up. 'I'm pretty dull, you know.'

'Did one of them tell you that?'

'Yes.' That was astute of her. 'How did you guess?'

'You're a bookworm, Paul; your friends are William Blake, Anais Nin, Celine, Wilson, Ouspensky, Frisch, Boll, Hesse, even Proust; you're not likely to make friends with people who have the same interest because they're all like you, their noses are buried in print. I've seen you get enthusiastic with some of our customers. They remain our customers because of you. You're the best read person I know. That's not being dull. But it is being a little unreachable.'

He picked at the hamburger, sipped the milk shake, ate the tomato; he didn't want any of it.

'I'm sorry, I'm just not hungry.'

'Don't worry. It's understandable. Don't talk if you don't want to either. I'm just trying to keep your mind occupied.'

He smiled at her, hoping it conveyed appreciation. His hands felt sticky and he wanted to go to the john.

'Will you excuse me a moment.'

He made his way to the washrooms desperately wanting to be alone, wanting to think things out. There was an emptiness in his stomach, a fear crouching there. He touched the black tiles above the latrines, ran his finger along the reliable squares. It was not knowing what would happen, not knowing who Warren was, not knowing where he was going now, what he would find there.

Mother dead!

As he zipped up his jeans he thought of Patty. Smiled at the Freudian slip. Patty always had her hand on his flies, when they'd gone to the movies anyway. 'It's called penis envy,' she'd said, and he had accepted that it was. 'You've got a sexy face too which'll make you vulnerable to older women. The young ones will just want you because you're strong and silent.'

Later she'd called him dull.

He glanced at himself in the mirror as he washed his hands. He'd had premonitions of death but never of love. Or was it that he had never recognised them?

An affair with Mrs Lidman?

His 'Graduate' to her 'Mrs Robinson'?

She didn't have a daughter he could run away with and she was younger. But would she dominate? He'd weathered her bad moods quite a few times when publishers had delivered wrong books, or several consignments arrived all at once. She had looked good that time her hair had all come down and she was crouching on the floor sorting out the invoices which had fallen out of the files. Otherwise he'd always seen her as an upright woman, a woman who crossed her legs elegantly when sitting down, a woman of poise. That time she had suddenly become human, sexy even.

If she didn't tell him to cut his hair or start buying him shirts he didn't like, it might be worth pursuing. He was conceited enough to believe that he had something to offer. His brain if nothing else. That store of quotes, the computer of authors.

She might divorce, he might marry her and inherit the bookshop.

Was that the sum total of his ambition, to own a bookshop?

He hadn't thought of that before either.

Would mother have left him any money?

Mrs Lidman was waiting for him by the car. The sun was hot, he slipped off his jacket. His arms were as white as his face, a pallid youth. He breathed in the fresh air, suddenly felt better.

'I haven't been out of New York for three years,' he said,

'It shows.'

'I'm pale?'

'You're pale.'

'Shall I, wasting in despair
Die because a woman's fair
Or make pale my cheeks with care

'Cause another's rosy are?'

'And who wrote that?' she asked, impressed.

'George Withers, early seventeenth century.'

He enjoyed quoting, he enjoyed most coming up with the right quote for the right occasion.

'I sometimes feel you're wasted,' Mrs Lidman said. 'On the other hand I suppose the shop does give you free access to all the knowledge you want.'

They got into the car and she drove back on to the highway.

'We should be there in a couple of hours now,' she said, glancing at the map. 'What do you think Warren's like. What are they usually like?'

'Male chauvinist executives on dirty week-ends with their secretaries.'

'All from the insurance company?'

'Mostly. She was getting near the top. Maybe blackmailing some for all I know,' he said.

Mrs Lidman laughed. It was the slightly bitchy laugh of a woman who had known similar circumstances. Had she been a secretary? Had she married her boss?

'Did you dislike your mother because she slept around?'

'No. I disliked her because she preferred the company of that type of man to me. She didn't appreciate me.'

'I appreciate you, Paul.' It was said flirtingly.

She had given him a present on his birthday, Painter's two volumes on Proust, hardbacks he valued very much. He had been touched, but had only seen the gift as an encouraging perk from his employer, though the blue ribbon and delicate wrapping paper had not been too business-like.

Was he awakening to something rather interesting that might have been staring him in the face for some time?

He glanced at her, the rich tanned skin of her arms, her slight wrists, her hands cared for with daily creams. She held the steering wheel with some delicacy. Those long fingers were exciting.

She saw him looking and smiled.

Could she read thoughts?

'You've got a nice tan,' he said. 'Where do you get it from?'

'You noticed? We have a garden and sit out in it week-ends.'

'You and your husband,' he said pointedly.

'Me and friends, occasionally my husband. He's away a great deal.'

She turned her head and looked him straight in the eyes again. The lady was making a definite pass, and he shifted in his seat.

'What does he do?' he managed to ask. 'I know nothing about you.'

'He's president of ISS, a subsidiary of ESCA.'

'Oh . . .'

'Baffled? ISS stands for Inter Satellite Services, ESCA stands for Electronic Sound Corporation of America.'

'That I knew. So he's in the space industries?'

'In its simplest terms. His company actually make metal screws for rockets. It's not as glamorous as it sounds.'

'Why is he away a lot?'

'Because he wants to be. We haven't slept together for two years.'

He felt the blush rising again. Thank God they were taking a bend and she had to concentrate on her driving.

What surprised him most was his own reaction. He went to the movies, had read virtually every erotic book that came into the shop, had weaned himself on Henry Miller and Frank Harris, why did reality unsettle him so much?

Had she noticed that he read erotica?

He hadn't noticed if she did.

But then he never noticed anything.

'Did that shock you?' Mrs Lidman asked when they were on the straight again.

'What?'

'Me telling you I hadn't slept with my husband for two years?'

'No . . . Yes. Not the fact, but that you were telling me. I don't get involved much in other people's lives.'

'What's your bedroom like?'

'My bedroom?' The question was odd.

'Yes, what colour walls do you have, is it full of books, do you have a single or double bed?'

'Just a single. Lots of books, a desk.'

'I always imagined you in a double bed usually with a very pretty girl.'

She was playing games, or making it so obvious what was in her mind that he was being pretty dumb.

What was he supposed to do, grab her leg? Put his hand up her skirt?

He turned in his seat to face her, his elbow resting out of the window, the wind blowing his hair. It was an attacking stance, a more aggressive position, but he couldn't think of anything to say.

'We're nearly there,' she said, pointing at a sign as they left the highway. Lake Champlain three miles.

She slowed the car down and turned to look at him.

'I was making conversation, Paul, to keep your mind off the reality you've now got to face. Don't take it too seriously.'

And she squeezed his arm, and he felt like a sixteen year old again, which was where he seemed to live most of the time as far as women were concerned.

'That's probably him there,' Mrs Lidman said, pulling into a large gasoline station complex.

A tall man, better looking than he had expected, better dressed, altogether more elegant than his mother's usual friends, was waving and coming towards them.

Mrs Lidman parked the car, stopped the engine and both got out as the man reached them.

'Paul Saralyn?'

'Yes.'

'Warren Hughes, administrative manager of East Coast Trust Life Insurance Company. I worked with your mother.'

Paul introduced Mrs Lidman, watched the two shake hands aware that the older man would know how to cope with a woman like that. She was certainly more fanciable than his mother.

'Have they found her yet?' Mrs Lidman asked.

'No, I'm afraid not. We'll use my car.'

'What exactly happened?'

'No one knows. And we won't know till the fire's been completely put out.'

'The place is still burning?' Paul asked.

'Yes. It's been kind of nasty.'

'Was it a hotel?'

'Private hotel, more of a club. Our clients used it for short vacations.'

'Were you with her?'

'Not exactly son. She came down with Gary Murdoch, but he decided to go fishing the other side of the lakes. So she was alone at the time.'

They got in Warren Hughes's Lincoln, Paul opening the door for Mrs Lidman then getting into the back. He'd been brought up well, knew his manners. For that he had to thank his mother. She judged men first by their manners. Expected to be treated like a lady.

'The house was originally built by an eccentric art dealer. A replica of a Tudor house in England, oak beams, gables, a lot of wood, that sort of thing. And being isolated the fire people couldn't get there too quickly.'

After a ten minute drive they could see smoke, strange pockets of it clinging to the trees and bushes as they turned down a lilac banked avenue. The smell was so strong that Hughes closed the windows. And then they were there, the remains of the house in front of them.

There were five fire appliances and a network of hoses everywhere, firemen in asbestos suits dowsing down the smouldering timbers. He'd never seen anything like it. A massive chimney stack remained standing in the middle of the blackened debris, twisted latticed window casings, charcoaled beams, broken water pipes. An ambulance was parked on what had been a lawn, the arched stone entrance still stood, stone lions on either side of the steps, evidence of ivy creepers on the remaining walls, incongruous flowered wallpaper, a pink wash-basin three floors up hanging upside down.

Hughes parked the car away from the official vehicles, stopped the engine and turned round to look at Paul.

'This was the second time your mother had been here, did you know that?'

'No,' Paul said. He didn't see the significance of the information.

'Was it some kind of health farm?' Mrs Lidman suggested, trying to ease Hughes's apparent discomfort.

'A home for alcoholics?' Paul then said bluntly, under-standing.

'You knew?'

'She was seeking treatment then?'

'She would have done eventually. Your mother liked drinking, you knew that. But she hadn't got to the stage yet where she saw it as a problem, though others did. The company ran week-end seminars here, dry-outs, to which people like your mother were invited. The idea was to break it to them gently that they were heading up the wrong path.'

So someone had been trying to help her.

They all got out of the car and moved towards a police van that barred the way further up the drive.

The local sheriff was leaning against his car talking to one of the fire officials.

'Anything yet, Barnie?' Warren Hughes asked.

'Nope. We know the fire started in the far left corner, and everyone has been accounted for except Mrs Saralyn.'

'This is her son, Paul.'

'Hi, son. My condolences . . . though we have no proof yet. The search may take some time, everything has to be sifted through. The men are working on it over there right now.'

Paul slowly moved away from the group. He eased himself from officialdom, from those who would be doing their job sincerely but cutting down on sentimentality because there was neither time nor reason to allow for it.

Mrs Lidman glanced at him, concerned by what effect the whole scene was having on him. He acknowledged the concern, nodded that he was all right. So far the tragedy hadn't touched him, his mother had not been found, she was not yet proved dead.

He wandered off down the lawns that sloped towards the lake. From where he was the whole scene could be taken in by a wide angle camera lens – the disaster area to the left, peace and tranquillity to the right.

What could have happened? His mother, drunk, starting the fire stupidly, pouring brandy on the carpet, the curtains catching fire, the timbers going up in flames?

He avoided going near the house, it wouldn't tell him anything. The officials would find something eventually, her wedding ring, if it hadn't melted, or her silver bracelet.

He wanted to be alone. Mrs Lidman had played with his

emotions. It hadn't upset him exactly, but he didn't need all that shit.

He stopped to watch four asbestos suited men raking the ashes where they said the fire had started. He could feel the heat from where he was some fifty yards away. The smell of burnt wood was incredibly strong, clouds of smoke puffed up occasionally as firemen hit a smouldering mattress with a jet of water. Charred beams cracked and fell, criss-crossing over the black debris.

He walked on down towards the lake, the grass soft and damp underfoot. There was a small pavilion by the water's edge, a jetty and a boat. He wanted to go there, see what the house looked like from there.

Then he stopped because it wasn't true.

He was being drawn to the left by something. From the moment he had got out of the car he had looked at the bank of lilac bushes and had wanted to go towards them, there seemed to be an arbour beyond, a wilder part of the garden which was beckoning.

He quickened his steps, but carefully, not wanting to attract attention, and as he got closer to the bushes he realised how tense he had become and stopped again.

What was happening to him? Why did he feel like this?

He knew he was going to see something unpleasant, that he was being drawn to it, that he had a sixth sense, *was* psychic. He had to admit it, accept it, act on it.

Now he went straight to the gap in the bushes, through into a small clearing of rough grass, and saw them standing there holding hands, looking at him with those strange penetrating grey eyes.

They were taller, older, more threatening than the last time. They were quite naked, translucent. The reflection of the sun sparkling on the lake's surface shining through them, and their hair was silver. The girl was nearly beautiful, she had a smile which conveyed anxiety for him, the expression wanted to help him. She was eight, nine perhaps, her hands stubby enough, her legs short enough to make her movements childish rather than sensuous, but he was aware of her nakedness. Then the boy, staring at him all the while, slowly raised his hand and pointed at a spot a few yards distance from where they were.

Paul followed the direction and saw a shape in the long grass a few feet away.

As he moved towards it the smell was so repugnant that he had to step back and cup his hand over his nose and mouth. He approached it again, aware that the children were watching him, and saw quite clearly what it was.

The black blistered arms covered the charred face and the singed wire wool hair; the clothing had been burnt off, so had the skin, showing the main tissues and muscles of the body. There remained the bones, yellow, covered with sickly mucous.

He looked up at the children. They had not moved, but just stood there staring at him, the boy, the smaller of the two, a finger in his mouth, seemed bewildered.

'Who are you?' Paul asked in a tight whisper.

And for just a moment he thought the girl was going to answer but she looked beyond him and behind him. Instinctively he turned, and saw Mrs Lidman, Warren Hughes and the sheriff hurrying towards him. When he turned again the children had gone.

In the seconds that followed the sight of the cadaver overwhelmed him, the sickening odour came up from inside and he choked and started vomiting in the grass.

He pulled a paper tissue out of his pocket, wiped his mouth, looked up at Mrs Lidman, then turned to point in the direction of what he had found.

Shouts, directions, firemen, police officials, all bounded past him.

A stretcher, a rubber sheet, Mrs Lidman looking on, then shielding her eyes.

'How did you find her, son?'

'I don't know . . . I was just looking . . .'

'Incredible. We searched around here this morning.'

'She obviously came running out and tried to make it to the water . . .'

'She came through there, must have been like a flaming torch, even the bushes got singed . . .'

Mrs Lidman put her arm round his shoulders and led him away.

There would be an enquiry, there would be questions and answers, right now she was taking him away, right away from the scene and Hughes suggested a hotel nearby where he was staying. The boy was not to be subjected to any more of this horror today.

CHAPTER TWO

'How did you know she was there, Paul? You did know because you went straight there, I was watching you, you left us and went straight there.'

He didn't want to answer, could not answer because he did not know himself, and could not explain it satisfactorily.

He was also tired of questions, of answers, of analysis, of theories. For ten hours he had been present at the preliminary enquiry with the sheriff, the fire chief, the doctor who had certified his mother dead, Mrs Lidman and Warren Hughes.

At one moment the argument had reached such a point of banality that he had excused himself and walked out of the court room to breathe some fresh air. Detectives were to be brought in, coroners, other doctors, other fire chiefs, then two funeral directors had approached him and he had collapsed in tears, allowed his nerves to break down.

So Mrs Lidman had taken charge.

She'd enjoyed it. He saw it in her face, and he was grateful because she took care of everything from the purchase of a toothbrush and toothpaste for the two night stay to the transportation of his mother's ashes to a suitable resting place.

Now, driving back to New York, forty-eight hours later, having spent a sedated night in Hughes's recommended motel, drugged to ensure deep sleep, he was being asked the very questions he could not answer himself.

The nightmares that everyone expected him to have, of reliving the horror of his mother's death, of being haunted by the calcinated figure in the undergrowth, held no fears for him compared to the sight of the opal children. Their very transparency was the fearfulness of dread.

Their eyes, their hair, their translucent whiteness, even in the bright sunlight of the afternoon their shapes had cast no shadows.

Were they entirely imaginary, phantoms of his mind, warnings, messengers of death? There had been no connection with any tragedy when he had seen them three years before. They had appeared in his bedroom, nothing more.

Why?

Why was he haunted by these figures, and what did they represent?

Had someone died three years before, someone he did not know, someone with whom he was distantly connected?

'I can't answer your questions,' he said eventually. 'It's not that I don't want to, it's that I can't.'

'But do you admit that you went straight to the spot where she was?'

'I just happened to go there.'

'I don't think you did. I think you were drawn there, drawn to that spot by something unnatural, whether you are aware of it or not, I'm not sure.'

'I don't understand.'

'I saw you leave us, I watched you all the time, you followed the line of the hoses going from the pumps to the lakeside, then, quite suddenly you branched off and very directly made for the bushes. There was hardly a path there. I couldn't see you completely because of the shrubs, but you seemed to stop as though . . . well, quite honestly, as though talking to someone. Then you made straight for the spot.'

Was there any harm in talking about them? She was the only person in the world to whom he could mention them. Was he frightened of being thought insane, or was he frightened of unknown supernatural repercussions? She understood more than most people, surrounded herself by every occult book imaginable, she could hardly be called sceptical. She might help, relieve him of his anxieties.

'Do you remember me telling you a long time ago that in a dream I saw the apparition of two children in my bedroom?'

'When you first joined me at the bookshop?'

'Yes. They were there. They were a little taller than when I last saw them, but it was them.'

'A warning then, messengers of death do you think?'

She was accepting the possibility of their existence completely.

'I don't know. There was no tragedy last time I saw them.'

'What of your other dreams? Your recurring dreams, do you still have them?'

'Yes.'

'The same ones, about being buried alive under a cannon during a battle, and people eating babies in a medieval chapel?'

She remembered what he had told her. There were worse dreams, nightmares of castration, of rape, he had not talked of them, they were so unsettling.

'Do you think I ought to see a psychiatrist?'

'No, but I think you should talk more freely to me when you feel you can. I am a friend and I know you. I also believe in the possibility of supernatural occurrences which a psychiatrist might not. You're not ill, you're perfectly sane, but you shouldn't bottle up, *that* could drive you mad.'

He wasn't sure. He wasn't sure he wanted to talk about it. And yet if he wasn't being haunted, if he wasn't being visited by child messengers and they were just his imagination, then it was insanity.

'What about coming back and staying with me tonight? I don't think you should go home or stay in your apartment alone.'

He'd thought of the empty apartment. He'd dreaded the idea of going in there by himself, of sleeping there alone. He was grateful for the offer.

And he accepted.

The Lidmans' house in Queens was pretty much what he had expected it would be, only bigger. Secluded, painted white, with a porch and steps leading up to the front door, it was a stock Spanish style successful executive's residence totally suitable for the president of a subsidiary of a multinational corporation.

The double garage opened automatically when the hatchback rolled up the ramp, and the doors closed behind them. For a moment they were in darkness, then lights came on and they got out. Two paintings hung on the garage walls, there were no tools or rubber tyres, or wheelbarrows or hosepipes around; it was the car's own drawing room, a hint at the shape of luxuries to come.

They went into the house through a sliding door, up some

narrow stairs to a blue and white tiled hallway with arches and an abundance of greenery. It was very fresh, very light. She led him into an L-shaped study room which was entirely walled with shelves of books.

'Make yourself at home, Paul, the drinks are in the cupboard on the left. I'd like a white wine; you'll have to get the ice from the kitchen.'

She sat down behind a leather topped desk and flicked a switch on the answer-phone. A number of messages came through, alternatives to appointments she had cancelled. He found the glasses, the wine. Pretending not to listen he went to the kitchen.

It was large, airy, with every conceivable gadget. In the freezer he found the ice, put some in the silver bucket provided.

'Hi, Sheryl, got your message. Hope everything's O.K. in the end and that the boy's not too shaken. I'll be in Chicago Thursday and Friday night, back Saturday morning. Don't forget we're invited to a Sunday dinner date. Love you . . . '

He waited for the next garble to come through before walking back in.

As he handed Mrs Lidman her wine, she stopped writing on a small notepad and raised the glass to him.

'Here's to health and sanity,' she said, then added, 'Jack won't be back till Saturday morning. That means we'll be alone for two nights.'

Was she playing games again?

He had no idea what to say.

'Well you can either run away now or take the consequences.'

It was a joke of course, he wasn't to take her seriously. Her way of helping him forget the tragedy.

He didn't want to go back to the apartment, that was certain. He wouldn't mind being surrounded by his mother's things, that he didn't fear, but he was frightened of seeing the children again; here, in these bright new surroundings with her he would be safe. He also had the feeling that she was a deterrent, her presence would keep them away.

'Thank you,' he said at last. 'I'll risk staying.'

'Good. Now how about some food?'

'I'm not too hungry.'

'But you should eat. I'm going to have a bath, then I'll cook you something. We can go out to a movie if you want.'

She was trying to keep his mind occupied, succeeding in a way, though unsettling him as well. He wasn't sure how to behave with her, what exactly was expected of him.

Probably nothing.

Because of the situation he had *carte blanche* to behave as he liked. He could make a bum pass and it wouldn't matter.

'Would you like a bath?' she asked. 'It would relax you a bit.'

Together?

His expression must have given away his thoughts because she went on to explain that there were three bathrooms in the house, one of which was part of the guest suite which he would be occupying.

Now he could relax.

She showed him the way, suggested he take his drink up with him. He'd also poured himself out a white wine.

The bathroom was green, Italian ceramics and mirrors, with everything provided including a matching bathrobe to wear afterwards.

She turned the taps on for him and closed the door after her. He thought of locking it, then decided it would be rude.

He undressed slowly, looking at his reflection, daring his image to change. Nothing happened, he just looked white, well . . . pale but interesting.

Perhaps it would help if he talked to Mrs Lidman about the burnt image he'd seen in his mind. Mention his feelings about the cremation too. The funeral directors had actually suggested a cremation. The charred remains of his mother would be incinerated. To make absolutely sure?

The insurance company was going to pay all expenses, Warren Hughes had assured him of that. He had also hinted at sums of money, insurance monies, coming his way, because all employees of East Coast Trust automatically had Diamond Key Life policies and with such a tragedy he would not only benefit from that, but from her accident policy as well.

Maybe he would be rich.

Maybe he wouldn't have to work for a while.

Independence.

Independence from Mrs Lidman and his mother all at one go.

Did he want that?

The bitter sadness which he had managed to suppress suddenly rose up from within him and a flood of tears clouded his eyes. The noise of the taps gushing hot water drowned the uncontrollable sobs which unexpectedly shook his body. He wanted to moan out loud, he had never wanted to do that, but the images of his mother, when she was younger, when he was younger, came flooding back, the desperate need to cling on to her, the admittance that though he did not get on with her, though they were poles apart in their daily life, they needed each other. He had needed her when he was ill, he needed her tenderness, had needed that person with whom he could be totally himself, and she had been grateful enough for his care so many of the mornings after the nights before.

He took a deep breath, wiped the steam from the mirrors to look at his tear-stained face, turned the taps off and blew at the surface bubbles of the foam bath. Then he heard the gentle knock.

'Paul, are you all right?'

Had she been knocking long?

'Yes, fine. I'm fine.'

His voice was tight, unsure, timid.

'I'm going to have my bath now, is there anything you need?'

'No. I'm all right. Thank you very much.'

And she went away.

She was just being the good hostess, the protective, caring substitute for . . . for someone he would never see again.

How unhappy had his mother been? How little had he understood her? Now of course it was too late to try and comfort her. He had never even thought about it.

Was he a selfish child then? Had he ignored her? Had she needed his love, his attention? Were the reproaches justified. 'Again with your books!' Maybe the jealousy of his reading had been unbearable. Had his indifference to her loneliness been the cause of her seeking the company of so many other men, of drowning her sorrows in drink?

He sank deeper into the bubble bath, aware for the first time also that he had not tasted much of the luxurious life. The surroundings were comforting to look at, the cleanliness, the thought out order, the plant at the end of the bath, the row of glass jars with green and blue salts, the green towels, the magazines on the small table. But what did it all cost, this luxury? Not in money, but in time and energy? How many maids did Mrs Sheryl Lidman employ?

And where was he going with her?

She had been incredibly kind, he had not had to spend a dime.

She didn't have a son, or a daughter, perhaps he was a longed for substitute, maybe she had been starved of motherhood. He would let events take their course.

He flicked the bath plug lever open with his toe and watched the surface foam very slowly go down, parts of his body appearing like islands in a sea of bubbles.

The wine had had its effect, it dulled the mind completely and made things seem quite amusing. A marvellous escape, alcohol, which was why his mother had turned to it.

He got out of the bath, draped himself in the huge bath-towel and acknowledged his Roman Senator reflection in the mirror.

The feel of his wet body against the soft towelling aroused him for a moment, and he stuck his tongue out as the thought occurred that maybe to lie with Sheryl Lidman in her no doubt massive bed might be quite an experience. Then, on hearing movements in the hallway, he realised that the reality would not be without embarrassment.

They both ate informally in the kitchen. A light meal, with a strawberry milk shake which he was told how to make using the mixer on the wall. It was domestic life, not husband and wife, nor lover and mistress, but mother and son. He could see her enjoying it.

And the questions started.

What was he going to do now? Had he thought about the future? With an intelligence like his surely he wasn't going to spend the rest of his life just selling books? What ambitions had he?

It made him appreciate his unenquiring mother. She hadn't

cared a damn whether he swept the streets or aimed at becoming president. She'd learnt to leave him alone.

While in his bath Sheryl Lidman had apparently been in contact with Warren Hughes and had good news for him. East Coast Trust would be paying him a good sum but not, of course, before all the legalities of the case had been cleared. Meanwhile, she or Jack, her husband, would help him out.

He listened politely, was well mannered, cleared the dishes and glasses up afterwards and put them away in the dishwasher, only to be told not to bother because Mary would be in first thing to clear up.

So now what did he want to do? Watch television or go to bed?

And before he could answer she had come up behind him and put her arms round his waist and squeezed him gently.

'Let's go to bed, my darling; I don't think I can pretend any more.'

She kissed the back of his neck, nibbled his ear lobe, and, as he froze, aware that his whole body was rudely tense, she slid her hand inside the front of his jeans.

'I think you could do with a little tenderness,' she said, and taking his hand, led him up to his bedroom.

His own excitement now took over.

As she kicked her shoes off, he kissed her, helped her undo the buttons of her dress as she undid his belt.

The wine helped, if he needed help. If she suddenly turned on him and accused him of misbehaving he could blame it on the wine. But Sheryl clearly wanted him.

Naked, they got into the large soft clean bed.

'Do you find me old?' she asked.

'No. Not at all.'

It wasn't true. The fact that she was conscious of her age, conscious about her looks made her old. And she'd got her priorities wrong. Her face was a different colour to her body because it had been treated over the years to so much make-up. Her body, in fact, was quite young. Nude, she was small, she depended on high heels for her superiority, and what surprised him most was how old *he* felt with her, how mature. Whereas with Patty he had felt like a child, an adolescent literally feeling his way to maturity, with Sheryl he was masterful, had to be because she played little girl lost. He became adventurous, did not hide himself under the sheets, was not shy about exposure. She had chosen him, she had chosen his physique, he had nothing to be ashamed of, so he acted a little wild, threw the pillows on the floor, pulled her down the length of the bed so that they could see themselves in the mirror, covered her whole body with the oil she 'timidly' suggested they might use, and once he got going he did not stop. She wanted a young man with energy and she got one, three times with glasses of white wine as refreshment in between.

He had no idea what it did to her, what dormant pleasures it awakened, but it made *him* realise that his mother had been right.

He should get out and about a great deal more, learn first hand by his own experiences and not by those of his countless authors who might well be imagining it all anyway.

'You're still restless,' Sheryl said. 'Are you going to be able to sleep?'

He wasn't sure. His mind was certainly revolving like a tombola.

'Take a tranquilliser, you need sleep.' And she slipped out of bed, was away a little while, and came back smelling of perfumed soap, holding a glass of water and a little white pill.

He put his head down on the soft, soft pillow, and when he woke up it was dawn and he was alone.

His mouth felt exceedingly dry and the sounds he made to himself were extremely woolly. After remaining motionless in the bed he slowly moved his limbs and eased himself out and went to the bathroom.

His clothes, he noticed, had been neatly folded, his shoes arranged side by side under the chair. He drew back the curtains and looked out into the suburban street; luxury cars were parked outside luxury houses where the double garages were already full. Down the road, over the hedge, he saw the traditional newspaper boy on his bicycle hurling the bundles expertly on to front lawns.

He had no idea what the time was and could not remember what he had done with his watch. He picked up his jeans.

His keys, the apartment keys, were for some reason in the

left hand pocket though he always kept them in the right.

Had someone been curious?

His wallet was intact, no money taken, but his keys had been moved. He then found his watch, six twenty-three. He pressed the date button and stared at the figure. It was the fifteenth, the fifteenth of the sixth. Had he been asleep a *whole* day then? Longer even?

He went back to the bathroom, looked at his face, felt his chin. There was more growth there than usual. A two-day growth.

Jesus, had he been asleep all that time? Was it now Saturday?

The newspapers would tell him.

He slipped on the bathrobe and crept downstairs and studied the padlocks and chains on the front door and gave up. No way would he be able to open that without waking up Sheryl. Then in the study he saw a briefcase, two glasses, a pair of men's spectacles.

Jack Lidman had come home.

He went to the kitchen to make himself a coffee. He'd slept over thirty-six hours, he'd lost a whole day, maybe two. He opened the ice box, found the milk, found the coffee in a cupboard, switched on the kettle. As he reached for a cup his sleeve caught a jar full of cooking utensils which overbalanced and the lot fell to the floor with a deafening clatter.

He held his breath, waited for sounds upstairs, then started picking everything up, ladles, spoons, forks, skewers, barbecue tongs. He put them all back, arranging them in the jug like flowers, and when he turned Sheryl was there in the doorway watching him.

'I'm sorry, I woke you up.'

'Did you sleep well?'

'Apparently. What day is it?'

'It's Sunday morning. You were beginning to worry me, but the doctor said it was normal and could do you no harm.'

He'd even miscalculated the day on his watch.

'Would you like a coffee?' he asked.

'I prefer lemon tea first thing . . . I'll make it myself. I know the way around. Wouldn't you prefer real coffee?'

The banalities of household awakening went on till lunch-time.

Jack Lidman came down yawning in his dressing gown bought in London at Liberty's. They shook hands firmly, avoided mentioning the mother's death, avoided mentioning anything, immersing themselves in the newspapers until over lunch, just the three of them, Paul said he thought he should go back to the apartment, just in case something had happened.

Neither husband nor wife objected to the idea. Sheryl Lidman volunteered to drive him back. He protested, but she insisted and, over coffee, as though it could not be broached before because business lunch traditions demanded it, Jack Lidman said he wanted to talk to him.

They went out into the small patio at the back, and under the shade of a parasol he gathered the purpose of the talk was to urge him to go abroad, lock up the apartment and go far away from everything he had known. Go to Europe, visit Paris, Rome, Madrid, London, have a good holiday. He and Sheryl had worked it out, the bookshop would pay him the air fare, other expenses could be met with part of his inherited insurance money. They had many contacts in Europe so he would in no way be lonely.

It was an idea which was not alien to Paul, he'd thought often enough of travelling, but he had never been able to afford it.

He protested, once more, politely about the bookshop paying his air fare, but Jack Lidman pointed out that this was one way of making sure he'd come back. Though it was not certain, there was the possibility of Sheryl opening a branch in San Francisco, which she would ask him to manage and his knowledge and experience would by then be invaluable.

They were handing him a secure future on a plate.

The apartment had an unpleasant smell about it, the garbage in the kitchen waste bin, decaying prawn shells of the last dinner he had had with his mother.

He could be melodramatic about it all, let the sadness envelop him again but he was strong enough now to overcome the temptation. He excused the untidiness, showed Sheryl into the sitting room and offered her a cup of instant coffee.

Then she did something which was quite surprising.

She said *she* would make the coffee and went straight to the kitchen as though she had been in the apartment before.

The keys had been in the wrong pocket, it was possible that she had come here while he was asleep.

But why?

He said nothing, hoping she would not be aware of her mistake.

After assuring her that he would be all right by himself and promising to turn up at the bookshop in the morning as usual when they would contact the Burlington police and make the final arrangements for the funeral, if the authorities released the body, he saw her down to her car, and climbed back up the two flights of stairs feeling relieved, released, free from the pressures of having to be polite.

Sleeping with her had not been his conquest, it had been hers, and he was aware that he was still boyish enough to 'score' as the expression so rightly had it.

He went to his room and looked around, trying to see a tell-tale something which might have been disturbed, and he noticed that a stack of old *Evergreen* reviews had been moved, not a great distance, a matter of inches, but they had been moved on the top of his desk.

He went to the drawer and found his five-year diary to the front. He had not written in it for nearly two years, had not looked at it for nearly as long.

He took it out, unclipped the catch, flicked it to the last few entries where it fell open naturally.

> 'I was visited an hour ago (3 a.m.) by a vision of two strange frightening beings. Children, a girl aged about eight, the boy maybe four. They stood by the corner cupboard and stared at me. They were translucent, not transparent, like opals. They were not like any other vision, daydream or premonition I have ever had before. They were not evil, but fearful.'

Why did he feel that this was what had interested her? Did she suspect him of being mad perhaps? Then why the suggestion that he go abroad and the offer to pay the fare?

None of it made too much sense.

He flicked back a number of pages, stopped at one of the recurring dream sequences he had written down.

'I am twenty-five and in Napoleon's army. I know this but do not know why I am so certain. We are fighting the Austrians near the Danube. A bomb or shell explodes near me and a vast mantle of mud envelops me and I realise I am going to be buried alive. I then surface, my mouth full of earth, only to feel a terrible pain and know I have lost a leg. I am pinned under the wheel of a 12-pounder Gribeauval. (I looked this up in *Arms and Armour of the 19th century*. Napoleon used massed batteries of General Gribeauval's 12-pounder field piece with effect at the pivotal battle of Friedland, 1807. Wagram, 1809. Borodino, 1812.) Am I then a reincarnation of a Napoleonic soldier?'

Paul went to his mother's room, to the desk drawers where she kept the family documents, her money, the receipts of the joint bank savings account from which he would now draw alone. It could have been disturbed, he had no idea. Then he wondered whether perhaps he had not become obsessed with suspicion. Because he was afraid of his visions he did not admit to them, and because he did not admit to them he was trying to hide them, keep them a secret and therefore feared discovery. From now on he would accept what the Lidmans wanted to do for him without question. They were simply kind, considerate people who genuinely wanted to help him.

Sheryl Lidman drove him to Kennedy airport and saw him as far as the gate, double checking that he had everything. Once through passport control he felt another wave of relief. He had allowed himself to be wrapped in cotton wool and had taken advice on everything for the last two weeks. Having slept with her gave her the right, she seemed to think, of expecting him to do what she asked. So he had done it. A while longer and he would have become her possession totally.

He looked at the magazine stand, bought three, enjoyed the fact that he could be uninhibited about money now. Within another eight hours he'd be someone else's property, the good Signor Capuela whom he was to visit on the Riviera, which was why his flight was direct to Nice and not Paris where he really wanted to go. But they were paying.

He sat down with other passengers to wait for his number to be called. No one but the Lidmans and five dutiful East Coast Trust executives had attended the funeral. They were now his only family, and he had vowed to accept them as such.

His new shoes pinched a little at the tips. He would have preferred to wear sneakers and jeans, but Sheryl had insisted that he would feel better in a suit in France. The Italians were extremely clothes conscious people and Signor Capuela came from aristocratic Florentine stock.

He looked at the indicator board; he was early. He'd rather rushed it through the barrier to get away, but she hadn't held back, had admitted she hated departures. Besides, their relationship had become a little strained, they had been lovers but not gone to bed again because of Jack Lidman being around. It had made him wonder whether he had been all that satisfactory after all.

He had ample time to go to the washroom, comb his hair, refresh himself for the journey.

He was going to Europe!

Was that believable? Nice, Rome, Paris, London. A whole itinerary had been worked out for him. Certainly he was living at a pace now. After twenty-two years of nothing, suddenly everything. Death, money and a new life had come to him.

Maybe his mother was somewhere up there watching him, guiding him. There was a desire to believe that she hadn't altogether left him. He still referred to her in his mind, he had had to stop on two occasions shouting out in the kitchen asking her if she wanted a coffee when he was making some.

He walked over to the washroom and pushed open the door. It was palatial: all tiles and piped music, empty except for the person in the far cubicle, who had left the door open.

There was a strange noise coming from it, a heavy irregular breathing, an embarrassing sound as though some old man was abusing himself.

Curious, worried that someone might in fact be ill, he moved towards it, then saw them again.

This time their faces were creased with pain as though in terrible agony, and the boy was clinging to his taller sister, his arms holding her tightly round the waist, the girl about to cry, holding him round the back, her legs open, the little boy between them. They were in such an unnatural position for children that it was repulsive and the boy was making hideous adult movements which, with every spasm, seemed to hurt them both. Then they stopped, their expressions, their features showing intense relief.

They disengaged, held their breaths, looked at him, and shook their heads. The girl then lifted her hand and drew it across the air, imitating the flight of a bird, or an aeroplane. The boy did the same, but with anguish in his eyes, and made his hand plummet suddenly, crash and explode.

The silence was shattered by the call bell, and a sharp voice announced his flight.

He looked at the children, both shook their heads as though pleading him to take note of a warning.

Someone came in, he slipped into their cubicle and locked the door.

He was now closer to them than he had ever been, so close he could touch them.

They were real now, these strange naked children, pressing themselves against the lavatory wall.

Their grey eyes stared at him and for the first time he realised they had no pupils.

He reached out, his fingers touched the girl's thigh. It was ice cold, hard, hard and wet.

The girl drew back as much as she could, *she* was frightened. He took his hand away.

'Who are you?' he asked in a loud whisper.

And as he looked at her he felt himself sink, a terrible sense of falling through space, of being sucked down into a vacuum.

And he blacked out.

CHAPTER THREE

The lavatory attendant, an airport official and two other men were standing over him when he regained consciousness.

'You O.K., son?'

'Yes,' he said, recovering.

'Have a sip of this water.'

He drank. Everyone was being kind, the black man more concerned, wide-eyed.

'You must have passed out.'

'I guess I must.'

'Ate something that didn't agree with you?'

'Fear of flying I expect.'

'Did you take some travel sickness pills? They don't agree with all people.'

He got to his feet, smiled, convinced them that he was all right, said he had to check his flight.

He hadn't been unconscious long, hardly a minute, but enough time for the children to disappear.

So what had it been, an omen? A warning not to fly? Not to take that particular flight.

He went out into the airport lounge and sat down again among the crowd of passengers. They were excited, talked volubly. He didn't want to stay behind, he wanted to go, but the vision meant something, he was quite convinced. The Lidmans would presume he had gone, Signor Capuela would be meeting him at Nice airport; such pressures were those that made weaker people ignore danger signals.

His number was called again. Last call. His suitcase would be on board now. Did it contain anything he really wanted? The new trousers, the jacket, the shirts, the other pair of shoes Sheryl had bought him. The leather toilet case he would never use. Why had he allowed her to take his life over?

He sat there, waited, knowing deep down what he was doing, surprised that he was doing it, waiting to see if he could carry it through.

Would they check the passenger list, call out his name?

He didn't want that.

He hurried to the desk.

'I'm sorry. I'm Mr Saralyn. I've forgotten something vital, a document, I can't take this flight. Is there any way my luggage can be taken off?'

'Not now sir . . . but we can make sure it is kept for you at Nice airport. Will you collect it?'

'If I don't I'll have someone else do so.'

And she took down all the details and struck him off the list.

It was possible that Mrs Lidman was hanging around outside waiting to make sure the flight wasn't delayed, that he wasn't poor little boy lost, so he darted quickly from the passenger lounge to the main hall, passing through passport control again, got out in the open and grabbed a cab.

'The harbour,' he said.

'What harbour?'

'The docks.'

'What pier?'

'Drop me at the Seaport Museum.'

'Seaport Museum pier!'

He had no idea who made his mind up for him, but something was motivating him. He felt relaxed, in control, sat well back in the seat and enjoyed the drive back across Brooklyn to Manhattan Island.

He had money, a cheque card, the world was his. He could do what he liked. He'd find out about boats, get a passage over somehow. Did one just get on to a ship? How did that work? He'd be adventurous, take the first boat out wherever it went, a cargo boat, maybe, to somewhere he'd never thought about before. An adventure, through the Panama canal to the West Coast, then across the Pacific, round the world!

'Do you know anything about ships sailing to Europe?' he asked the cab driver.

'Nope, but I know someone working for a freight company who has all the schedules at his finger tips.'

'Can you put me in contact with him?'

'I'll take you to him. The offices are in Front Street.'

They crossed the East River over the Brooklyn Bridge,

turned left and got down in the maze of dockland warehouses.

Sheryl had told him he should now forget his mother and act independently, make his own decisions, not rely on others. Well he was doing just that. Breaking loose.

The man at the Freeland Marine Freight Company offices was in his thirties, bearded and had a limp. There was an acknowledgement in his eyes the moment Paul told him what he wanted. Europe by sea, peace and tranquillity, no planes, no speed.

He had various directories stacked on shelves to consult, schedules, timetables, manuals, itineraries.

'It works like this, some cargo ships take passengers, some don't. Those that do don't guarantee a direct route, it all depends on their cargo. Two boats should be leaving for England in the next three days, one's Scandinavian, docking at Southampton, the other's Russian, going to Leningrad via London.'

'Which sails first?'

'The Scandinavian line. The MS *Bjornstjerne*. Takes twelve passengers. They're usually fully booked in advance but we sometimes get cancellations. I'll find out for you.'

Paul sat quietly looking at the dusty office. It was straight out of a 1930s movie, only the telephone was modern.

The man knew the booking clerk at the other end personally. Contacts, that was all that was needed, contacts and a little money to push in someone's direction.

'Sails Friday, one berth cancelled yesterday. You may have to share a cabin.'

'I don't mind.'

The man wrote down the shipping line's address, gave him directions on how to get there.

He walked the seven blocks, under the East Side Elevated Express Highway, found the building, got to the eighth floor and found the clerk who was expecting him.

Three days in New York as a tourist, then Europe.

He was tempted to go back to the apartment but knew he'd get caught up with neighbours. He'd said his goodbyes, had done the whole departure bit. Instead he would stay in that small homely hotel not far from Central Park where he'd stayed one night with Patty, and from there do all the things he'd always wanted to do but never done.

With all he needed in way of personal belongings in his shoulder bag, he got a cab to the hotel, booked in to a single room, and lay down kicking his painful shoes off before picking up the phone.

He'd ring Sheryl Lidman and tell her what he was doing, he couldn't be that ungrateful; besides it was unfair to have Il Signor Capuela stand by at Nice airport waiting for a non-passenger.

She wasn't at the bookshop, she wasn't at home, but the answer-phone was, begging him to leave a message. So he hung up and thought about what he'd say. In fact he got his pen and notebook out and composed the message carefully.

> 'Premonition warning against Nice flight. Sailing instead for England Friday. Very happy. Enjoying freedom and self reliance as you said I would. Apologies to Signor Capuela, will contact him on arrival Europe. Thank you for everything . . . Paul.'

He rang it through, felt tremendous relief when he'd done it and flung himself backwards on the bed again, pressed various buttons for the television set to switch itself on, and tried all the channels for the news.

The children had warned him about the plane. Would it have crashed yet?

He wanted to know but realised he would have to be patient. He'd hear about that soon enough, but now was not the time to worry. Now was the time to enjoy being a tourist.

He went to a movie, had a large hamburger and an ice cream sundae, looked into a few doubtful bars and dives, didn't feel it was for him, saw another movie and went back to the hotel.

He slept well that night, enjoyed waking up to the new surroundings, then went down to have breakfast in a café with the morning papers. There was nothing about any air disaster. Dissatisfied, he went back up to his room and rang the airport to enquire about the flight. It had landed on schedule at Nice airport local time.

So it had not been a premonition, or would in only have crashed had he been on board?

Maybe he'd never know.

Anyway, he wasn't going to think about it any more. He was on vacation, he had enough cash in hand to enjoy himself. He'd spend the money he had and when it started showing signs of really disappearing completely he'd act. For a month he'd live like this, at least. His tastes weren't Ritzy; he could probably exist for years on very little.

He bought himself some new jeans, a couple of T-shirts, a sweater. He saw a bargain coat with sheepskin lining, he bought that, and a bargain suitcase to put them all in. He wanted to travel light. If he lost any of this it wouldn't matter. He bought himself some new sneakers, which made him feel really great and delighted the boy who served him by giving him his Italian super shoes.

He saw another two movies, one off-Broadway show, bought a couple of books which he read during the night and took a walk round Central Park. Then on Thursday night he paid for the room and asked to be given a call at five.

The morning dawn in New York was beautiful, the air comparatively cool, the smells quite different from the night. After a light breakfast he got a cab and went to the docks, presented himself at the right pier, went through customs along with other passengers, elderly couples it seemed, one young girl. It was a huge world dominated by the warehouses and the cranes and the massive ships towering above everything else.

Up the gangplank, the smell of diesel; a uniformed officer greeted him, checked his ticket, ordered a younger steward to take him to his cabin.

'My name is Lars, sir. I look after all you passengers. I think you are fortunate, you have the double cabin to yourself. A married couple had to cancel, and one other traveller.'

Paul wasn't sure whether to tip him or not, decided not. That would come at the end of the voyage. Anyway they were about the same age. It wouldn't be expected.

The cabin was compact. One bunk over the other, all metal. A heavy iron door opening into a tiny bathroom with shower, washbasin and lavatory, everything solid, bulky, spotlessly clean. He looked out of the porthole, at the dirty grey sea of the docks and the floating garbage, a few white seagulls squawking, diving, even floating among the broken fruit boxes and bubbled-up plastic bags.

There was a thin carpet on the floor, three good lights, one central, the other two next to the bunks. He wasn't sure which bed he'd take, decided on the lower one just in case the seas got rough and he fell out.

He unpacked, put everything neatly away in the lockers provided. Home for the next six or seven days. Safe, looked after, yet far away from everyone. It was the best decision he'd ever made.

He went up on deck to look around and find out the size of the ship. His steward was there looking down at things happening on quay.

'What's the routine?' Paul asked. 'Where can one go?'

'Anywhere which does not say "No Access to Passengers". All meals are served in the dining room. There is a small lounge on A deck. Were you expecting entertainment?'

'No, not at all,' Paul laughed.

'There is one pretty girl, a Miss Morrow, in cabin 6. She is sharing with another Miss, who is a lot older.'

'Thank you,' Paul said, and the steward winked.

He was a tall, handsome Nordic type with curly blond hair and bright blue eyes. He wouldn't try to compete. But he wondered all the same what a young girl was doing alone on board such a ship. Afraid of flying as well perhaps.

The ship moved off at nine. Chains wound in, men in dark blue heavy knit sweaters and heavy canvas trousers ran about. Whistles blew, a deep blast from the funnel made the air vibrate, someone on the quayside waved to someone on the ship. Paul was sailing away!

He went along the deck as far up the bow as possible but passengers had 'no access' on to the fo'c'sle. He was disappointed not to be able to see the sea ahead except by leaning over the side, however it took a long time getting out and away past the Statue of Liberty. Looking back on Manhattan, the coastline, he found that everything seemed so immense. Then, unexpectedly, the ship started to dip and rise and roll and he began to feel unwell.

He had not thought about being sick. It was something alien to him. He had only been sick a few times in his life, after silly drinking at parties, smoking for the first time, once at a fair after eating ice-cream then going on the swings and roundabouts. This was a similar nausea.

He didn't want to be seen, to be laughed at, so he quickly made his way back to his cabin and thankfully stepped into the lavatory to stand over the basin and grip the metal handles he had previously thought unnecessary.

He didn't know how long he stayed there, but found comfort in the closeness of the bowl and in the antiseptic smell of the cleanser. He retched a few times, was actually sick once, after which he went to lie on his bunk holding the towel, propped himself up on the hard pillow calculating how long it would be before the ship stopped rolling. Six days, one hundred and forty-four hours, eight thousand six hundred and forty minutes, every one of which seemed like a lifetime.

He should not have had the fried eggs for breakfast yesterday, nor all those hamburgers, nor tried the various flavours of milkshakes where that artificial blonde waitress had smiled at him so much.

Some time later in the morning, the steward came in to enquire whether he had wanted lunch and offered his sympathies. He could give him a pill which would help, but after a day, or two, he'd get used to it.

Paul accepted the pill, forty-eight hours of vomiting was not why he had bought his ticket.

The drug made him feel drowsy after a terrible hour or so and the rest of the day and night passed in a nightmare of queeziness and thirst.

Mid-morning on the second day he found he was able to drink the tea brought him and keep it down. He in fact felt that the ship had stopped dipping and rolling and that he had finally got its rhythm. He felt hungry too.

It was a bright morning, blue skies, brilliant sun, sparkling green sea and he went up on deck, happy to be alive.

Then he saw her for the second time. She was petite, shortish curly chestnut coloured hair, unassuming in dungarees and bright red polo neck sweater. Her nose was freckled, she had large brown eyes under eyebrows that seemed to be constantly surprised.

'Hi!' she said, coming towards him, dancing her fingers along the siderail. 'You must be P. Saralyn of Cabin 3. Feeling better?'

'Yes thanks,' he said. His seasickness was obviously general knowledge.

'My name's Cathy Morrow.' She put out her hand, a tight, friendly grip. 'You seen the other passengers?'

'No, I haven't seen anyone. I hid in my cabin from the start.'

'Wise. It's a geriatric ship. Even the captain's over fifty.'

She looked up in the direction of the quarterdeck, then turned and leaned on the guard rails and looked down at the sea.

'It's pretty magnificent in its immensity, isn't it? I mean, just imagine slipping through and falling into that. Not much hope.'

The white spume buffeting the side was impressive.

He wanted to say something, not appear dumb, but couldn't think of anything clever. He could quote *The Tempest* of course . . . 'Now would I give a thousand furlongs of sea for an acre of barren ground . . . ' but it would make him sound bookish. He looked at her, smiled. She looked at him, critically, he thought.

Ask questions, if you're interested, ask questions. Nobody minds having someone interested in them.

'Where are you from?' he asked.

'New York, New York via London, England.'

'Is that where you're going?'

'Yes,' she said, through a deliberately long sigh.

'But you don't want to?'

'No.'

If you're interested ask. Go on asking.

'Why not?'

'You want my life story?'

'It's a six day voyage.'

'I'll tell you mine if you'll tell me yours,' she said comically. 'But it's none too warm up here, where can we go?'

'My cabin?' he suggested bravely.

'Who else is in there?'

'Nobody.'

'You have a cabin to yourself?'

'Yes.'

'You rich then?'

'No, just lucky I guess.'

He led the way, a little unsteadily along the deck as the ship rolled, but he managed to keep a degree of dignity.

They reached his cabin without mishap; he opened the door for her and followed her in.

'Cosy! And with a view of the sea from above,' Cathy said, going to the porthole. 'I'm stuck at water level and have to have it closed all the time. Also there's an octogenarian in there who snores. We're the only two unaccompanied women aboard and she's the one who's frightened of being raped.'

She sat down on his bunk, drew her legs up, hugged her knees. 'This could be quite a pleasant trip after all.'

'I've nothing to offer you. I don't smoke and have no drink.'

'I don't want anything. Just company. Where're you from?'

He told her, he told her more than he had told anyone before at one go, about his mother dying, about working in the Village bookshop, about his hopes of doing a grand tour of Europe as in days of old.

He didn't tell her how his mother had died, he didn't tell her about the opal children, he didn't tell her about Sheryl Lidman.

In two weeks he had acquired some secrets.

'I'm a middle class British subject,' Cathy said, stretching out on the bunk very much at home. He sat down in the armchair facing her.

'My father and mother are both boringly alive, he's connected with shipping which is why I got this ticket. Our family seldom fly, we sail.' She paused and studied her nails; her hands were not large, but she looked after them.

'I fell in love with a shit, a real creep, and the real pain is not that he never loved me, or indeed that I wasn't as fond of him as I thought, it's that I had to call up my parents for help because I ran out of money! I came over to live with this asshole, believed it when he told me we could carve a life out for ourselves on the West Coast. All *he* wanted was his fucking passage back to the States from Angleterre!'

It was mock bitterness with enough edge to it for him to take her seriously. She'd been hurt.

'When I rang up Pa I could hear the joy in his voice. I was going to ask him to send me money, instead I just said "Can you ship me back? You've been proved right." He came up trumps with this barge! But I wanted six days alone, so far two's been enough!'

'Your boy friend was American?'

'An all-American college boy from Berkeley, California. His parents took an instant dislike to me and he wasn't even a good screw.'

He reacted. Tried to hide it, but she saw him flinch, tighten up.

She smiled.

'Did that shock you? I used to shock him. I couldn't believe how sensitive some of you American people are. You're really easily shockable.'

'There are a lot of us around and not all of us can live like in avant-garde movies.'

'Is it the word "screw" that shocks, or the fact that I do. Or the fact that I talk about it so disconnectedly?'

'Yes, the last.'

In that respect she reminded him of Sheryl, the openness with which she was ready to talk about her sex life, *wanted* to. He liked a little mystery. Maybe he was really old fashioned.

'You're a romantic.'

'I'm nothing. I'm not yet fully mature and aware of it, that's why I've come on this voyage to learn about life and meet people I wouldn't meet normally between Prospect Park and Waverly.'

'Do you write?'

'No.'

'But you'd like to write? You speak with such un-American turns of phrase.'

'My mother was half English, she was brought up in Canterbury, and she taught me how to speak. I also read a great deal.'

'What about your father?'

'Killed in Vietnam when I was a kid.'

They talked about what she read, what he read, there was a

small area of contact but she was no bookworm. She preferred the movies, considered herself a film buff.

'What are you going to do when you get home?' he asked.

'Find a job, and try and find somewhere to live in London. Convince my parents that I *can* look after myself, but until I'm actually twenty-one, which is in a couple of months, they're not going to allow themselves to believe that.'

'You're a Scorpio then,' he said.

'Oh wow! Are you into that?'

And he was on home ground.

Oh! Was he on home ground.

After experiencing the early premonitions when he was in his teens he had spent a good deal of time learning the ins and outs of the Zodiac. *The Modern Textbook of Astrology*, which was not modern at all, had been his Bible. While his shyness with the opposite sex was a setback to getting the girl he wanted, his unexpected knowledge of the future had won him more than just admiring attention. Martha, who had begged him to read her palm and about whom he had predicted a life abroad, had gone to the Argentine the following semester. Anne, losing her mother's gold bracelet and finding it, on his instructions, in the back seat of her boy-friend's car. Ruth passing her exams when she was sure she would fail. After such successful readings he had known that it wasn't luck or coincidence, but a genuine gift. Then he had seen death when reading Jackie's tarot cards, an unmistakable series of disasters, had been reprimanded by her parents for frightening her and they had all been killed in a coach crash.

He had soft-pedalled then, been cautious when reading hands, seldom tried the tarots.

'What sign are you?' Cathy asked.

'I don't believe so much in astrology,' he said. 'But I do a bit of palm reading.'

'You do? What's heading my way?' And she held out her hand, and he stretched out and took it.

She was warm, the lines were very clear, but he did not go by the lines. He did not know what he went by, his imaginings, he supposed, inspired by the obvious.

He concentrated, both fell silent so that the throb of the ship's engines dominated the cabin.

She had been lying about her boy-friend, he got that. She had been lying about her parents as well. An anxiety about her image perhaps, nothing serious. They existed, but weren't of paramount importance to her. He couldn't tell her that right now.

'I'm sorry, I'm not getting anything,' he said after a while. 'All I'm aware of at the moment is the movement of the ship. I'm not really in the right mood.'

'But what do the lines indicate. You didn't look.'

'I don't go by lines,' he admitted. 'I go by psychometry.'

'Psychometry?' The word was not familiar to her though she pretended to know what it meant.

'Second sight. I know things about people by touching them, or about objects by holding them.'

'You're clairvoyant?'

'Sometimes. But I never know when. I can't turn it on like a tap, nor am I ever sure I'm right.'

'Don't people tell you?'

'It's not something I talk about. I've never wanted to be regarded as a freak.'

'A freak! It's a *gift*!' She sat on the very edge of the bunk and started opening her small knitted bag. 'Can you tell me anything about this?' She handed him a short gold propelling pencil; it had a silver tip and a little ring at the other end to hang it from a chain.

He took it, studied it. 'Eversharp 14 carat gold' it read, a 1930s bauble which business men stuffed in their waistcoat pockets along with a gold timepiece and champagne swizzle sticks.

He looked at it, let it lie flat in the palm of his hand. Then he gripped it fairly tightly, let himself fall back in the armchair and closed his eyes.

He knew she was looking at him with interest, scepticism, amusement, disbelief, but liking his act. He was also aware that if he wanted to impress her he would have to be right, pick up the first feelings and describe them immediately. That was how it had worked in the past, instant reactions before other influences could come through. Not let the image remind him of something *he* had actually experienced.

An image came through gratifyingly clear.

'I'm in a restaurant,' he said. 'In a large room, a huge room, a theatre, the auditorium of a theatre perhaps, gold, blue ornamentation, but there are tables. I'm in a restaurant, a banqueting room. I'm at a banquet surrounded by men in tuxedos, in dinner jackets, white tie and tails, the women in long dresses, jewellery, there are long tables, a series of long tables, flowers, waiters in black jackets with long white aprons, there's a band playing . . . I can't hear the music. Now a man, a small man with a pointed beard and pince-nez, wearing one of those solid shirt fronts . . . he has grey hair . . . but balding in the front. He is standing up and there is something about royalty . . . there is talk of the Prince of Wales, the King . . . people are standing, the man with the beard is standing, he is fingering his beard very nervously . . . '

A loud hollow noise in the cabin pipes startled him. He opened his eyes.

Cathy was sitting looking at him wide eyed, her mouth open.

'Can I have the pencil back a moment please?'

He handed it to her.

'Shit!' she said, dropping it. 'It's hot!'

He picked it up. It was hot. Not burning hot, but hot enough for her to react. He handed it back to her a little unsettled himself now.

She held it by the ring, looked at it, studied it.

'How did you know?'

'How did I know what?'

'How did you know about my grandfather meeting the Prince of Wales?'

'I didn't.'

'Grandad went to his banquet, he was chairman of his company or club, or something to do with the City Fathers. I'm not sure, and he was host to the Prince of Wales . . . that was in 1935 before he became King then abdicated . . . '

'I didn't know anything about it, English history isn't exactly my forte.'

'But you must have known something.'

'Second sight. That's all.'

'Can you do that with anything?'

'With any object that has been cared for, loved you might say. People usually give you something that they value and that means that their vibrations get attached to these things. Somehow I pick them up. We all do, only I have this faculty developed more than other people.'

Cathy dug into her bag again but, unable to find anything quickly, she tipped all the contents out beside her on the bunk. Comb, hairbrush, diary, purse, powder compact, lipstick, lighter, address book, cigarette packet, eye shadow, rouge. She held up the blue plastic lighter.

'That any good?'

'You bought it on 76th Street at the corner kiosk,' he said jokingly.

'It was given me by someone who bought it in L.A. But how about this?'

She held up a folded piece of paper.

'What is it?'

'You tell me. I want you to tell me. Can you? It's something pretty powerful.'

'I can try.'

He had never done it before with paper. Rings, brooches, metal objects yes, but he had no idea what would happen. The gentle roll of the ship, the peace and guaranteed tranquillity of the cabin might however be conducive to a surprise.

He layed the folded piece of paper on the flat of his hand, placed the other hand on top of it and held it up to his forehead as though praying. He wasn't sure why he did that except to impress her, yet he had done it rather naturally, the gesture had been instinctive.

Words appeared in his mind, a name, 'Bill', 'Dear', then not so much strings of words, sentences or paragraphs, as the clear message of sadness, anger, revolt, dismissal, contempt. The word 'despise' was singled out, the signature Cathy.

'It's a letter written by you,' he said, 'to someone called Bill. The exact words do not come to me exactly but the mood is angry, hurt, yet I feel that what is expressed is false, overall the vibrations tell me the writer was insincere. It's a copy of your goodbye letter to Bill.'

He opened his eyes.

She was astonished.

'You're a magician. That's absolutely incredible.'

He was surprised, yet not surprised.

'How *do* you do it?'

'I have no idea . . . Except that some time ago I accepted the fact that we all have the ability to develop ourselves, that we have the mechanism. I have never denied that belief, I let things happen and do not analyse. In short I force myself to be simple. Mediums and people who claim to have psychic powers have always been regarded as simple people, because they do not question. I have forced myself not to question. An image comes into my head, I release it, I don't keep it in there to try and work out why it came. Images, visions, ideas come to you through some form of vibration. You try it.'

He slipped his watch off his wrist and handed it to her. 'Just hold that and tell me immediately what you get from it.'

Cathy took the watch, closed her eyes tight and remained silent.

'I'm not getting anything. My mind's a complete blank.'

'The mind is never really a complete blank.'

'O.K. so I'm thinking that I'm sitting here on your bunk with my eyes tightly closed holding your watch. The vibes are purely in the present.'

He was disappointed, he had hoped she would reveal something.

Then the bell on the tannoy sounded, announcing the evening meal.

'I'm really hungry, are you?' Cathy said, handing him back the watch and collecting her things together. 'Are you well enough to eat in public? The captain's table is nearly fun. Specially the Bourbon Dragon.'

And as they made their way to the dining room she gave him a description of their fellow passengers. All ten straight out of an Agatha Christie whodunnit, and dating from the same period. There was the silent couple, the Christian couple, the Bourbon Dragon who drank Bourbon, the two queens who were terrified of their awful vice being discovered and three civil engineers who only talked amongst themselves about engineering and their part in the Far East during the war.

All were already sitting down waiting for the steward to serve the food. The Christian couple were pointedly clasping their hands in prayer and whispering Grace to make everyone feel guilty, the Bourbon Dragon stared at them in disbelief and after they'd finished bawled out 'What the hell difference does that rubbish make to the meal could you tell me? We're all eating the same garbage, will yours taste any better?'

To which the Christian gentleman softly replied in fear and trepidation 'We are not expecting better food, we are thanking the Lord for providing it.'

'The Lord didn't provide it, we provided it by paying an exorbitant fare for the privilege of coming on board this steamer!'

At that moment the last passenger came in, Cathy's octogenarian cabin mate who was so deaf that she did not hear the strong reprimand from the Bourbon Dragon for keeping them all waiting.

'You can serve the hor's d'oeuvre now, Lars,' she screamed. 'And recharge my glass. Christ, what a crowd of lousy bums you all are!'

'Paul is no lousy bum,' Cathy decided to say. 'He's psychic.' Which he found extremely embarrassing.

'That's all we need on this trip. Two Jesus freaks, a deaf and dumb cripple, two closet queens and a medium. Can you get in contact with my husband and ask him why the hell he left all his money to my sister?'

'No, but I can tell you that the 26th of August is a day of danger for you,' Paul answered, to his own surprise.

'How the hell do you know that?' She leaned across the table at him and stared him in the face. She was a little drunk, enough to overact the part of the alcoholic, which she wasn't. But the pose helped her. 'Why should it be dangerous for me?'

'I can't tell you. All I know is that the 26th August is meaningful to you. I suspect that it is something that may have already happened, something unexpected, something which shocked you.'

'I'll tell you something sonny. It means nothing to me at all!'

'I'm sorry.'

And he was.

While looking at her and listening to her insulting the two Christians, the date 26th August had come very clearly into the mind.

Then he noted that the Christian couple were looking at each other, the husband trying to restrain his wife from saying something, but it was stronger than her.

'The 26th August was the day we embraced the church,' the husband said quickly before his wife could speak.

'It was the day our little boy died. The 26th August last year. He had leukemia,' the wife corrected.

'Oh, you characters have a way of making people like me feel really shitty,' the Bourbon Dragon said, and she got up and left the dining room.

Cathy looked at Paul amazed. How could he have known anything about these people?

The two queens were fascinated by his display of intuitiveness and immediately asked him a number of questions about clairvoyancy. The captain and the first officer then joined the table, the conversation changed and he was spared any further need to demonstrate his capabilities.

All the same he was again surprised by what he had done. One day, maybe, he would get used to the idea that he was truly psychic. For the time being it was still rather like a hobby.

After the meal he strolled along the deck with Cathy, pleased that he had been wise enough not to eat too much and that, so far, it seemed he would keep it all down. The weather, however, had turned stormy, the ship was rolling, the wind was gusty and it started to rain.

He put his arm naturally round Cathy as they zig-zagged along the deck, then she looked up at him.

'Shall we go to your cabin?'

He turned her round and guided her towards the steep steps leading below deck.

He switched on the cabin light, held the heavy door open for her, but as she came in she switched the light off and moved towards the porthole.

'Let's look at the sea.'

She settled by the porthole, kneeling on the locker. He stood behind her, waited for his eyes to get accustomed to the darkness. The sea was like a mass of black ink swelling and dipping, the ship's light highlighting the white foam, a wave occasionally thundering against the thick glass leaving a trace of salt when the water had drained away.

Her hair smelt of lemon, sweet lemon, lemon and honeysuckle maybe.

'It's nice here,' she said quietly.

There was a warmth about her closeness that he was afraid of wanting. He feared rejection. His timidity was incredible. Another man would have asked her outright, 'Let's go to bed,' or, 'Let's screw.' He couldn't say things like that. He did not know how to.

'Can I stay the night?' she asked.

'Of course.' He put his hand on her small shoulder. Was he reading her mind or his own?

'Let's get into bed then, I'm cold,' she added.

She broke away and started to undress.

By the little light that came in through the porthole he could discern the whiteness of her skin as she pulled off her thick sweater and took down her jeans. She was right there next to him in the dark, nude; he could not see her breasts but he could sense them.

'Which is your bunk?'

'The bottom one.' His voice sounded high.

He slowly undid his shirt, thanked God for the dark; if there was something he really couldn't handle it was undressing in front of a girl for the first time. Sheryl had been different, he'd been half cut anyway. Right now he was stone cold sober. He took off his own sweater, his T-shirt, dropped his jeans, hesitated for a moment, then took down his briefs. He was already in too high a state of excitement to pretend he was blasé about the whole business.

'I hope the sea is going to get really rough,' she said a little nervously as he slipped into the narrow bunk beside her. The sheets were coarse and now he could feel this young, warm, silk-like skin beside him.

'Why?' His throat was so tight he could not have said another word.

'Then we don't have to do much . . . just lie here and the ship does it all for you.'

The bunk was very small so they lay facing each other, their lips glued together, his arms holding her tight, her arms holding him. He became aware of the rolling, the sudden dipping when he didn't expect it. The motion unsettled him. For a moment he thought he was going to feel unwell, then she moved, trying to get under him and, as he lifted himself up, the ship dropped again as though into an abyss, leaving his stomach behind. The acidity of the captain's wine came into his throat, he knew his breath would smell, then the ship climbed right up and dropped again and he knew he wasn't going to be able to live through it.

'Sorry,' he managed to say, and got out of the bunk.

'What's happening?' she asked, disappointed.

He couldn't talk. He made it across the cabin, over into the lavatory, and the dinner came up. The pickled herrings, the smoked fish, the overstewed lamb and all the fat he hadn't wanted, the ice cream . . .

He moaned because it helped, wanted sympathy, was cold, knelt down in front of the pan again, retching. He tried to close the door but when he moved he was sick again.

Exhausted, he eventually stood up only to feel the ship lurch again, and his stomach tighten.

'Sorry, Paul,' Cathy called out, 'but one of the things I can't take is someone being sick.'

And he was half aware of her dressing quickly and leaving the cabin.

He was too wretched to care. He was thankful in fact that she had gone. He didn't want her to see him like this. He found a towel, held it to his mouth, switched on the light and made it back to the bunk where he lay down and waited for the next spasm.

It came. Two dips and two upward heaves and more of the billiousness flooded his mouth. He stumbled back to the lavatory and stayed there most of the night, shivering, damp eyed, staring at the bowl which should have been one of the most unattractive sights in the world but somehow provided him with more comfort than anything else he could imagine.

In the middle of the sickness, in what seemed to be the dead of night, he became aware of a quite sudden and remarkable calm, a total lack of movement. He heard whoop-like sirens some distance off answering each other across the expanse of sea. It was quite warm, still, the atmosphere ghostly.

Carefully he got up and went to the porthole to look out. Some two hundred yards away there loomed a huge tanker with only a few lights showing, and some distance beyond another was silhouetted against a reddish sky. The sea was pitch black, moving, yet not.

His sickness had vanished, his stomach totally settled, he wanted some fresh air, wanted to walk up on deck, so he dressed quickly and left the cabin.

Outside there was complete silence as though the sea around had been enveloped in a shroud and there was light coming from the starboard side. He moved across. More ships sailing close by. They were in a convoy, going *through* a convoy, for all the other ships were heading in the opposite direction. Then there was a frightening flash of whiteness which lit up the whole sky, followed by a thunderous boom. It was as though a giant mallet had struck the side of the ship next to them and he saw a yawning hole in the steel and the sea surging in and flames leaping up from a fierce fire within. All around flares lit up the sky, men were throwing themselves off the burning ship, lifeboats were being cut from the davits and went crashing down to the water. He watched as this huge mass of iron and steel bubbled down into the sea, swallowed up like a toy boat in a bath.

He turned round to see who else was with him only to realise that he was alone. Was no one else aware of what was happening? Or was he dreaming? He took several deep breaths, looked at his hands, bit his lip. It hurt, he was awake, very awake.

He went up to the quarterdeck, tried to find the door into the wheelhouse and saw the quartermaster at the helm, apparently totally unaware of what was going on around them. Then the radio operator came out of the radio room.

'Evening, sir. Passengers are not truly allowed up here, please,' he said in a strong accent.

'I know, I was wondering why it was so calm?' And as he said this he realised that it was not calm at all, that there was quite a wind and that the ship had started dipping and rolling again.

'It is not that calm, sir. It is probably that you have found your sea-legs.'

'Is that what it is?' Paul said, now playing dumb. He could guess what had happened to him. A dream, another vision.

'Come in out of the cold anyway now you are up here. This is the quartermaster, Sven.'

Sven smiled. 'Come to join the middle watch? What is happening, Sparks?'

'I've got another one of those signals, the third tonight.'

'What is it in this time, German?'

'No. English. "SS *Sandpiper* hit on port side. U-boat spotted east-south-east starboard . . ." '

'In morse?'

'All but this last one. I heard a voice.'

'What did that German one read again?'

' "15.23. 60 degrees north. 01.17 degrees east. Range 880 yards, estimated speed of tanker 6 knots. One torpedo fired. No. 2 tube. Explosion heard, damage caused by hit aft of funnel. Upper deck buckled. Ship now appears to have a five degree list, and sinking." '

'Any identification codes?'

'Market Garden.'

'Doesn't mean anything to me,' the quartermaster said, shrugging his shoulders.

'Shall I log them?'

'Yes. Best log them.'

'What is unsettling,' the radio operator went on, 'is that the position given is right here, as though we were in the middle of a convoy, considering the interference I am getting.'

Paul watched the bows of the ship dip down into the black sea and white spray splash over the bows.

They had been through a time warp, the convoy belonged to the past, but if he tried to tell them they would never believe him.

He asked, however.

'Don't you sometimes pick up radio messages belonging to the past?'

The radio officer turned to look at him, his blue eyes studying him carefully.

'If we do, we do not usually like admitting it. Are you a journalist?'

'No. Not at all.'

'Well, I have heard of radio operators picking up strange signals, even television programmes in mid-Atlantic, but never messages from the past. That belongs to legends like the *Flying Dutchman* and the *Marie Celeste.*'

Paul shrugged his shoulders apologetically and made for the door.

'Or the Bermuda Triangle,' the quartermaster added.

CHAPTER FOUR

Cathy was standing over him when he woke up. She might have been there some time. He was lying on the bunk propped up by a pillow, his head thumping, his mouth thick and dry.

'Are you still feeling sick?'

'Better, thanks.'

'You look terrible. You're green.'

The steward came in with a cup of tea which she had obviously asked him to bring. Paul sat up and took the cup gratefully.

'It was a bad night, Force Seven. Pretty well everyone was sick, except you of course,' the steward said turning to Cathy.

It wasn't much, but enough for Paul to pick up on. An exchange of intimate humour. The look of two beings attracted to each other and promising to do something about it.

'Best leave the patient to rest,' the steward suggested and opened the cabin door wide for Cathy.

He had been an excuse for them to meet, he felt.

She looked over her shoulder, smiled a goodbye, but nothing more. Their intimacy of yesterday was over, forgotten, he had been seasick at the wrong moment and the penalty was to miss out on her altogether.

Until she got bored and came back to him for more psychic demonstrations perhaps?

But she didn't get bored.

She didn't return to see how he was, and when the sea had calmed down and he was well enough to walk the deck again, he looked for her everywhere, but she was nowhere to be found.

Eventually he asked the Bourbon Dragon if he had seen her. 'Playing checkers with that blond adonis, sweetheart, and if I had a body like hers I'd do exactly the same thing!'

He ventured down to the crew's quarters, beyond the 'No

Access' notice, down one passage, then another and heard her laughter, her giggles coming from a cabin.

It hurt.

He hadn't expected that.

But it hurt.

She wasn't fickle, she wasn't a brainless girl, she was intelligent, they had much in common, which was why it stung. She preferred the company of a Mr Macho to him.

Because he'd been sick?

He went up on deck again, admitted that he still didn't feel strong enough to stay up and look at the sea, so went back to his bunk to lie down.

The evening supper bell rang and, though he wanted no food, he forced himself along to the dining room to see if she would be there, to be with her, to pick up the threads. But she never turned up.

Mr Macho was there, smiling as always, serving up the chicken gruel, insisting that it would do Paul good to get something in his stomach. He drank it down, it helped, but he swore that he would never go on a ship again. He could have flown. Or was it perhaps Sheryl Lidman, psychic herself, sticking pins into a Plasticine image of him because he had deserted her?

He couldn't eat any more, excused himself from the silent company and walked around the deserted ship, then went down to the steward's quarters again. Bravely he knocked on the door.

'Yes?' She was in there still.

He opened the door. Cathy was lying nude in the steward's bunk just covering the top of herself with the sheet, eating supper from a tray, a bottle of champagne in a bucket by her side.

'Hi! How *are* you?' She was delighted to see him. No apologies, no recriminations, to her it was all very natural. 'Feeling better?'

'Yes, thanks.'

'Want some of this?' She offered him a glass of champagne. 'It's all free. Lars has got just about everything you could wish for down here. Certainly knows how to please a lady.'

No mention of last night, no allegiance, no loyalty. She'd

slept with Lars, hopped from his own bed to the steward's in one go. He hated her.

'Why are you looking at me like that?' she asked.

'Like what?'

'Like a hurt husband.'

'I'm probably jealous,' he said honestly.

'Oh . . . I'm sorry. I just don't like missing out on a good thing when it's handed to you. You must agree he's quite a catch, though he dyes his hair. He's not really blond, just feels he should be. Want a piece of chicken?'

'No thanks, I'm still not feeling a hundred per cent.'

'I don't think boats agree with you.'

'No,' he said, then left as she picked up a piece of lettuce and dipped it into a silver sauce boat of mayonnaise.

Not only did boats not agree with him, but the people on boats did not agree with him, and slowly he realised that he was incredibly angry, an anger that was building up inside him and doing him no good at all.

With all his knowledge, with all his psychic gifts, she preferred to lie with that . . . Lars!

He returned to his cabin.

His bunk reminded him of her, the sheets were cold when they could have been warm with her body. He'd had her there next to him, naked, and because he had been sick, because he had a weak stomach, she had left him.

He understood her up to a point, but could not swallow that she was enjoying the other's company.

Christ! If he had any psychic powers worth their salt, if he could conjure up any evil, then he would do so now!

He switched off the light and kneeled on the locker to look out of the porthole at the sea shining in the moonlight. Now that it was calm, now he was fit, and she was lying in someone else's bunk!

Was it her he wanted to hurt? Or him?

It was the steward because of the smirk on his face, the constant hint that only men with a capital Macho could take the sea. Well he wanted to inflict sickness in the man, wanted him to suffer exactly the same as he had, willed Lars to vomit on her. That would teach them both! If there was anything in him that could inflict discomfort from a distance, he wanted to test it now. Like Faustus he was ready to give his soul to the Devil in exchange for a sign. Not his soul, nor the Devil either, but he promised the void around him that if he was shown some sign that he had kinetic powers at his command, he would work on himself and achieve whatever was wanted of him.

He found his way to the bunk, lay down on it fully clothed and concentrated hard on an image of the steward Lars coming in with his white jacket, handing him the tea, smiling, leaving. Lars at lunch serving them all at the captain's table, Lars giving him a particularly fat ration of lamb to make him sick, Lars eyeing Cathy. God he had been slow on that uptake!

Then he concentrated on them both lying in the bunk, hairy chest, tattooed arms, with Cathy nestling close to him, and like a camera lens he moved down the length of his body to his stomach, saw the steward's navel in his mind's eye, the black hair coming down from the chest, up from the pubic area which Cathy had been so proud to hint at; he then imagined laser rays going into that stomach, penetrating that white belly. Then he sat up and shook his head.

He was going mad.

He was living a comic strip cartoon and going mad.

He had no idea what time of night it was but he was woken up by a frantic banging on the door. He switched on the light and shouted, 'Come in!'

It was Cathy in a terrible state. She wore a T-shirt, jeans, no shoes, her hair was a mess and she looked pale, terrified.

'Paul, something awful has happened . . . '

He blinked, sat up, got off the bed. 'What?'

'Lars . . . ' This time she rushed to the bathroom and was sick. A violent sickness through groans and whimpers. When she turned she looked even worse, her eyes puffed with tears of fear.

'What's happened, Cathy? Tell me, what's happened?'

'It's so horrible I can't . . . Look . . . ' she held out her hand, it was red with blood. 'The bed's seeped in it. He had a haemorrhage . . . we were making love and suddenly . . . he had this convulsion. Oh God, Paul . . . ' She flung herself at him, talked into his shoulder through shivers. 'He was having these convulsions and I thought he was . . . and . . . then I felt something sticky over my stomach, and his whole body became rigid, his whole body solid like a log of wood . . . and his face froze into his death mask, and when I looked down there was just blood everywhere.

'We'd better go . . . '

'They're all there,' she said. 'The captain, the acting ship's doctor, the whole crew's there. He had some sort of internal haemorrhage . . . I just had to talk to someone who . . . I could . . . trust.'

'Try and calm down, take a deep breath.'

'Will you come with me? All my clothes are in there. I'm not even sure I was supposed to be with him. I don't know what they'll think . . . Jesus!'

'Put these socks on,' he said, handing her his own pair. 'Or you'll catch cold.'

She led the way down the familiar steps to the crew's quarters, along the corridor to Lars's cabin. Two seamen were standing outside talking. They made way for them on seeing Cathy.

Paul looked in.

Lars was lying flat on his back, naked. His body had been laid out full length on the bunk half covered with a sheet. On the floor in a corner were other sheets stained with blood.

The ship's doctor looked up.

'What happened?' Cathy asked.

'Not sure, a haemorrhage, something very wrong inside. Maybe he was in a fight and someone hit him very hard below the belt. There are bruises in the lower part of the abdomen. Won't be able to tell much till we have the result of an autopsy.'

Paul looked at the body. 'Maybe someone had hit him below the belt. There were bruises in the lower part of the abdomen . . . '

God! He really didn't want it to be true.

The captain invited them up to his cabin where he offered them both tea.

'There'll have to be an official enquiry when we get to Southampton of course, but it would help me if you were willing to answer a few questions now, and maybe make a statement.'

'Of course, anything.' Cathy was desperate to help.

The captain sat down behind his desk, found his glasses, a pad. 'I'll just make a few notes.' It was obvious that the idea of cross questioning Cathy was unsettling. Men falling overboard, knifing each other in the boiler room, a mutiny, hanging them from the yard-arm, keelhauling them was perhaps routine, but questioning a twenty year old on why she had gone to bed with one of his crew was something else.

'Perhaps you could tell me what happened?'

Cathy had asked Paul to accompany her, to help her get through the interview. They had asked if the captain minded and he had been delighted, somehow another man present helped the situation. The captain didn't know that Cathy was one of the girls with whom one did not have to pull punches.

'I became friends with Lars during the first two days and he invited me down to his cabin to have some champagne.'

The captain raised an eyebrow, but said nothing.

'I accepted. One thing led to another as I fully expected it would, we got into bed and when we were making love he had this sort of fit . . .'

'Had you been to bed with him before? I am asking that not to pry into your private life, but simply to know whether you had any prior knowledge of his health.'

'No. It was the first time. I knew nothing about him really. Nothing at all.'

'Did he mention to you that he frequently had visitors in his cabin? I mean, did he give you the impression that this was something he did often?'

'Yes, I suppose so. I mean he seemed very casual about it.'

'He was in no way disturbed, said nothing to you about pains in his stomach or having a quarrel?'

'No, nothing at all. It just happened very suddenly, like a bolt out of the blue.'

And after they left the bewildered captain, making their way back to Paul's cabin, Cathy said, 'It was as though you'd wanted to get your revenge on me for deserting you when you were sick. It was as though you'd willed him to be ill just as we were making love, to get your own back.'

They docked in Southampton on the morning of the seventh day. They had been watching the coast coming up for some time and it was now comforting to see the solidity of land, of greenery and buildings, though all much lower than he had imagined.

'They don't have skyscrapers in Europe,' Cathy explained. 'Or only a very few. Anyway that's the Isle of Wight, not the mainland proper yet.'

They had discussed their immediate plans, both were going to London, she would help him find a cheap room somewhere, though it wouldn't be easy, and when she had seen her parents and settled everything she promised they would meet again.

As they approached the harbour, the excitement of docking rose to fever pitch.

As Paul and Cathy leaned on the guard rail looking at all the activity of the quayside below, the radio officer tapped him on the shoulder.

'Could you spare a moment, sir? The captain would like to have a word with you.'

'With *me*?' Paul, puzzled, exchanged looks with Cathy, then followed the officer.

The captain, sitting behind his desk, smoking his pipe, genial, all smiles, got up when Paul came in and offered him a chair.

'Thank you for coming, Mr Saralyn. Please sit down. This is not official at all, just a personal curiosity I have about you.'

Paul sat down, still surprised.

'Yes. I have made this crossing many times, indeed I have been on the high seas for most of my life, but never have I had two such strange incidents as have occurred on this voyage.'

'Two?' Paul said.

'Three if you count Lars's death.'

The captain turned back a page of the log book in front of him, studied it, then looked up.

'During the night of the 8th numerous strange noises were heard over the radio. They were the sounds of war, of ships being torpedoed. Signals were received from four vessels all with 1939–40 codings, we even received a description of a sinking in German. It was as though we had intercepted the past . . .'

Paul said nothing.

'You were in the wheelhouse during the middle watch that night, as those interferences were being received.'

The captain smiled, did not seem to expect any comment. Paul let him go on.

'The following night, approximately an hour before Lars the steward died, Mr O'Keefe, the second mate, reported seeing two small children on the passenger deck. They were transparent and quite naked and stood in a high wind holding each other's hands but in no way showing signs that they were cold. He believed them to be ghosts.'

Paul managed not to show surprise, yet not be indifferent.

'Would you have any explanation for that?' the captain asked him directly.

'Not unless your ship is haunted.'

'Or somebody aboard was psychic?' The captain got up and came round to the front of the desk, then paced the small cabin, looking down at his boots. 'My grandmother was a medium, Mr Saralyn, which is why I asked you to come and speak with me. Many of us sailors think differently to land people because we are alone much of the time and have time to contemplate life, death and the supernatural. I happen to be interested in the occult. At sea one has plenty of time to read and think and one is much closer to the elements and under the constant surveillance of the universe. Your trick at dinner about the date of the 26th August was not a trick, and it was very impressive. I would be grateful if you could cast some light on the events I mentioned.'

The captain really expected an answer from him, respected him as a mature psychic.

'The convoy could have been an anxiety trace. There is a theory that when a number of people suffer a tragedy they leave traces of their anxieties in the ether around. Sometimes it is picked up by sensitive receivers.'

'Such as radio receivers?'

'Yes.'

'Or mediums such as yourself?'

'Possibly.'

The captain took one big stride towards his desk again and picked up a diary. 'I took this down from a book I was reading about the mysteries of the Bermuda Triangle. I read . . . "Reports tell of shining and pulsating lights seen in the night sky or beneath the sea, glowing fogs, the inexplicable loss or gain of time on air flights as well as the well witnessed appearances of 'phantom' ships appearing and disappearing in complete silence. Many of these reports touch on previously unreported phenomena which, although apparently unrelated, may be relevant to the overall mystery of psychic activities at sea . . ." '

Paul realised that the captain just wanted to talk, just wanted him to know that they were kindred spirits.

'And what of the ghostly children?' he asked.

'That I couldn't explain,' Paul said. 'Unless they were a warning of death?'

'The reason I ask you, Mr Saralyn, is that they were seen to be standing outside your cabin door. I thought you should know.'

They cleared customs by four o'clock and Paul was thankful Cathy knew her way around. He was too stunned by the captain's interview to be able to do more than just carry her bags as she led the way to the railway station, found the right train, sat him down in the right compartment, then went to ring up her parents, and get them something to eat.

She came back with some sandwiches and two burning cartons of tea. 'Paul, they're meeting me at the station, in London. I'd like to give you a lift, even invite you home, but under the circumstances I really can't. I hope you understand. I mean, leaving with one American and coming back with another . . . '

'Just point me in the direction of a hotel before we part,' he said.

She sat down next to him and he took her hand and squeezed it to reassure her that they were friends. She had been badly shaken by Lars's death, and her parents were obviously more of a problem than he understood.

'There's a small hotel in Paddington, which is quite a nice district, where you can get a comfortable room cheaply. It's in Sussex Gardens. It's more of a boarding house, called the "Bramber". Try that. The tube's nearby, and it's very central.'

And he said he would, and took his first sip of real English tea.

It was in the National Gallery that he saw the man for the fourth time and became suspicious.

He had been in London for five days, staying at the 'Bramber' as Cathy had suggested and had made out his own tourist schedule, the monuments, the museums, the art galleries and had become aware of the man at the Victoria and Albert, then the Tate, then at Harrods in the food department and now again in the Crivelli Room directly in from the main entrance.

The man looked very much the tourist, it was possible that he had by coincidence followed the same schedule, but it was too unlikely and it unsettled him.

Why would anyone want to follow him? Because of what had happened on the ship? Had Lars's death been recorded as murder, was he a suspect?

He stayed quite a time studying the paintings, noting that the man, a camera hanging from one shoulder, a small hat, a white raincoat, looked Scandinavian.

Paul deliberately left quickly, passing him as he walked out, made for the Charing Cross Road, up past the theatres on the right, to the string of bookshops he had already visited.

He paused several times to look at second-hand paperbacks displayed on the stands, looked in the plate glass window at the reflection of the shops opposite, and there he was across the street.

Cat and mouse time.

Every detective movie he'd seen had given him a lesson on what to do. Move slowly without drawing suspicion of knowledge, then dodge down a side street and into the subway.

He could lose him, but he was curious. He wanted to make absolutely sure that this was not an illusion.

He felt hungry, needed to eat, so retraced his steps down to Leicester Square with all its cinemas, and went into a hamburger bar. He sat down at a table by the window and ordered his meal, with a Coke, and watched the world go by. In among the world was his shadow. He got a really good look at him this time, black shoes, blue trousers, a blue sports jacket under the raincoat, pale creamy shirt, greyish tie. A man in his late forties, Mr Interpol himself.

Mr Interpol walked past the hamburger bar, got lost for a moment among the people crowding the pedestrian precinct, then disappeared, probably to hide round the corner.

Paul finished his meal, drank his Coke, and waited to pay the bill. He could of course concentrate on the man's belly and have him explode.

It was a sick thought. Distasteful, frightening. He had managed to avoid thinking about the whole episode and even the remote possibility that he had such powers.

He paid the bill and left, not looking back but making straight for the Piccadilly Underground. He queued to get a ticket on the Bakerloo Line for Paddington, then went down the escalators.

Two years before a hundred or so people had been massacred down here when an IRA bomb had gone off. He wasn't sure why he knew about this, something he had read in the papers and remembered. Unless it was an anxiety trace . . .

Down the escalator and along the access tunnels, it was nearing five o'clock, rush hour time. He pushed his way through to the platform, studied the advertisements then looked up and back.

Mr Interpol was there hiding behind a newspaper in good private eye tradition. It was unbelievable.

The train came in, the rush of air, the noise, the chaos. He did the *French Connection* trick, got in, then got out again just as the doors were closing. The train moved off and for a brief moment the platform was empty and he knew he had lost his shadow.

Hearing a train coming in on the next platform going in the opposite direction, he rushed through and got on to that. After three stops he got off, then took a cab to a cinema.

Because his small residential hotel was part of a terrace of houses set back from the main thoroughfare reached by a private roadway, cabs always had difficulty in getting to it due to the line of parked cars. So he stopped the taxi where it was convenient and walked the rest of the way.

It was purely by chance that he saw the man sitting in a beige saloon car some twenty yards past the hotel. His shadow again, hatless, but somehow unmistakable, just sitting there behind the wheel facing his direction so that he could be seen arriving.

He went into the small hotel, up the musty carpeted stairs, into his first floor room, was about to put the light on, but did not.

He went to the window, very gently, very quietly opened it and leaned out. It was getting dark, he looked down the roadway at the car but couldn't tell whether there was still someone in it.

Was he allowing his imagination to run away with his guilt? For that was what he felt about Lars – guilt. He could not be certain that he was responsible, but *that* was one hell of a coincidence. And the apparition of the children to a total stranger, a warning then to others that he, Paul Saralyn, was dangerous.

He went to lie down on the bed.

Had he inadvertently killed someone when they had appeared three years ago? Had he been responsible for his mother's tragedy by a subconscious death wish?

And what was he worrying about now? That the authorities – whoever they might be – were keeping an eye on him?

He needed to talk to someone.

Sheryl Lidman?

Cathy Morrow?

Well, not the former. He had shaken her off and didn't want to get involved with her again. Anyway it was a good excuse to contact Cathy.

It was ten o'clock. He couldn't ring her because that might complicate her life. It would be best to go down to her place in the morning, a reason for adventure. She lived somewhere south of London. It would be interesting.

He closed his eyes and tried to imagine what she was doing. An image of her slipping out of her jeans that first night with her in the cabin came to mind. The thought of her excited him. If he could attract her somehow, he would really like to be with her.

Then he got a clear picture of her standing in a bright blue and white kitchen, in a white T-shirt, jeans, but wearing a Snoopy apron. She was on the telephone and looking horrified.

She hung the receiver up on the wall and turned to him. 'Daddy's just had an accident!'

He sat up.

A premonition he should warn her about? Or wishful thinking drama that would make him more important in her eyes.

He lay down again and made his mind a blank.

He awoke an hour or so later feeling cold, and hungry, thirsty, uncomfortable and restless, and a plan of action started forming in his mind.

He got up, crossed to the window and looked out very cautiously. The beige car was still there. Nearly midnight now and he was still being watched.

In the dark he moved away from the window, found his shoes, reached out for his money on the dresser, his passport. He stuffed them in his pockets, it was all he would need, the joy of travelling light.

In the silent blackness he tiptoed downstairs and waited, holding his breath. He then eased the front door open and slipped out, stood on the steps in the shadows of the portico.

The man was still in the beige car presumably satisfied that his prey had gone to bed. Would he go home now, or would he stay there all night?

Paul waited some five minutes, then darted across the roadway to hide between the row of parked cars and the bushes. Through the back windows and windscreens he could still see the man. The beige saloon had a short-wave aerial, which meant the man was probably not working alone.

Tense, but stimulated, Paul stealthily moved back along the row of parked cars intent on making a getaway, but the beige car door opened and the man got out.

It was a warm muggy night, he only wanted a smoke in the fresh air. Paul crouched down and waited. He could not move, could not give his position away. Cramp set in, so he carefully took his weight on his hands and sat down. He could not see the man now, but could hear him pace up and down. Slowly the man came along the roadway, paused right outside the hotel, then went back to his car.

He could stand up suddenly and make a dash for it down the road of course, but that would only give away the fact that he knew he was being watched, which was not the answer. He wanted to get clean away without the spy knowing.

Then a car turned into the roadway, its headlights casting clear cut shadows under the parked cars. Paul froze, the car passed him, an identical model to Mr Interpol's only black, with a short-wave aerial.

The night relief?

Whoever it was having him screened obviously considered him important.

Would his room be bugged as well?

He watched the second car draw up next to the first, the two men exchange greetings, information, then the beige car started up, moving out of the way to let the second take its place in the row.

Paul waited.

The first man let his engine run, got out and had more words with his successor. Paul took the opportunity of the diversionary noise. Making his way quickly in the gutter between the bushes and the parked vehicles, he reached the main thoroughfare, walked calmly along the pavement under the bright street lights and took the first turning off.

For the rest of the night Mr Interpol II would believe him to be in bed asleep. He had time to put distance between them.

He had time to get to Cathy.

CHAPTER FIVE

He asked a taxi to take him to a reasonable hotel in the Victoria area where he knew the railway station was for the south. He spent the night in a much more comfortable room secure in the knowledge that he was no longer being tailed.

After a hearty English breakfast in bed the following morning he rang up Cathy at nine, feeling that at that hour she had the right to be phoned by friends, American males or not.

He told her it was vital that he should see her and she brightly, happily suggested he should come down for lunch. Both her parents would be away for the day and they would have the house to themselves.

She gave him all the instructions he needed on how to get there, including the times of trains to a place called Redhill, which was the nearest station. And he left the hotel.

The journey through the southern suburbs of London, with the rows of neat low houses and gardens backing on to the railway line was as silent as it was extraordinary. He had a whole carriage to himself, enjoyed looking out of the window. Though some of the scenery was untidy, with the debris of manufactured goods in the yards behind small factories, parts were beautiful, expanses of green fields, lush heavy trees, cows, farmhouses, then back again to suburbia.

At Redhill station he got out and walked alone down the exit steps, meeting only a few late commuters going to their offices in the City.

He followed Cathy's directions. It was not far enough to warrant a taxi, though a good walk. It was a pleasant sunny day and he started off at a brisk pace, asking twice if he was heading in the right direction.

Lodge House could be seen as you came up the hill on the left, Cathy had said. 'A low white two storey house, the name is on the gates.'

He saw the name on the gates, and just as he turned in to walk up the gravel drive he also saw the dark blue car with a man sitting in the driver's seat minding his own business too much, and a short-wave aerial at the back.

She was being watched.

He managed not to hesitate but went straight up to the house, to the front door and rang the old bell-pull.

She came to the door quickly and threw her arms round his neck, genuinely pleased to see him. She had tied two little bows in her hair above the ears, pulling her curly hair back, which made her look even younger. She wore a white T-shirt, jeans, and a Snoopy apron.

'Are you hungry?' she asked, leading the way in.

'Fairly . . . '

'I'm ravenous. I prepared spaghetti, was waiting for you to come before starting. Could we eat now?'

'Sure.'

'I've opened one of Dad's bottles of wine. Not his best but I hope you like it.'

The kitchen was bright, modern, painted blue and white with low windows overlooking a pleasant garden with a lawn leading down to an apple orchard between high privet hedges which hid it from its neighbours. A white telephone hung on the wall by the door.

'Have you lived here long?'

'I was born here.'

'In this house?'

'In this very house. In the room above us in fact.'

He sat down at a large round table, white, with a spotlight shining down on it. It was clinical rather than romantic.

'How is it all going?' he asked. 'With your parents, I mean.'

'Fine. I've been forgiven in exchange for good behaviour. Providing I give them the impression I'm settling down, which means staying at home nights and watching television with them, all is well. It's lunacy isn't it? I mean I can go up to London during the day and get screwed for five hours, but if I'm there next to them when the sun goes down, then butter doesn't melt in my mouth.'

She placed a steaming bowl of spaghetti on the table and started dishing out.

He poured out the wine enjoying the domesticity of the little scene.

'Thing is, I've been offered a job in France. Monte Carlo, no less,' she said.

'What sort of job?'

'Travel agency. Nothing too exciting, but imagine living down there!'

'Do you speak French?'

'Un peux, mais pas beaucoup. That's not the point. It's because I speak English they want me. Friend of Daddy's, of course.'

'When would you go?'

'Pretty soon. Like the end of the month. You could come too, I thought. Maybe we could share a flat or something? I couldn't afford one alone, rents are astronomical, but we could live in the back country.'

He liked the idea. He'd even be able to pay Signor Capuela a duty visit without getting too involved.

'Have you been out at all?' he asked.

'To London, you mean?'

'No, just around. Out of the house, shopping?'

'Yes, of course. I'm not being kept a prisoner.'

'Have you noticed anyone following you?'

She stopped chewing the spaghetti which was half in half out of her mouth and cascading down her fork. She sucked in, munched quickly.

'Why do you ask?'

'Someone's been shadowing me for the last two days, maybe longer, and I think they're shadowing you.'

'Jesus!' she said, but did not seem *that* surprised. 'Come with me,' she added and got up.

Still with her mouth full, quickly taking a sip of wine, she grabbed his hand and led him up a flight of carpeted stairs to a very well converted attic room cosily furnished as a bedroom. From the dormer window he imagined you could see the driveway and the road beyond.

'Just stay there a moment,' she said, stopping him in the middle of the room. She approached the window and cautiously looked out. 'Right, come over here . . . '

He joined her, looked out. The front garden, the driveway, the road beyond he had walked up.

'Do you mean that man in the blue car?'

'Yes.'

'He's often out there. Security. Pa's head of a multi-national company and since the IRA started threatening the lives of VIPS, he's often under surveillance.'

'But your father's not here today.'

'True.'

She led the way back down to the kitchen, seemingly a little disconcerted.

'Why would *I* be tailed?' he asked.

'Are you sure you have been?'

'Positive. I was followed across London by a man all yesterday . . . ' and he gave her all the details of what he'd done during the night and that morning, while she finished her spaghetti.

Cathy fell silent.

Something was troubling her.

'I wonder if he's having me watched? And by me I mean you?' she said, thinking aloud.

'Your father?'

'Yes. He could be checking up on me, and on you. He might have heard about the Lars business and he could be having you checked out.'

'How important *is* your father?'

'He's chairman of the NPG . . . the National Pharmaceutical Group. They have a finger in every pie, politics, army, shipping. I think they even make napalm.'

'I had a premonition about him,' Paul said, 'which was another reason why I wanted to see you.'

'Tell!' she said, excited.

'If you promise me one thing.'

'Your word is my command.'

'How many telephones do you have in this house?'

'God, I don't know, five . . . six?'

'If the telephone rings while I am in the house, do not answer the one in here, this kitchen one on the wall. Nor are you to wear that apron when you pick up the receiver.'

'Why?' She was wide-eyed.

'I had a premonition that you received bad news when answering that phone wearing that apron.'

'You saw me in this apron in this kitchen?'

'Yes.'

'But you've never been here – and I only bought Ma this apron two days ago for her birthday.'

'I *am* psychic,' he said simply, but sternly.

He was surprised at how forceful he was being, but in a way she was behaving rather childishly and not taking him as seriously as he had hoped.

'While we're waiting for the call,' she said, hinting that he needed to be humoured, 'Tell me about this . . . '

She went to a dresser, opened a drawer, brought out a brooch and handed it to him.

'Is there a reward if I get it right?'

'A kiss.'

'Is that all?'

'You get everything if you can wait till we get down to Monte Carlo and you're not sick.'

'Would we fly or go by boat?'

'That's up to you.'

He studied the brooch. It was a diamond paste clip, made up of some twenty-five small diamonds and a large one in the centre, a heart shaped design. He took a sip of wine, leaned well back in his chair, held the clasp tight in his cupped hands, closed his eyes, thought of the design, then concentrated on the feeling in his head.

An image came, a thought, very quickly, which was ridiculous; it was a cinema, the outside of a cinema, then the inside, the auditorium, empty but just filling up with people. There was music and the curtains were white, highlighted in pink spotlights; the music was military.

'Well?' Cathy asked after a long time.

The moment she spoke he lost the image, it just went, he opened his eyes.

'I saw a cinema, modern, empty, filling with people, and they were playing military music. Period.'

'How were the people dressed?'

'Quite elegantly.'

'Was it inside or outside the cinema?'

'Both.'

'Were there many people outside?'

'Yes.'

'What about a name up in lights?'

He concentrated on what he had seen, tried to remember. 'No. The entrance was brightly lit, it could have been a first night, I suppose. Something like that.'

'My mother wore it at a preview of *A Bridge Too Far,*' Cathy sighed. 'She'd never been to a preview before and was really excited by the whole thing. It fell off her dress and they had to wait behind afterwards to look for it, which embarrassed her. It had fallen under her seat. I find it quite incredible.'

Paul himself was fairly pleased. It was not what he had expected. It seemed that whatever he touched he could get some vibrations, or then she had been thinking about the first night and it was telepathy.

'Is that what you expected me to say?' he asked.

'No. I expected you to tell me about my grandmother. It was hers. Grandad had it made specially in 1923, a replica of the real thing in the bank. It was for their diamond wedding anniversary. Your reading was much more impressive.'

They fell silent for a while and Paul saw Cathy glance at the telephone once or twice expectantly.

'You could find out who that man is, I suppose?' she said at last.

'How do you mean?'

'By touching his car perhaps. I mean you are capable of getting messages from inanimate objects.'

'I don't think anything as large as a car would fit in my hand.'

'Have you ever thought of finding out about beds?'

'Beds?'

'Lying in a bed and getting a sense of who was last in it?'

'No.'

'Would you like to try?'

She was being flippant again, not taking him seriously, but if this was going to be her way of passing a dull suburban afternoon, he'd go along with it. He needed to be taken outside of himself, needed someone to make fun of the world he was living in.

He got up, took a deep breath, put on a mystic expression and said, 'Yes, I'd like to try, but will need an assistant. One of the double beds upstairs should be right for my first experiment.'

'No,' Cathy said. 'Try the chaise longue in the sitting room. That must have history. Go and lie on it and I'll bring the coffee through.'

He went to the sitting room dutifully, lay down on the red velvet chaise longue which was hard and not at all comfortable. He closed his eyes, let his mind drift. He saw a lot of criss-cross patterns on the inside of his lids, was aware that they were negative imprints on his mind of his immediate surroundings, the lined wallpaper, the ceiling, the door, the square frames of the pictures. He heard noises from the kitchen, smelt lavender, opened his eyes to see a bunch of dried lavender in a copper bowl in the chimney. He stroked the red velvet, the mahogany woodwork, but nothing came to him.

When she came in he closed his eyes and spoke in a deep, soft whisper.

'This is French . . . I am in France in a red room, the walls are hung heavy with red silk. It's an early Edwardian setting, a young man in an extremely expensive suit with embroidered waistcoat, sideboards and a curly moustache is sitting on the very edge of this chaise. Now she's come in. Quite entrancing, her hair up, wearing a pink evening dress and boa. She looks very much like you. She is undressing now, and he is reaching out for something on the wall. Ah yes . . . a whip . . . a riding crop . . .'

'You're joking!'

'She's slipped off her dress now and is wearing black stockings; on her thigh there is a silk rose, a red rose. She looks over her shoulder demurely at him, and he points to the chaise longue. Now she is taking down her long frilly underskirt and presenting her posterior. He crosses the room, raises the whip and *ouch*!' He gave a little yelp.

'You are a shit, Paul.'

'It's an Edwardian chaise longue which saw long service in a brothel in Paris.'

'It actually came from a vicarage in Suffolk, if you want to know.'

And she sat down next to him and looked him in the eyes.

'You've got very strange eyes, did you know that?' she said.

'It's the man who pays the compliments, usually.'

'I'm serious. They're quite evil sometimes.'

'Evil?'

'Maybe evil's the wrong word, penetrating, and all-seeing.' She kissed him lightly on the lips. 'Am I forgiven for what I did on the boat?'

'I think that depends whether I get any good vibes from the double bed upstairs.'

She took off her apron and lay down alongside him on the chaise, clinging to him tightly so as not to fall off, and he kissed her and her mouth tasted of bolognaise sauce, but he didn't mind because her body felt small and vulnerable and excited under her T-shirt, and the back of her legs were taut and flexed inside her tight jeans.

They drank their coffee quickly, then went upstairs.

'Do you want a king-size double bed, medium-size double bed or a single bed? There's a choice of six.'

'What size is yours?'

'The single. I like to be cosy when I'm alone. Will you excuse me for a moment? I have to go to the loo.'

And she left him on the landing to disappear round the corner.

He peeped into one room which was all flowered wallpaper with bed cover and curtains to match. He looked into what was probably a guest room, different colours but similar, then someone came in at the front door downstairs.

He stood on the landing looking down, and saw an elderly man, very respectably dressed in a dark grey suit, carrying a black dispatch case and an umbrella. The man stopped in front of the hallway mirror, stuck his umbrella in the stand, patted his grey hair, then, sensing that he was being watched, looked up and Paul gasped in horror.

His face was a skull.

There was no skin on it, no eyes, just a white skull which seemed to acknowledge his presence with a deep understanding.

The man then walked on into the house and disappeared.

Paul rushed down the stairs to check, as Cathy came out of the bathroom.

'What are you doing?'

'I thought I saw your father come in.'

'You can't have done. He's in Brussels for two days. Besides, you've never met him . . . '

'The umbrella . . . '

'It's been there all the time. Why? What's the matter, you look as though you've seen a ghost.'

'Describe your father to me.'

'Oh come on, Paul, are you serious?'

'Yes, absolutely. I just saw a man come in through the front door, he stopped to look at himself in the mirror, put his umbrella in the stand, his dispatch case down, patted his hair, and walked on in.'

Cathy ran down the stairs. 'Daddy?' She looked in the living room, drawing room, dining room and in the kitchen. 'Daddy?'

She looked at Paul.

'There is a smell,' she said, sniffing the air. 'Like his after-shave. What was he wearing?'

'Dark grey suit.'

'You're very unsettling, Paul. Do you realise that every time I get a little bit excited by you something happens? First you're sick, then you see ghosts!'

'I'm sorry.'

She led the way back into the living room. The moment had passed. Both knew it.

'Mother'll be back soon,' she said.

'Would you like me to go?'

'I'd like to know when I'll see you again and we can have a few relaxed hours together . . . ' And as she moved towards him warmly, the telephone rang.

She froze.

She looked at the telephone, searched his eyes for advice.

'Answer it,' he said.

He had no idea what the call would be.

She moved across the room, picked up the receiver.

'Yes?'

From her expression he knew it was bad news, from the way she closed her eyes and bit her lower lip.

He turned away, looked out of the window. There was no reason why he should be held responsible for what he foresaw, he did not cause tragedies, he instinctively sensed them ahead of time.

She murmured a few words softly, put the phone down and there was silence.

'Father's had a heart attack.'

'Serious?'

'I don't know. That was his secretary.'

She looked at him in a very strange way and, though she did not move, her attitude changed, her expression, as if she were curling up on herself, cringing from him, her eyes registering little less than terror.

Nervously she picked up the phone again and dialled a number, waited, watching him.

He could have been a rabid dog the way she stared at him, ready to flinch if he raised a hand, ready to run if he took a step forward.

The other end of the line answered.

'Polly?' she said simply. 'Yellow Ten,' and put the phone down.

She made no attempt to explain what the words meant or to whom she was talking; it was a code, Paul realised, possibly a cry for help. Certainly she was calmer when she moved cautiously across the room and sat down on the end of the chaise longue.

'Daddy's dead actually. How could you possibly have known?'

'I have no idea. I am not in control. I am sorry.'

'People die like flies around you, don't they? Your mother, Lars, now Daddy . . . '

'Are you afraid of me?'

'Yes.'

He turned to go towards her, wanting to comfort her, wanting to give her confidence, but even at that distance she recoiled. 'No, please. Stay where you are. I'm sorry, but you're something I don't understand and you frighten me.'

'What was that strange telephone call you made?'

'Yellow Ten?'

'Yes.'

'You weren't to know this, but my American boy friend was on hard drugs – so was I. It's a code, a call for assistance. They'll be coming here soon, the doctors.' She smiled bravely, nervously, toyed with the corner of her shirt.

'Why are you afraid of me? I mean you no harm,' he asked.

'That's just it. I don't think you know what you're carrying. You're like some sort of box full of radiation, innocent outside, God knows what inside. It's not personal, Paul . . . I just think you're lethal!'

He said nothing more.

She had been through Lars's death because of him. Maybe she was right. But he hadn't consciously threatened her father.

The silence was broken by the sound of a car coming up the drive. It was a low, metallic grey, performance car, a symbol of youthful wealth, and Paul watched the driver get out, black hair, heavy tweed suit, loud check shirt. The doctor perhaps, a small untidy man, early thirties, who moved with a purpose.

'Karl Wiser,' Cathy said just behind him. 'An old friend of the family. He must have heard the news.'

And a few seconds later another car came up the drive, a sedate chauffeur driven saloon. In the back a neat woman with blonde hair.

'And mother . . . she must know as well.'

Then came the doctor.

'I'm afraid Cathy is not too well. She needs a rest. She was very close to her father, you see. Could I offer you some sherry?' Cathy's mother said with stiff upper lip.

Paul hesitated, not knowing whether it would be rude or not to accept, till Karl Wiser nodded, suggesting it would be all right, the conventional thing to do.

'Thank you,' Paul said.

There was a great warmth about this man; though his lips did not move, his eyes smiled. Don't worry, they seemed to say, you did right by staying, just be yourself, act simply.

Only a few minutes after letting Karl into the house and greeting her mother with a sad kiss, Cathy had quite suddenly turned quite pale, then facing Paul had spat out at him like a cat. 'How did you get in here?' she had screamed. 'Get out! Get out!' And before anyone could do anything she had dropped to the floor, curled up on herself screaming hysterically. 'Get him out of here! Get him out of here! He killed Daddy! He killed him like he killed Lars . . .'

Paul had remained rooted as Karl, and the doctor who had

just come in, took hold of her and led her out of the room, the chauffeur coming in from the kitchen hovering around, unsure what to do.

Karl had closed the door, listened to Cathy sobbing as she was led up the stairs. He had stared at Paul for a moment, then said quietly, 'What was that about?'

'I don't know,' Paul had lied.

'You do know but you don't want to talk about it.'

'Well, I can guess, but it's all a bit unbelievable.'

'You're a clairvoyant, aren't you? You're the Paul she met on the boat?'

So probably everyone knew about him, about Lars even. Cathy a drug addict, unbalanced, unreliable. He'd felt drained. Then her mother had come in, all British, stiff upper lip, offering sherry.

'I'm going back to London,' Karl Wiser said. 'Can I offer you a lift?'

'Thank you.'

He'd go back to the Bramber in Paddington, that dim little room with the spies outside. He felt very lonely now, very insecure. And he listened politely to Wiser reassuring Mrs Morrow that Cathy would be all right and that if she needed anything to be sure to give him a ring.

They left.

Wiser said nothing till they were on the main road where he used the car's power to the full.

'Will you have dinner with me? I'm extremely curious about you. I presume that that outburst was because Cathy thought you cast a spell on her father or something. She is not too stable. We are childhood friends. We would have married but luckily found out that we weren't physically suited. Cathy is a bit like that, an experimenter, a goer. The drugs scene naturally got all her attention, hence this.'

Paul told him about the telephone call with the code word for emergency treatment.

'Dramatics,' Wiser said. 'She lived in a fantasy world when a kid, made inventions become reality. I suppose meeting you must have come as a shock, because you're virtually a magician!'

Paul said nothing. It was obvious that Cathy had talked about him a great deal more than he had imagined.

As they came into London and crossed over Battersea Bridge, Wiser said, 'We'll call in at the office first if you don't mind, then go and have dinner. We work late hours.'

The office was a recording studio, Wiser Studios no less, further up the Charing Cross Road than he had ventured, where it becomes Tottenham Court Road, a truly radio-active centre.

The studio was impressive, a complex on two floors, ground and basement. Wiser showed him round quickly, young men in jeans like Paul himself locked between earphones behind aquarium windows nodding their heads and signalling with hands and fingers, flicking countless controls while wired up musicians pounded out deafening rhythms.

'I can't interrupt the sessions, but later on you must come and listen to a group recording. It's fascinating. If you're interested in music that is. Here they mix the tapes,' Wiser said, taking him from one room to another. 'In here they cut the discs. In here I sit down and talk on a telephone to people who complicate my life.'

Over dinner in a small Italian restaurant next door, Wiser cross-questioned Paul about the incident on the boat, how Cathy had got involved with the steward in the first place, how he thought the man had died. Paul felt he was talking to Cathy's older brother, he was so protective and curious about her.

While they were having coffee and brandy Wiser slipped a gold watch from his wrist and handed it to him.

'Can you tell me about this?'

For a moment Paul felt he was singing for his supper – it was Uri Geller time and he rather wished the hands of the watch would double up on themselves or the spring inside snap loudly.

He took the watch, studied it. Modern, expensive, it had a clear cut face, the numbers were delicate, the case light, flat. He closed his fingers round it, did not hold it in both hands in prayer fashion, aware that the people at the next table were watching him. He felt embarrassed, knew that nothing could come of it.

'It's very hard for me to concentrate here, you must understand.'

'Of course,' Wiser said, holding out his hand ready to take it back.

'It was probably used by a referee at a football match,' Paul said jokingly.

'Why do you say that?' Wiser had taken him seriously, but enough surprise registered on his face for Paul to check why he *had* said it.

When he'd opened the palm of his hand a feeling had come to him that he was in the middle of a football field surrounded by boys in black and green sweaters.

He clasped the watch again, closed his eyes and saw the players more clearly. The colours of their shirts were distinctive, apple green and black, burgundy red and blue. A goalkeeper in the distance wearing a yellow polo neck sweater. But they were boys.

He told Wiser all this, then explained that it didn't always work, so many other influential images could come to mind. The trick was to recognise the valid ones. Everyone could do it.

'I can't.' Wiser said. 'If you give me something of yours I won't get an image.'

'Try,' Paul said, and handed him his key ring. He had bought it himself in a Manhattan store.

Wiser went through the motions of clasping the key ring firmly, shutting his eyes and concentrating.

'I get the feeling of cold metal warming up in my hand and am now imagining my own key ring, and my own front door, which is an association of ideas,' Wiser said.

'Go on,' Paul urged, wanting to believe that everyone could do it. 'Progress the association of ideas.'

'A bicycle chain . . . there's a little chain there, a chain saw, logs being sawn . . . fir trees . . . fir trees in Surrey. The house of a friend. I'm in an English village . . . ' He handed the key ring back to Paul. Paul handed him back the watch.

'It doesn't always work. Your watch was hardly a referee's watch.'

'But it was. Admittedly I expected something different, but in fact I used it to referee a game at school on the first day it was given me. I was so worried that it would be kicked, that I held it tightly in my hand throughout the game. The colours you described were those worn by opposing house teams. And you couldn't have known that, not in a month of Sundays. You are an extraordinary clairvoyant and you should capitalise on it in one way or other.'

'A freak show?' Paul said, amused.

'No, not at all. You could help people find things, missing things, missing persons even.'

'Like Peter Hurkos, the Dutch psychic.'

'He's done valuable work.'

Wiser was staring at Paul in an unsettling way, as though he were studying a piece of electronic equipment which might be beneficial to his studio.

'Would you like another coffee?'

'Thanks.'

As Wiser looked round for the waiter, he was surprised to see one of his people from the studios. 'Larry?'

'Ah . . . sorry to interrupt the meal, something's gone wrong with the Delta tapes.'

'What do you mean wrong?'

'Very wrong . . . like wiped out!'

'The master tapes?' Wiser was incredulous.

'Yes. Yes, the master tapes. Nick would like you to come as soon as possible.'

'Mind if we skip the second coffee?' Wiser said, and got up, summoning the waiter. 'Crisis. Can I have the bill?'

'Immediately, sir.'

Paul drained his glass of brandy, felt mellow, pleased that he was not involved in the panic that was about to break out.

He watched Wiser deal with the bill, signing it, adding the tip, and once out in the street he suggested he should leave.

'No . . . no . . . stick around, unless you've got something better to do.'

'Not really, but won't I be in the way?'

'No. Come and see how a big recording studio fucks up three months of a client's work. Because that's what it amounts to.'

They burst into reception. The girl behind the desk tried to stop Wiser with phone messages, but he brushed her aside. Down the carpeted stairs they went, along the panelled corridor to Studio One, burst in there. Five technicians were listening to some very strange sounds. Wiser stopped dead and listened too.

'Is that it?'

'That's it,' the one called Nick said. 'That's the Delta master tape.'

'What happened?'

'No idea. I can't figure it out.'

Suddenly the speakers vibrated with a heavy beat, which was then interrupted for about forty seconds by unidentifiable noises.

'What are those sounds?'

Nick reversed it, and they listened again.

There were voices, sounds of tapping.

'Typewriters?'

This time when the music should have come back in, there was a distinct sound of traffic, the acceleration of a motorbike, the deep hum of a diesel.

'Now what! We're losing it as we're playing it back!'

'It must be the machine,' Wiser said.

'No it's not. We've tried it on another. Same thing.'

'Which one?'

'Number two.'

'Try it on the others.'

They went to Studio Three, interrupting an editor who was frowning at what was coming out of his earphones.

They played it again; different sounds, different noises came through, the definite clatter of plates, the clinking of glasses, the general low hum of conversation.

'It's the restaurant next door,' Nick said.

'Through three feet of soundproofing and God knows how many feet of bricks and mortar?'

'Have you got a copy of this original Delta?' Wiser asked.

'Yes. Two copies. This happens to be the master. They need editing, but they'll be O.K.'

'Thank God for that. Let's try Studio Four.'

In Studio Four they got the restaurant sounds again.

'Nick must be right, we're on the restaurant side. Get a blank tape, see what happens.'

The engineer got a blank tape, switched on, let it run.

They watched the spool go round slowly for a minute in

silence. The engineer rewound it and then listened. More clearly the sounds of the restaurant came through, definite cutlery and glass noises, even the shout of a waiter giving his order to the kitchen.

'Incredible.'

The editor for Studio Three came in. 'Mine's erased out now. It was completely wiped when you were in the room.'

'How do you know?' Wiser asked.

'I just worked it out . . . Come and listen. I noted the number I was on when you came in. Played it back . . . gone!'

Wiser was beginning to enjoy the challenge, but as there were seven now in the small studio and Paul could contribute nothing, he tapped him on the shoulder and said he was going.

'O.K., mate, give me a call, keep in touch . . . Must talk some more.'

Paul made his way up the stairs, smiled at the receptionist on his way out, but heard Wiser calling his name as he reached the door.

'Paul!' Wiser came bounding up the stairs. 'Are you in a hurry? I mean are you going anywhere in particular?'

'No . . . just back to my hotel.'

'Can you just hang on a second? I'll run you home. Have a coffee, Maisie here will get you one. It's just something I want to suggest to you.'

Paul sat down and looked out of the window.

It was still light, an articulated lorry had somehow got stuck across the road taking up nearly all the room and a number of people were discussing how it could best reverse. A policeman had parked his motorbike on the kerb and was suggesting to the driver that he should never have come into that street in the first place.

Maisie brought him a very hot black coffee in a mug that burned his fingers. He put it down on the table and watched the steam curling up in the still air. He was unsettled by Wiser, it was the same feeling he had had with Sheryl Lidman, that such people thought he could not look after himself and that he needed help. Maybe the world was populated by those who thought it their duty to look after him.

He was kept waiting so long that Maisie offered him another cup of coffee, by which time it was dark, and getting well on for eleven o'clock. She was so concerned for him that she went down to see for herself what was happening only to return with the news that they were still trying to find out what had gone wrong with the equipment.

'They spend more time repairing and making adjustments down there than recording, if you ask me,' she said.

Paul learned from Maisie that she was disillusioned by the recording business. She had wanted to go on stage and sing and thought the job of receptionist in a studio might lead somewhere. It led nowhere. It was all very technical.

Eventually Karl Wiser came bounding up the stairs, smiling happily. 'I think we sorted all that out, the KTXs. Come down to Studio Four, we'll be more at peace there.'

Studio Four, thickly carpeted and cork-lined, was cosy; the panels of instruments with flickering lights and a thousand and one switches placed him in a space age atmosphere to which he did not belong, but which made him feel secure.

'I've got a number of problems with the business and I sometimes over-react when things go wrong,' Wiser said apologetically, sitting down behind the console in a deep comfortable chair. He occasionally flicked a switch, pressed a button, which did not seem to do anything particular. Paul sensed he was a rich young man with an expensive toy which he could not yet fully operate himself.

'A little while ago someone tried to sabotage this place,' Wiser went on. 'In fact they managed to ruin an important tape. It's easy to do. That's what I feared had happened again.'

'Who?' Paul asked because he felt he should.

'We're a small company, small but successful, and very effective, so we tend to annoy larger companies, the corporations. They want to buy me out, and I won't sell, so occasionally they put on the pressure, a little heavy handedly. Of course I have no proof.'

Paul had no idea why he was being told this, how he came into the picture, if indeed he came into it at all.

'I'm fascinated by your powers,' Wiser said suddenly, leaning forward.

'I wouldn't call them powers,' Paul protested.

'I don't suppose you would even acknowledge them, but I

think you should. Tell me more about yourself, your childhood. Where were you born?'

'Syracuse, upstate New York.'

'And both your parents are American?'

'No, my mother was English.'

'Your father died in Vietnam, I believe, how old were you?'

'Seven.'

Wiser had lost the urgency in his voice. Whatever he had had in mind, whatever he had been going to suggest seemed to have been forgotten. Then he suddenly swivelled round in a complete circle and flicked a few more switches. A buzz came loudly over two of the speakers inset in the wall, then the engineer's voice.

'Yes, we've got more. I'll put it through.'

'Put that earlier one through as well.'

At first Paul thought Wiser had simply recorded their conversation for fun, playing games, but it was neither of them speaking. It was the indistinct voices of a man and a woman.

'Brazil to Trinidad . . . plane from Sao Paolo . . .'

'Is . . . direct? . . .'

'Morning . . . 5.38 . . . Campinos Airport . . . Aerolinas Argentinas . . . schedule . . .'

'. . . am . . . nervous . . . always . . .'

'No need . . . Comet Four . . .'

There was a pause over the speakers, then quite different noises were heard, again the restaurant sounds, plates being piled on one another, a further pause then traffic sounds. After a further short pause the engineer's voice came over saying that that was it and the speakers were cut off.

Wiser swivelled round in his chair again and turned to face Paul.

'Those recordings were piped in from Studios Two and Three. Do you know what they are?'

'No . . .'

'They're takes which are coming on to our tapes, whatever we are trying to record, because you are here. You seem to be some kind of static receiver. We tested our equipment when you were upstairs, everything checked out positive. Yet now we're getting these restaurant noises again. You are pulling sound waves out of the atmosphere and transferring them to tape. The strangest thing of all is that you are pulling out some sounds from the past.'

Wiser paused, studied Paul, who was trying to look more surprised than he was. It was the M.S. *Bjornstjerne* business all over again.

'Larry thought of it when listening to those flight schedules which we cleared on the earlier tape, the first one that gummed up the works on the Delta recordings. He checked up with London Airport authority who gave us information which ties up with the fact that this building was occupied by the Argonaut Travel Agency, over eighteen years ago. That conversation between the man and the woman concerned a flight on a 1961 timetable. What is even more extraordinary is that on November 23rd 1961 an Aerolineas Argentinas Comet 4 crashed approximately one mile from Vivas Copos airport after take off. It was a total loss. Forty passengers and twelve crew were killed.'

CHAPTER SIX

Karl Wiser brought Paul a morning cup of coffee.

'Did you sleep well?'

'Great, thanks.'

'I've got to go out and do a few things, make yourself absolutely at home. I'll be back at about ten, and I'll collect your things from the Bramber.'

'I haven't paid . . . '

'We'll settle up later. Have a rest, after yesterday you deserve it.'

Wiser had suggested to Paul that he should move in with him during his stay in London. He had a large flat, he could have his own bedroom, even his own washbasin. It had sounded very pleasant at one o'clock in the morning when they had finished listening to all the tapes at the studios, and Paul had accepted.

The flat was well appointed with views out on to well cared for gardens. Three bedrooms, a living room and open plan dining area, all carpeted except for the kitchen, it was furnished with well chosen antique and modern pieces and again there were plenty of books. Not surprisingly Wiser had an incredible audio equipment set-up, every conceivable electronic toy, the kitchen itself seemed to be computed. All you had to know was which button to press and you more or less got what you wanted.

'Electronics were my hobby then I turned it into my business,' he had explained showing him around. 'I built all this for my wife, then she became an earth-mother and left me to live in a country commune. Infra-red grills and ultra-sonic foodmixers are not for vegetarians. I couldn't impose my way of life on her, and she could not impose her diets on me. We were the most ill matched couple ever to marry.'

His bedroom was stark compared to the multi-coloured papered guest room Paul now occupied, untidy with clothes hanging everywhere. So much so that Paul had decided just before going to bed that a woman would do him no harm whatever diet she imposed.

Now he sat up with the morning sun coming in through the windows, having again fallen on his feet with the well off taking care of him.

He had a bath, a shave with the guest electric razor provided, a guest electric toothbrush, weighed himself on a digital weighing machine and made himself an amazing breakfast from deep-freeze to oven without touching anything but a tin-foil tray. It didn't taste too much in fact, but it was fun.

Wiser turned up at ten as he had said he would, also with Paul's belongings from the Bramber Hotel.

'You owe me sixty-one pounds eighty pence including VAT, but I'll take that off your salary,' he said.

'What salary?' Paul asked.

'Let's talk about it in the living room.'

Paul followed Karl. Perhaps he would be following people all his life. Or was it that the people he was meeting were just older?

'Now then,' Karl said, settling down to light a pipe with a match, which Paul thought out of keeping with all the gear around. 'By pressing this button here in this specially constructed cabinet I can record any voice in any part of this room. I've had several people sitting here and talking all at once and have managed to isolate each separate conversation. Six mikes strategically placed, and each records on an independent tape.'

'Are we being recorded now?' Paul asked.

'Yes.'

'But then if your theory is right, all the tapes will be blurred, erased, wiped?'

'Possibly. Whether they are recording our conversation or what is being projected out of your mind is something I want to find out. Shall we see?'

He pulled open the drawer of a cabinet revealing a miniature control panel. He flicked two switches and hidden speakers behind the wall panels gave out a crackling sound. The noises went on for quite some time.

'Well we certainly haven't been recorded, but there is some activity there.'

'Perhaps there's nothing close by to pick up?'

'Charmion stop it!' A woman's voice suddenly blurted out.

'God! How do you explain that?' Karl said.

'Who was it?'

'My wife, telling our three year old off. Neither have been in this apartment for three months.'

Then there were noises, movements, a drawer being opened and closed, liquid being poured into a glass.

'Me, do you think, coming home and having a nightcap?' Karl suggested, fascinated.

'Oh, this is beautiful,' a foreign female voice said.

Karl raised his eyebrows, smiled.

'Have you lived here long?'

'A few years.' Karl's voice. 'Would you like a liqueur?'

'No, thank you. I have drunk enough . . . all these books . . . these paintings . . . are you married?'

'Divorced,' Karl's voice said. 'Come and see the kitchen, an electronic wonderland . . . '

'Is it near the bedroom . . . ? An electronic kitchen is so much more original than etchings . . . '

A door closed.

Karl switched off the tape, got up quickly, went to a desk and brought out a diary, flicked over the pages.

'Janine. January 7th. I entertained her here for one night only. Haven't seen her since. When you're present the tapes pick up past sounds.'

'Past sounds of tension,' Paul added.

'You think so?'

'There seems to be a reason.'

'But is it when *you* are tense, or when the people who are recorded were tense? Last night's traffic sounds for instance, don't tell me the cars were tense?'

'No, but the people driving them were. There was confusion outside the studios last night when a lorry got stuck in the street. In a restaurant there is always tension, the woman in the travel agency was anxious. When I heard the warships . . . '

'What warships?' Karl asked.

And Paul told him about his experience aboard the M.S. *Bjornstjerne*.

'Have you had many other experiences like this?'

'No.'

'Look, let me switch on the machines again and you tell me everything about yourself. We'll record and we'll play back. If we pick up something, good, if not I'll be learning about you anyway.'

Paul talked for two hours.

Reclining full length on the sofa, occasionally given coffee, a drink, he let his mind drift back into the past and told Karl about his childhood days in Syracuse, the white painted timber house he lived in with his mother in Lorraine Avenue, a respectable suburban area, the respectable school, his respectable friends. Then a sudden change in fortune, his mother having to sell everything and get work in New York, the move to the city, the apartment in Flatbush, his incessant reading coupled with his dreams, his visions, his nightmares.

Karl was interested in these, begged him to elaborate.

He'd had fearful nightmares since he was seven, waking up in the middle of the night screaming. His mother concerned, trying to console him. Then the repetitive dreams had started. The struggling in the mud after an explosion during a battle, emerging from under a cannon with the broken leg. The hideous visions of a baby being boiled in a cauldron, and the nightmare of castration, his own, and yet not. For he would watch this gaunt man being pulled up against a sun-baked wall with chains and a small woman grabbing his testicles, squeezing them and a knife flashing in the sunlight and the sight of his genitals flying in the air like a bird across the blue sky to land in a bloody basket with a flat, sick, wet noise. Seeing his own entrails dripping on the sand with the knowledge that the now dead man was him seen through the eyes of a woman whom he had also been.

'Can you date these visions?' Karl asked.

'No,' Paul admitted, 'not really. The cannon battle I feel was Napoleonic, the boiling baby much earlier, medieval, but I don't know why. The castration is among Arabs, in a desert town, a kasbah, the Sudan, Egypt, Morocco. I have no idea.'

'But what do you think these dreams are? How many times do they recur?'

'Often. Very often. I've had them as often as one recalls a happening in one's life. I think they're inherited memory.'

'You're reliving some of the horrors your ancestor went through you mean? Have you tried to find out who your ancestors are?'

'Yes, but I only got as far as mother's grandparents who lived in Kent.'

'What if we went down there? Have you any names, any contacts we could follow up?'

'It might be from my father's side, and I know very little about him.'

He told Karl about his premonitions as a child, about the more recent episode in the bathroom when he saw himself with burnt skin prior to his mother's death.

'Were you close to your mother?'

Hardly. She had sent him to a psychiatrist when he was fifteen, a heavily built Hungarian woman in her forties, Doctor Berkzic, whose personality had totally overpowered him. He often dreamt of Doctor Berkzic, but those were real dreams, real nightmares, not inherited memories. He had expected kindness and sympathy from her and he had got a sneer for his stories. She had interviewed him across a desk, not on a couch, had questioned him as though he were a lying schoolboy telling tales, then quite suddenly she had changed her tactics and become very gentle and understanding and had explained everything to him. He had to accept that he was a hypersensitive young man, that he had imagination which had no outlet, that what he should do is keep a diary of everything he saw, everything he imagined, that every morning he should write down the dreams he had had. He should note down those which were imaginings, those which were dreams and those which he thought were reality. They had met every week after that, and she had read through his diary with him, and encouraged him to go on. He had felt better, the sessions became monthly, bi-monthly, then eventually she had suggested he should not hide himself away so much in his studies but go out and get a job. It was Doctor Berkzic who had found him the position with Sheryl Lidman at the Greenwich Bookcase. A few months after that Doctor Berkzic had gone back to Europe, and somehow Sheryl Lidman had taken her place, advising him what to read, but he had developed his psychometric abilities alone, had realised his possible potential, delved into the psychic world and because of this had become more and more distant from his mother.

'You seem to have three gifts then,' Karl said, 'Precognition, psychometry and this effect on sound tapes. Is there a common denominator? Are any of these connected?'

'Anxiety,' Paul suggested. 'I pick up anxiety traces, I don't know why, but I do?'

'Anxiety traces of the past *and* of the future?'

'It seems so.'

'I looked through all the books I have here on the subject last night, especially concerning affects on tapes, and the only thing I came across, which *is* similar is a paper written by physicist working at Longwood College, Virginia who was involved in plotting satellite pictures. I'll read it to you . . . ' And Karl got up to pick out a book which he had earmarked from his shelves. 'Here it is . . . For the last two years – this is from the mid seventies – the National Oceanographic and Atmosphere Administration (NOAA) noted that polar orbital satellites at an altitude of eight hundred miles have frequently malfunctioned BUT only while over the Bermuda Triangle. Of pictures taken by satellites, clear and taped, the taped signal often ceases transmission when the satellite enters the Bermuda Triangle area and telemetric and electronic pulses from the satellite are also *wiped out*. He attributes this to some kind of enormous magnetic field in the area that is *erasing* the magnetic tape on which the visible pictures are stored. It does not, however, interfere with the orbit pattern of the satellite. With a magnetic field strong enough to erase a tape eight hundred miles above the earth, it should definitely affect the ease with which the satellite goes through space, but this does not happen, *so we are talking about a force we don't know anything about.*'

Karl slammed the book shut and threw it down on the carpet, then slumped down in an armchair.

'If I had the equipment I'd monitor your brain. Do you sense things in the present? I mean, if you are in danger, do you sense it?'

'No. So far it has never been personal. When I was being shadowed, I got no presentiment about it. I became aware I was being watched because I kept seeing the same man.'

'What shadows, what are you talking about?'

Paul told him about the two Mr Interpols, and the third outside Cathy's house. 'Her father's security friends, she said. I was watched since I landed at Southampton.'

'The whole family's neurotic,' Karl said, dismissing the issue. Then decided to play the tape back.

There was nothing. Flicking the fast-forward switch so that the tape played through rapidly yet still gave out sounds, it all proved completely blank. Nothing, not even their conversation had been recorded.

'It seems that when you are concentrating, when you are talking, you do not act as a receiver, though you wipe out. Maybe it's only when your mind is unconcerned, void, that you pick up the past? I'd like to carry out a few experiments. How are you off for money?'

'Not too much cash, but I have traveller's cheques.'

'I'll give you a hundred pounds this afternoon ...'

Paul started to protest.

'I'm going to employ you, Paul. I don't yet know how, but I can't believe that a person like you with your capabilities can't be put to some use.'

'Commercial use?'

'Every use. I'm offering you a job. Do you want it?'

'Yes ...'

'Good. Let's agree on a hundred a week and a month's trial.'

Karl got up and took Paul's hand to shake on it. He then disappeared out of the room, coming back with a briefcase.

'I've got a business lunch date for which I'm already late. See you this afternoon. There's food in the kitchen, or you can go out. Plenty of restaurants in the main shopping centre up the road. Bye.'

Paul waited for the door to close, then got up.

Luck? Guidance?

Why not earn money while on holiday? He liked Karl Wiser, trusted him; at least he was not pretending that he would not try and make money out of him.

Besides he might actually find out what was making him tick.

Karl returned at four in high spirits.

'I've closed the studio from five onwards, cancelled two

sessions so that we can have the place to ourselves. No interruptions, no one else around. We can work in peace and in secret. Have you ever affected television sets?'

'Not to my knowledge.'

Driving to the studio Karl slammed a cassette into the car's stereo system, reversed it, played it back. No problems.

'There must be a pattern, there must be something which sets you off affecting tapes. I've a close circuit television in Studio Two which clients use for rehearsals. I'd like to try it.'

The place was empty, Karl locked the front door behind them and took Paul straight down to Studio Two. It was the largest of the four, equipped with a small TV-camera and monitor.

Paul watched Karl set it up, offered to help.

'Just sit in that chair. I'm going to interview you.'

Various signal lights went on, the monitoring screen in front of him blinked and a grey picture came up. Karl adjusted the camera on its stand, the picture came through, Paul himself, very clear in blue and white. He turned his head to see the side of his face, it was better than a mirror, but it wasn't what he thought he looked like, his head bulged more at the back than he thought.

'O.K. Now, it seems that we're getting a perfectly normal picture. Will you look directly into camera.'

Paul did as he was told.

'You realise I'm risking thousands of pounds worth of equipment having you here at all. Now, close your eyes and think of something, a house, a tree, some simple object.'

'Are you trying to turn me into a Ted Serios?'

'Ted Serios! How about him! Prints images on film straight from his mind by looking into a camera lens. Weird. We should try that too.'

There was a moment's silence. Paul couldn't think of anything, he tried to remember trees, thought of a lake, saw the one where he'd found his mother, changed direction, didn't want to think of that in case the children showed up.

'What are you thinking of?' Karl asked.

'Trees, a lake . . . '

'Nothing coming up is there. Frighten yourself. Get your mind back to one of those dreams.'

Paul closed his eyes. A very clear image of the opal children came to him now, standing in his bedroom, the first time he had seen them. A shiver ran down his back.

'Did you get anything then?' he asked. Karl had moved the monitor. He could no longer see it.

'Nope. Just you sitting there with your eyes closed. But carry on. I'm going to switch a tape on at the same time.'

Paul sat well back in the chair and closed his eyes again, tried to think of a tree, saw one very clearly suddenly, an old gnarled gum tree with a particularly sinister branch sticking out at an odd angle. It was a tree he knew, and then saw the man hanging from it, a thick rope round his neck, his legs hanging down apart, then the scene getting dark very quickly and the moon there behind the tree and the two witches appeared breathing heavily as though in a trance, carrying a heavy wooden table between them. Slowly, as though it was a ritual, they started taking off their clothes and first one, then the other stepped up on the table and, pulling down the dead man's trousers, started to use him because he was in a state of rigor mortis. Paul wanted to help, wanted to go and hit the witches, he wanted to hit them violently because the man had been a friend, and as he approached them they both turned on him and stuck their tongues out at him wriggling them sensuously, jumped down from the table and started running towards him. He turned and fled, the ground uneven, bushes scratching him, he caught his foot in a root, fell headlong into the dust, doubled up, then felt someone helping him to his feet.

It was Karl.

'That was some performance, what happened?'

'I . . . I can't . . . '

'Past, present, future?' Wiser insisted.

'Oh past . . . past . . . but God knows when or where . . . '

He sat back in the chair, looked at the reassuring surroundings of the studio, at the television camera, the back of the monitor.

'Anything on there?' he asked.

'Not visually, no, I'm just going to play back the tape.'

Karl slipped out and went behind the glass panel where the main controls were. Paul heard the reel skimming backwards, the high pitched screams of reversed voices. Something was on there. The witches' yelps? His own screams?

Karl switched the tape forward and rushed back to join Paul.

For a while there was just a humming, a strange flutter like bird's wings, then it became louder, clearer, a regular mechanical sound, machinery working at a regular pace, a hissing, a stamping, like a printing press. It stopped. For a while silence, then a voice, a man, followed by a woman's.

'It's coming out quite nicely now.'

'Oh yes, the Baskerville Old Face looks better, less sad, but is the card rather large?'

'No, it's standard.'

'It shouldn't be larger and folded over?'

'This is traditional.'

'All right then. Go ahead.'

There was a pause and the hissing and stamping started again, the machinery took over all the sounds. Then it ended.

Karl went back to switch off the tapes, returned, pensive.

'That may come from a little printer's a few doors down. It is just possible that this wall backs on to theirs, though I don't think so. We should find out anyway. Anything direct would be a breakthrough in this endless mystery. They were printing something small, a visiting card but bigger, Baskerville Old Face type. The name of the woman? A boutique perhaps, an invitation card. Something traditional anyway. Come on, let's go. They'll be closed, but we need a break.'

Paul liked the way Karl lost no time. An instant man, an immediate man. Snap decisions, snap action.

As they walked out of the studio and down the street he told him about the 'memory' he had had. Karl was astounded.

'It seems though that you pick up voices regardless of what you yourself are thinking, or imagining, or dreaming. But this time there is something different!'

'What's that?'

'No anxiety.'

'We don't know that yet.'

'They didn't sound anxious to me.'

'Anxiety is personal. She might be very anxious about having these cards printed.'

'Like not being able to pay for them, you mean?' Karl suggested.

A door next to a radio shop had a nameplate – Tottenham Court Printers, 1st Floor. Steep stairs led straight up.

'If this is the place you're not even receiving at the same level. And we're a whole block down.'

They went up the stairs surprised to see a light on so late in the evening. The door at the top with the same nameplate shielded them a little from the thumping of the printing machine. They knocked, but no one answered, so Karl went in.

Inside a large press was hissing and stamping. Watching were two people, an elderly man in a stained overall and a middle aged woman dressed in a sombre suit. Both looked up surprised to see anyone at this late hour.

'I'm sorry,' Karl said. 'Are you open?'

'No, not really. But can I help you?'

'I'm from the studio down the road, just round the corner, do you know it, Wiser Studios?'

'Not really,' the man said. 'There've been so many changes around here lately I've lost touch with the neighbourhood. Photographic studio is it?'

'No, sound recording.'

The man looked politely interested.

'I wanted to know two things. One was whether you had heard any disturbing noises coming from us, the other was an estimate for a print job I want.'

The man thought it was quite amusing that anyone should be worried about noise. 'We've had more complaints about this machinery than you'll ever have. As for printing, what sort of job was it?'

'Four colour off-set litho.'

'Don't run to that. Small business. Very limited. Your best bet is Bell's at No. 73. We just do this sort of thing.'

The man handed Karl the card the machinery was flicking out. It was the announcement of a requiem mass for a Colonel Stobart who had died the week before. 'We do weddings and Christenings too. Parties, receptions, anything small. Line drawings as well.'

'How far do these premises go back?' Karl asked.

'Just this wall. Backs on to the Relton warehouse.'

'Relton?'

'Relton. Rag trade. Bales of cloth. Apart from anything else, that deadens sound, so I wouldn't worry about you disturbing us!'

'Thank you.'

Paul followed Karl out, and Karl handed him the card.

'There's your anxiety then. The death of Colonel Stobart. Any relation by chance?'

'No.'

'Tomorrow I'm going to take you out in the field, so to speak. With a portable recorder I'm going to take you to somewhere in the City where horrible things have been known to happen.'

'What?'

'The Black Death. The Plague. When they dug down some years back to sink the foundations of a new high riser, the builders found the sites of old plague pits. If you don't react to that sort of anxiety, then . . . well then I don't know what.'

The next morning they drove to the City. In the shadow of St Paul's Karl turned into an underground parking area under a magnificent new office block, all glass, reflecting the blue and greys of the cloud peppered sky.

The car park attendant stopped Karl, recognised him as a regular visitor it seemed, and told him the place was virtually empty. It happened to be Saturday.

Karl parked the car in a bay, got out and took various pieces of portable recording equipment from the boot which he painstakingly set up, three microphones placed in key positions.

'They found the plague pits just under here. Hundreds of skeletons, some preserved in clay. You should get pretty unpleasant anxiety traces from them.'

'Except that dead men aren't usually anxious.'

'But those that buried them were, specially those that knew they had the plague themselves.'

Paul thought about it, remembered a passage he had memorised when at school from Defoe's *Journal of the Plague Year*. Perhaps he had always been morbid. 'Looking upon her body with a candle he discovered the fatal tokens on the inside of her thighs. She was a dead corpse from that moment for the gangrene which occasions the spots had spread over her whole body . . . ' he recited.

Karl turned and looked at him aghast.

'I'm only quoting,' Paul said. 'Defoe. 1665.'

Karl returned to fixing up his equipment.

'The main thing to do, I think, is talk,' he suggested. 'If possible *not* about the plague. To get your mind off the present and the past, to get your subconscious blank, because that's where things are happening. Let me tell you about this building. It was finished about two years ago and only half of it is occupied. Arab financed of course, and four floors, believe it or not let to a North Sea oil company . . . '

He heard the footsteps echoing on the concrete floor round the corner. Car keys rattled, the sound amplified by the hollowness and emptiness of the space. A car door opened, a man's body brushing on the leather seat was clearly audible. The car door closed, the sudden roar of the engine as it started up, the gears being shifted, the car reversing and driving off very slowly.

Now he saw it.

Curiously the man did not go down the exit lane but cruised very slowly to the end of the car park in the opposite direction, reversed and backed right up against the wall. In front of the car was the whole length of the garage like a runway between the massive concrete supporting pillars.

Paul stared, aware that Karl had stopped talking and was watching him. It was a large black saloon car, a Daimler-Jaguar, Paul thought, a diplomat's car, or executive's company car.

The man revved up, then suddenly, like a maniac, accelerated to career down the runway at full force. As he neared the sheer wall in front of him he made no attempt to brake, but let go of the steering wheel and put his hands up to protect his face.

The impact was fearful, the noise terrible, the car concertina'd, then caught fire. Not a massive explosion, but a belch of black smoke and a roar of flames.

'Karl! For Christ's sake!'

He started running towards the car and felt Karl tugging at his sleeve to stop him. He tore himself away, he couldn't let the man burn.

Then Karl's voice screamed in his ear, and he stopped because, of course, the car was not there, the smoke, the flames, the man, nothing was there; ahead of him was an empty corner of the garage.

'Paul, what's happening to you?'

'Didn't you see?' He held his breath. Another imagining, another vision. He crouched down on the cement, exhausted, aware that Karl was patting him on the back. 'It was a vision Karl, that's all,' he said.

'Of what?'

'Of a man committing suicide by driving himself into a wall.'

'Over there?' Karl enquired, pointing at a blackened area of the garage.

'Yes,' Paul said. He had not noticed the blackness when they had come in.

'Christ!' Karl said under his breath turning away, afraid, it seemed, to look at him.

'Why?' Paul asked.

'Cathy's father didn't have a heart attack . . . ' Karl spun round to face him now. 'He had a brainstorm and killed himself. This is the National Pharmaceutical Group office block where he worked. I had no details but heard it involved his car.'

'Is that why you brought me here – not for the plague pits?'

Karl nodded. 'I knew you could be put to some use. You can confirm everyone's worst fears of the past!'

Paul spent the rest of the day in bed, a mental exhaustion overwhelming him. Karl could give him no explanation as to why Morrow had died like that, all he could tell him was that he had deliberately gone to the office block to see if an anxiety trace could be recorded.

On the tape, Paul learned, he had subconsciously reproduced the sounds of the crash.

It was a major breakthrough. It meant that he could produce evidence of events from the past. Karl naturally saw limitless possibilities – from solving crimes to re-writing history – but by the time they had got back home Paul just wanted to sleep.

Over-concerned for his well being, Karl insisted that he should take a sleeping tablet so that he could really rest and called up his secretary to come and watch over him and look after his needs should he wake up. He couldn't baby-sit himself, as he put it, as he had to make sure the business would run without him during the oncoming weeks.

Paul had become a priority.

The next day Paul was awakened early by an excited Karl dressed in even heavier tweeds and a fishing hat.

'I'm taking you to Devon for a couple of days trout fishing,' he said. 'I need the break, you need the break. Besides, you haven't seen anything of the English countryside since you arrived.'

Paul got up rather reluctantly, it was nothing that he could get particularly keen about, though getting out of London would be interesting.

As he was getting dressed the front doorbell rang and he heard Karl rushing to open it.

'That'll be them. We'll be leaving in five minutes!'

'Who?' Paul asked.

'The girls. I've invited two friends of mine to come with us, Suzy and Phoebe. We can't fish at night and must have some sort of entertainment.'

Paul instantly froze. A blind date. The effort of having to be nice to someone he might not like, or worse to someone who might not like him, was something he would dearly have liked to avoid.

He heard the girls' voices in the sitting room.

One spoke with a strange accent he had heard around London, the other had a lilt in her voice which sounded oriental.

When he had shaved and dressed he made his appearance in the sitting room and was pleasantly surprised. Both girls were petite, one was blonde, the other brunette, the one with the lilt clearly oriental, Burmese perhaps, or Chinese.

It took them the best part of four hours to get down to the fishing village in Devon Karl eulogised about most of the way, and, if it had not been for the rain, it would indeed have been lyrical. The girls were neither equipped for, nor impressed by, the weather or the surroundings, and when Karl checked them all into the hotel the only one to react to the fact that he had booked two double rooms was Paul.

Was he to sleep with one of the girls, or Karl?

They went up to the rooms to freshen up from the journey and the oriental girl behaved as though she had done this sort of thing before. It was so taken for granted that they would share the same bed that night, that Paul wondered whether she had been hired. It would not be untypical of Karl to arrange such a thing, and it would certainly make things easier. Diplomacy, however, forbade him to ask.

She was certainly very pretty, and her casualness as she changed her dress to put on satin trousers was exciting to say the least.

Thankfully Karl decided it was too wet to go fishing, so instead they went into the quiet and sedate lounge to have a traditional tea, with scones and jam and Devon cream, and had a game of cards by the log fire till dinner when both girls went to change again.

'Are they old friends of yours?' Paul asked.

'More or less.'

'Real friends or hired friends?'

'Well, they're hostesses old chap. I mean they'll want a little present, but I'm taking care of that. Does Suzy suit you?'

'Yes,' Paul said. 'Thank you.'

'Tomorrow night we can swap if you like.'

Paul did not want the remark to upset him, but it did. He wanted most of all to be loyal to someone he slept with, for at least the period they knew they were going to be together. Karl's attitude reminded him of the men who took his mother out. He respected girls more than that. They were not objects of desire to be cast away after the desire had been satisfied.

They had a few drinks in the old beamed bar after they themselves had gone up to change shirts, and went in to dinner aware that they were a source of entertainment for the other hotel guests, not only because they were younger than anyone else both in age and spirit, but because the girls were, considering the surroundings, somewhat bizarre.

They all went to bed when the bar closed at eleven, though they could have stayed up longer being residents. Paul's head was however swimming with alcohol and when Suzy tightened her grip on his hand as they walked up the creaky oak stairs he felt that adolescent ripple of excitement which had thrilled him at early teenage parties when he had made a conquest.

His first Chinese night was yet another experience. The Sheryl affair, brief as it had been, had taught him not to be inhibited.

The next morning, after a breakfast in bed, he sat back against the pillows, watching the pouring rain splash the windows, Suzy's head resting on his chest, her arms hugging him tenderly. There would be no fishing again today, which was welcome news.

Then Karl came in and said that Phoebe wanted to see Suzy. Paul thought him a little abrupt, as though he wanted to remind them that it was the man who paid the piper who called the tune. But he had a reason for wanting her out of the way.

When they were alone Karl got down on his hands and knees and reached for something under the bed. It was a canvas box; inside it was a recording machine.

'I haven't been taping lewed noises, Paul. It just struck me that you might be at your most relaxed and most clear-headed after sex. I hope you don't mind.'

'So all this is another experiment?'

'I'm afraid so.'

'You never let up, do you?'

'Never. If my theory's right we should have a recording of what was going on in the next room between me and Phoebe. Poor thing, I talked into the night, even while we were making love. So much so that she fell asleep during it!'

He switched it on.

The sounds were strange, undulating hums, then clear cut noises of breaking glass. This was followed by a long silence, then light breathing, short intakes, equally short exhalations. Then a very young voice, a child's voice saying, 'I want to go back.' There was an echo in the voice, as though it were in a long tunnel, then another voice, also a child's, lisping slightly saying, 'I think it's all right this time. I don't think he's in danger.' Footsteps as though someone were walking on broken glass, the undulating hum, then nothing.

Total silence.

Karl waited patiently for the spool to run right through, switched off the machine and looked up.

'What the fuck was that then?'

Paul stared down at the machine.

He knew what it was about.

He knew only too well.

They had been in the room during the night, the children. They had visited him. They had said something which sounded protective.

That at least was comforting.

On the other hand it could also mean that something horrific would happen again soon.

CHAPTER SEVEN

By a unanimous vote they all decided to go back to London after lunch. They got into the car, Suzy cuddling up to Paul in the back, and drove off along the cascading country lanes, the rain pouring down relentlessly from blackened skies.

'Mind if we stop at Stonehenge?' Karl said. 'Paul's never seen it.'

'What is it?' Phoebe asked.

'You must have heard of Stonehenge!' Suzy was hurt by her friend's ignorance. 'It's a circle of massive stones where ancient Britons used to perform sacrifices by moonlight.'

'I also want to record some sound effects of whistling winds for a client, something haunting,' Karl said.

Paul saw the winking in the rear view mirror. What did he hope to hear, Druid ghosts chanting?

By the time they had got to Salisbury Plain the weather had changed. It was still very overcast but the rain had stopped.

Stonehenge was a disappointment, much smaller than Paul had been led to expect from the photographs he had seen in countless books and magazines.

Suzy was fascinated by the place, allowing her imagination to see her ancient Britons sacrificing their womenfolk to various moon gods. Phoebe looked bored seeing nothing but the stark blocks of grey stones.

Karl handed Paul the portable tape recorder, suggesting he should wander off on his own.

He was happy to do so, circumnavigating the circle of megaliths to get as far away as possible from the few tourists who were visiting the monument that day. He liked the wind, the forceful fresh air, the dramatic sky. He was close to the elements and realised he would much prefer to live in the country.

The sudden roar made him spin round.

Like a gigantic bat, it thundered only some hundred yards above him, totally blacking out the sky with its massive wing span. The noise was ear-splitting, its jet engines throwing up a hurricane of stones and dust, its heat burning the earth. Quite suddenly the air above him glowed red, a bright, very vivid scarlet, then white so intense that it scorched the eyes. The noise was deafening.

The blast hurled Paul to the ground. He rolled over on his stomach, covering his head with his arms. The screams were hideous. He dared not look up for fear of seeing human torches twisting in the agony of the holocaust. Then there was a silence followed by a tearing sound as though a forest of trees were being felled at one blow. He looked up, saw the buckled black wreckage of the aircraft impaled on the red hot stones.

'Paul, are you all right?' Suzy's voice. She was crouching over him.

He looked up.

All was quiet, comparatively peaceful. Karl ran up, knelt down next to him.

'What happened, Paul? You look terrible.'

'He passed clean out,' said Suzy. 'I saw him, he just fell to the ground.'

Paul sat up unable to speak, looked in the direction of the disaster. There was nothing. Undulating countryside splashed with vivid greens and golds, the Stonehenge circle untouched, solid, defying history.

He had been warned, the children had come to him in the night to tell him. It was a premonition.

'You're trembling and sweating, Paul, what's the matter?'

'I saw a plane crashing. It exploded over there. A huge military aircraft.'

Karl switched on the recording machine, reversed it impatiently, played it back.

Paul's voice came through very clearly, a little tense, a little high pitched, encanting the strange quatrain in perfect French . . .

> '*Entre les dents des hommes historiques*
> *Mourira en flames celui qui vole.*
> *Cercle de pierres rouges et calorifiques*
> *Tombes de se qui veulent changer de roles.*'

All looked at Karl who seemed to be mesmerised by what he'd heard.

'What on earth is that?' Paul asked.

'It was your voice,' Karl said. He reversed the tape and played it again.

'Between the teeth of historic men,' he then translated, 'Will die in flames the one who flies. Circles of stones, red and hot . . . Tombstones of those who wish to change their roles . . . their way of life . . . '

The girls were totally baffled, Paul still unsure what it all meant.

'It's like a Nostradamus quatrain,' Karl said. 'A premonition of an air disaster which will happen here. Do you know of Nostradamus, the 16th century French clairvoyant? He predicted the Second World War, the Kennedy brothers' assassinations, all sorts of things.'

'Why should *my* voice speak, then?'

'God knows!' Karl said. 'At least I hope He or someone does.' Then he added, 'I think we'd better get back.'

Leaving Paul to recover from his singular experience, he led the girls away, whispering something to them as he put his arms round both.

By the time Paul had got himself together and joined them at the car, it had been agreed that Karl would drop Suzy and Phoebe off at Salisbury where they could catch a train because he had decided to visit someone locally on business and it would take time.

Karl drove like a madman, overtaking dangerously to get to the station quickly. Once there he was pretty ruthless, taking the girls' luggage out of the boot and handing it to them, not accompanying them to the platform let alone checking whether they would have to wait long for a train.

Suzy hugged and kissed Paul as though she really cared for him and felt some deep sorrow at the parting. Karl then got back into the car and drove off, only to stop at the first convenient spot, a lay-by on the outskirts of the town.

'So tell me all about it.'

'What did you say to the girls?' Paul asked.

'I told them you had a history of mental instability, that it was not serious but that I would take you straight to a hospital.'

'Thank you very much. I was getting on well with Suzy.'

'They're a penny a dozen those girls. Come on. Tell me what you experienced.'

Paul explained what he had heard, what he had seen, what he had felt. He described the whole accident.

'Sounds like a Vulcan bomber, probably from the RAF station at Woolcombe Fields. We'd best go there.'

'What for?'

'Check that they have those types of planes.'

'But what was that recitation in French? And whose voice?'

'Your voice, you idiot!' Karl said, pulling away and accelerating down the road. 'Tense, high pitched, not too recognisable – but your voice.'

'I don't speak French.'

'Your ancestor did though. Inherited memories, inherited tongues, a premonition from an inherited mind. You're a link, Paul, a link in a family line of clairvoyants that goes back to the 16th century psychic Nostradamus. Someone, somewhere has a file on you, and that file is very important. But *I've* got there first! Jesus, I had absolutely no idea who you were. No idea. Now I understand a great deal.'

'I don't,' Paul protested.

'You will. I promise you, you will.'

At the gates of the Woolcombe Fields RAF Station, Karl stopped the car and asked the security guard for the Station Commander. He mentioned someone important he knew in London, and the security guard went into his box to use the phone. After a brief conversation the gate was lifted and Karl drove through.

'I happen to know a Wing Commander who is connected with RAF recruitment. They made a demo-tape at the studios some months back.'

As Karl swung the car into the parking area, Paul saw a plane inside a hangar which was like the one that had crashed.

'It was that one, the same as that one.'

'A Vulcan,' Karl confirmed. 'Come on, it's believe it or not time.'

They went into the main building and made their way down a long corridor to the door Karl was looking for. In his usual manner he burst in and charmed the uniformed secretary with his smile.

'Group Captain Brendle, please. I have an appointment, security rang through.'

The secretary got up, reluctantly, because she preferred sitting behind her desk, poked her head into the main office and opened the door wide. They went in.

'Group Captain Brendle, this is Paul Saralyn, my name is Karl Wiser. I helped Wing Commander Gigham-Browne with a recruiting campaign a few months ago . . .'

They shook hands and sat down on the suggested chairs.

'I'm going to be very brief. Message first, explanation afterwards. We believe that one of your Vulcan bombers is going to crash on Stonehenge.'

The Group Captain, who up till now had been amicably pleased to see them, lost his composure.

'When?' he asked.

'We don't know,' Karl said simply.

'Could I ask where this information comes from and whether you are talking of sabotage or a terrorist act?'

'You're not going to believe this,' Karl said, 'but neither of us would be here if we didn't think you should be warned.'

'Try me,' the Group Captain said, regaining his geniality.

'Would you give Mr Saralyn a small object which you know he could not possibly have been in contact with before?'

'I don't follow . . .'

'Mr Saralyn is psychic. I first want to prove to you that he is not a charlatan and that we are not wasting your time, and that we think a number of people are in danger.'

Paul was taken aback.

'I can't perform in a situation like this, Karl. I'm not a circus act. I'm sorry. I don't think we can do more than register our fears. It's up to them to act on them or not.'

'I think you have the right idea,' the Group Captain said, getting up and moving swiftly to the door to open it. Clearly the man thought them lunatics.

Karl was visibly shaken by the way he was being treated, then he shrugged his shoulders in a way of apology, and both left.

Three armed aircraftsmen were standing close to the car by the time they got to it, two more at the entrance gates which were wide open. Karl waved at the security officer who had let them in. He did not wave back.

'Are you willing to try more experiments?' Karl asked when they got home. 'It means with *everything*, radio, television, recording devices, telephones, drugs, girls. I want to put you through every human emotion possible and record what happens?'

Paul nodded. He had already agreed to be a guinea pig for a month. 'You promised to tell me more about Nostradamus,' he said.

'I will,' said Karl, 'after the experiments.' And went on, 'We'll start straight away. One strange pointer is that you had this premonition *after* sleeping with Suzy. Sex generates a powerful lot of moods and I think this may be significant. How did you get on with her?'

'I liked her.'

'Felt at ease with her?'

'Yes.'

'Then we'll ask her back.'

Karl started to organise everything immediately. 'If we don't crack this nut after three days I'm giving up. But I'm going to have a damn good try.'

He rang up Suzy and asked her to come round as soon as she could. Paul's own room was to be the laboratory, stripped of everything but essentials. The double bed was the centre piece and Karl set up all the electronic equipment he had available: at the end of the bed a large television set with a VT 5000 video recorder, in one corner the close circuit camera from the studio with a monitoring screen on the opposite side.

He placed battery and mains operated cassette recorders under the bed, four speakers and microphones in each corner, spotlights overhead with dimmers and different coloured bulbs, brought in the telephone and answer-phone, fan heaters to alter the temperature upwards, and ordinary fans to cool.

When Suzy arrived she was told they were carrying out sex-dream experiments for one of Karl's clients. She didn't care, the money was good. She didn't believe them either but thought it was something to do with Paul's mental instability.

Paul decided that she wasn't far from wrong, only it was Karl's illness, not his.

A swivel chair was set up by the bedside for Karl to sit on and take notes, but over the evening meal Paul made it clear that a voyeur would disturb him and, though he did not mind his actions being recorded for the sake of the experiments, he did not want to be watched by a physical presence.

Karl agreed.

For the next twelve hours Karl left the couple alone. It was raining outside, they had no desire to do anything, so they lay in bed watching the television, playing the cassette tapes and making love while drinking a selection of wines and spirits. Suzy slept a good deal more than Paul who read while she did so.

After thirty-six hours Karl decided that Paul had been through as many moods as was possible under these particular conditions and Suzy was paid off and sent home. She had asked a great number of questions but hadn't got any answers.

Paul and Karl then spent the next day listening to every tape and watching the video recordings.

There was nothing unusual.

Paul felt somewhat embarrassed to see himself in bed with Suzy, but the lighting was so poor that he was more of a restless shadow than an erotic stud.

Having drawn a blank on that series of experiments Karl suggested that he should take a large dose of valium. At six that evening he took 30 milligrams and got into bed.

The sleeping pill made him feel drowsy and he was very content to lie in the large bed alone, looking at television, with Karl sitting next to him, noting down what was switched on in the room.

They were looking at a Western when the screen suddenly went blank. Both sat up, Karl very highly strung and excited. The announcer came on immediately, however, to apologise for the break in transmission, but this was a newsflash.

A Vulcan bomber of the RAF Research Establishment Squadron at Woolcombe Fields had crashed shortly after take-off in a hillside close to Stonehenge on Salisbury Plain. A number of people were reported killed. Further details would be given in the nine o'clock news.

Paul should have felt excited, should have shared Karl's astonishment, but the valium was taking effect and nothing seemed to be of any importance any more. Karl calculated the exact time between the premonition and the crash, then tried to ring the RAF station and talk to Group Captain Brendle.

Paul fell asleep.

He was awakened occasionally by Karl's movements in the apartment, by Karl telling him excitedly that the Press were going to take notice, then he heard the front door bell ringing, went to sleep again deeply and woke up to find the room full of men he had never seen before.

They were kind, considerate, asked him to get dressed, enquired if he had been drugged. They were curious about the equipment round the bed, what had been going on and Paul realised that Karl had disappeared.

He did not remember going down the stairs but was now conscious of being helped into a large car and of being thankful that he could sit down in comfort. On either side of him were these men; the driver, he noted, was wearing a policeman's uniform.

'Who are you?' he heard his own voice ask in the distance.

'Friends, Mr Saralyn, we're friends.'

He turned to glance through the rear window feeling they were being followed, but not knowing why it should concern him, then realising his eyes could not cope with the street lights and headlamps of the oncoming traffic.

'What time is it?' he asked, not really interested.

'Four in the morning. When did you take the drug?'

'Can't remember.' His mouth was thick, his words slurred.

He fell asleep again to wake up in a small office lying on a leather sofa covered with a blanket, a white pillow under his head. A policewoman was sitting at a desk reading a newspaper. She looked at him and smiled.

'Good morning. How are we feeling?'

'Where am I?'

'In a safe place.'

'Where's Karl? Mr Karl Wiser?'

'He's all right. Don't you worry.'

She had obviously pressed some sort of buzzer for the door opened and two men came in, one a doctor who immediately crouched down over him, examined his eyes and took his pulse.

'How do you feel?'

'A little drowsy.'

'Is he fit enough?' asked the other.

'After a meal and plenty of water. Feeling hungry?'

'Yes, a bit . . . '

The policewoman, on a nod from the doctor, picked up a phone, got through to a canteen and ordered a three-course meal, and a large jug of iced water. Also black coffee.

And both men left.

It was light outside, but overcast. Late morning, noon perhaps, Paul felt. The office was well furnished but in no way luxurious. There were no pictures on the walls, no portraits or maps or photographs to give anything away. He had no idea where he was.

Not long after a uniformed man came in with a tray, soup, roast chicken, boiled potatoes, cauliflower, and a pudding, and the policewoman suggested he should sit at the desk to eat.

'Am I allowed to talk to you?' he asked.

'Of course.'

'Where am I?'

'You're in London, not far from Trafalgar Square. A building of the Home Office.'

'Am I under arrest?'

'No, but they want to question you.'

'Who are "they"?'

'The authorities.'

He started eating, found he was hungry, drank all the water and felt much better. After a meal he was given an old newspaper to read which was entertaining enough to pass the time. He was very aware of how indifferent he felt about his situation, due, he presumed, to the valium.

The telephone rang and the policewoman asked him to follow her.

They went up in a lift and down a corridor to another office. It was much brighter, the sun was shining now. The man who had come in with the doctor sat behind a desk, Group Captain Brendle in an armchair nearby.

'I'm sorry we kept you last night, but it was important for us to make sure you recovered. You were apparently under a heavy dose of drugs which could have been dangerous. You've met Group Captain Brendle, I believe. Please sit down.'

He exchanged glances with Brendle. No great warmth came from him, no sympathy.

'We've prepared a statement for you to read, and if you are happy about it we'd like you to sign it. You are of course under no obligation to do so and if you wish you may consult a lawyer. We only need the statement for our own records, however, and you are in no way held responsible for what happened.'

He pushed a typed document across the desk, and Paul picked it up.

I, Paul Saralyn, American citizen, Passport No. 9376310 temporarily residing at 112 Greenwall Gardens, London NW3 confirm that on July 5th at 3.45 p.m. when visiting the Stonehenge monument on Salisbury Plain, saw a Vulcan bomber crash on to the monument, explode and cause the surrounding area to burn like an inferno. I further confirm that this was an imagined vision which I believe to have been a premonition of the disaster which subsequently occurred on July 8th.

Paul read it through twice, slowly, could see nothing in it that was untrue or that admitted anything illegal, the facts were correct. He could think of no reason why he should deny this straightforward account of what had happened. He reached out for the proffered pen and signed.

Both men then stood up, shook him by the hand and saw him to the door.

'The lifts are to your right.'

'What of Mr Wiser?' Paul asked.

'Mr Wiser is at home,' he was told.

He was apparently free to go.

So Karl would be waiting for him. As he took the lift down to the ground floor and walked out of the building he realised how dependent he had become. Again he was leaning on another person. Anyway Karl must have given them all those details, because he certainly had not told anyone else what he had seen.

In the fresh air he looked around; no one was watching him. He was not sure where he was though he could hear Big Ben chiming. He saw a telephone box and decided to ring home.

Home! Is that how dependent he had become?

There was no answer.

He rang the studios.

'Mr Karl Wiser, please.'

'Mr Wiser is away for a few days, can I take a message?' It was Maisie.

'This is Paul Saralyn. Have you any idea where he's gone?'

'Oh, Mr Saralyn, I have two messages for you. Mr Wiser apologises but he had to go to the States for a few days. He said for you to go on using the flat. And would you please ring Miss Morrow?'

'Miss *Morrow*?'

'Yes, Miss Cathy Morrow. I have a number for you.'

She gave him the number, a London one. He hung up and rang Cathy.

'National Pharmaceutical Group,' a voice answered.

'Miss Cathy Morrow, please.'

'Hold the line. I'll put you through.'

He held the line, waited. Various noises, a girl answered. 'Cathy Morrow's secretary.'

'I'd like to speak to Miss Morrow, please,' Paul said.

'Miss Morrow is in a meeting at present, can I help you?'

'Yes. My name's Paul Saralyn. I was asked to ring her.'

'Ah yes, Mr Saralyn. Would you please hold on, I'll get her for you straight away.'

He waited. He was important, but she was important. Her own office, her own secretary, her father's company . . .

Cathy's young voice came over the other end.

'Paul!'

'Yes.'

'Paul, can you have dinner with me tonight? There's a restaurant called *Le Joffrin* in Walton Street, could you meet me there at eight o'clock? I'll tell you everything then. Are you all right?'

'I'm fine.'

'See you at eight, then.'

Again he would do as he was told. He was like a tennis ball being volleyed from one player to another but thankful all the same that he was not alone right then.

And Karl had never told him of the great revelation. The meaning of that strange French recitation.

He was pleased he was going to see Cathy. She was his only real friend, however terrified she had been of him. She had recovered from that, it seemed, or the job had been given to her in way of psycho-therapy. But the Lars incident, accident, tragedy had brought them close to each other, it was an experience they shared, and would go on doing so for life.

He took a taxi back to Karl's apartment, looked out for tell-tale men in parked cars but saw nothing outside the house. He let himself into the flat and went from room to room, hoping to find a note from Karl, but there was nothing. He'd made a quick decision and acted on it immediately, which was typical.

He tried the phone; the line was dead. He went back to his own room, untidy with all the equipment, somehow feeling uncomfortable.

It was five o'clock. He would have plenty of time to clean himself up and go to the studio before meeting Cathy who had to know something about it all.

He started shaving and as he looked at his tired reflection in the mirror he heard a very strange sound, like that of a bird flapping its wings, but flapping its wings in desperation. He went into the hallway, listened some more. The sound was inside him, the feeling he had was that he was a huge bird falling, then a vibrantly clear picture came to him of a tower block in all its immensity. Flashing past floor by floor at great speed, he looked down and saw the flat black tarmaced roof of a lower building coming up towards him. He doubled up for the impact. He had time to realise that he was not seeing his life in flashback as predicted, but only time to understand with horror that it was too late, the impact was near, the end now! He instinctively stretched out his hands, they were not his hands, they were Karl's hands – nausea, an awakening into reality, a feeling of sickness. He went to lie down.

Karl was going to fall from a great height then?

Karl had fallen from a great height?

Le Joffrin was a small select restaurant in a small select Chelsea street, with a centrepiece of flowers and cold buffet surrounded by some ten tables, blue tablecloths, matching napkins, polished silver and crystal.

He was early, there was no one else there except the waiters who were all charm and smiles. He asked for Miss Morrow and they showed him to a table for two in one of the corners by the window.

He had a white Cinzano, which they suggested, and he waited, nervously.

He wanted to be active, did not want to have time to think. Thinking meant going back over all the experiences he had been through and they were beginning to build up into something totally unmanageable. If it were not for that constant feeling that somehow, from somewhere, he was being looked after, he would probably go mad, if indeed he was not mad already. How did one know?

And were those children his subconscious guardians?

How could he know that?

And the fact that he was someone whom Karl knew about, who was on file somewhere?

Had Karl taken everything with him?

Cathy arrived ten minutes late. She had changed considerably, was carefully turned out, prettier, more efficient, not the crazy hippie he had met on the boat.

'What happened to *you*?' he asked.

She was wearing a white dress and he had never seen her in a dress before.

'You'll never guess. I landed the most incredible job! I'm head of public relations – U.K. division – of NPG. Can you believe it? Not only a whacking great salary, but expenses as well. So we can eat here! I also have a little apartment across the road, and they're paying for that too.'

She ordered a Campari and suggested what he should choose.

'What happened to Karl?' he asked.

'He sold out! NPG had been trying to buy him out for

months. He was terribly stubborn, as I understand it, and I'm not management so I don't know the details, but then he suddenly agreed and rushed over to New York to do another deal.'

Connected with Paul? Was Karl throwing himself headlong into psychic research because of him?

'You've changed a lot,' he said to Cathy, unsettled. He did not feel too much at ease with her, and she was being too matter of fact about everything. Barely ten days ago her father had died and she had reacted violently to Paul's presence.

'I've been through a fair amount since I last saw you and I owe you an apology. I now know that you had nothing to do with father's death, that you were only trying to warn me. I'm sorry.'

She put her hand on his across the table.

'I flipped my lid, as they say. One doesn't realise it when one does. You go through these traumas, these fears, and, though at the very back of your mind you know that you are ill, it is reality to you, and it's the reality that affects you. I was just frightened of everything. It was as though someone of great authority, like the God one believes in as a child, really appeared at the foot of your bed in a white gown and friendly white beard and said: "You are being deceived by everyone, you are even being deceived by me," and flashed! or something as ludicrous as that. The bottom falls out of your life. You can no longer trust anyone.'

'What pulled you out of it?'

'Mother. British stock you know. Stiff upper lip stuff.'

They ate, had a really good dinner. The dishes she had chosen were rich; they tried each others, he enjoyed that, but when he tried to talk more about Karl she changed the subject.

She offered him brandy, a cigar. He had two brandies, didn't smoke, started to relax. The warm glow in her eyes, the dare started to excite him. She suggested they leave.

Outside the restaurant she hesitated, not sure where to go. He suggested 'I'd better look for a taxi.'

'Don't be a loon, you're coming back with me. You don't think I've spent all this money on you just to let you go home. And what's home anyway? Come on, I've got a magnificent view of London looking West. It's a bit like New York at night, and the whole place is very respectable, I should warn you.'

They crossed the road, walked along the line of different coloured terraced houses, then turned left into an apartment block, through the well oiled swing doors and into a carpeted silence. They took an elevator to the top floor, went down a corridor and into her studio flat. It was hardly larger than a hotel bedroom, cupboard-sized kitchen, cupboard-sized bathroom and a bed-sitting room with a window that afforded a panoramic view of London, as she had said. The recessed double bed was unmade. She switched off the lights she had put on, and stood behind him as he gazed out at the night lights. She stood nuzzling the back of his neck, then he felt both her hands slide into his pockets.

Sheryl had behaved in a similar way.

Perhaps they all did.

But it was instant excitement, and she felt it. He turned round and grabbed her and both fell on to the bed. By the orange hue of the London sky they undressed and made love. At long last he had this thin, white, energetic girl in his arms and was controlling her lust with his now taut, sinewy, youthful body. She felt different to Suzy, to Sheryl, to Patty of long ago, he wanted this girl all to himself. He was infatuated with her.

He loved her.

'Why don't you go and collect your things and move in?' she suggested over breakfast the next morning. 'There's not much room, but then you haven't got very much.'

'What will I do with myself all day?

'Help me? I don't work regular office hours. Like today I'm organising this exhibition stand at Earls Court. You could come up with a few ideas. I could even pay you as a consultant.'

What had he to lose? The more involved he got with her and NPG, the more likely he was to learn what had happened to Karl.

The exhibition was not large, the general atmosphere fairly dull, humdrum, with a smell of dust, new carpets, fresh paint, but he enjoyed being occupied with something which had nothing to do with his inner feelings.

Cathy's stand was displaying a computer system. It was not

new, but was on show to keep the company name in the limelight. He met a number of important people who were totally unimportant to him; they liked him, his slight American accent fitted in with the corporate image they liked to project. He was hired for the week as stand host.

His legs hurt after the first day. Cathy's legs hurt too, so they lay in the hot bath together, sipping cold white wine before going to bed where they consumed smoked salmon sandwiches stolen from a reception at another stand.

For Paul it was the domestic bliss he had searched for all his life, love for Cathy, love for London, love of being free now to enjoy it.

On the last day he was arranging handouts on a table when a deep feminine voice purred his name behind him.

'Hallo Paul, remember me?'

He turned.

It was Sheryl Lidman, with Jack.

CHAPTER EIGHT

They were as delighted to see him as they were surprised.

Jack was in London for the International Space Year conference, they were staying at the Dorchester, why didn't he join them for lunch the next day?

As it happened, Cathy was leaving for a trip up North, the idea of which he hated, so being alone he took up the invitation.

He met the Lidmans at their hotel and they chatted about old times asking him without reproach about his trip over and how he liked London, how he was getting on, his plans for the future.

They were going down to the South of France to see their old friend Signor Capuela, why didn't he come too? He could then return to America with them if he had had enough of Europe and take over the management of the bookshop, Sheryl having decided to do other things.

He wasn't sure about that, he would have to think about it, meanwhile Jack left him with Sheryl to go to a meeting and so they went shopping. As she had in New York, Sheryl insisted on buying him clothes he did not want. 'You'll need that on the Riviera,' she kept saying, and he kept protesting that he hadn't decided to go yet.

He went back to the tiny flat where it was lonely and smelt of Cathy's scent. He was in love, wanted her for ever, would do anything she asked.

The phone rang. It was her.

'I'm stuck Paulie. I've got to be here the whole week, if not longer. It's awful.'

'I'll come up.'

'You can't. I'm sharing a room with a female colleague for one thing, and for another you'd hate it. There's nothing for you to do. Why don't you go off on a trip somewhere?'

He told her of the Lidmans' Riviera suggestion, and of their bookshop management offer.

'Go! For God's sake go! Why think of staying?'

'For you.'

'You're joking! If you ran the bookshop you could give me a job. I don't want to be doing this sort of thing for the rest of my life, and I'd love to live in New York. And you already have an apartment!'

He could see a future now, Cathy and himself running the Greenwich Bookcase, living in the home he would provide. He would grab the opportunity with both hands, make the most of the Lidmans. Why not? They wanted him to.

The following morning he tried to contact Karl Wiser. He rang the studios, but they had no idea where he was, nor did the people he had got to know at NPG seem to be aware of his existence.

He wrote him a letter giving him forwarding addresses and decided that once back in New York he would somehow find him. Since meeting Karl he had not been shadowed, since the Vulcan bomber incident he had been left in peace. Now perhaps he would be able to live a normal life.

He took the 11.35 flight from Heathrow airport for Nice with the Lidmans. Half way over France it occurred to him that this was the flight that might crash, the one he had been warned against. But then for days now he had been so removed from psychic impressions that he controlled the thought and, when the low cloud base cleared and he could see the green and brown landscape of Provence, he forgot his troubles.

The Tristar flew over the clear deep blue sea, banked back, came in low and landed at the small clean-cut airport with its palm trees and white buildings, perfumed air and suntanned people.

Giacomo Capuela was waiting for them at the customs barrier. He was an elderly, portly man, with a dark but powdery skin and receding white hair. He was dressed in a light beige suit, white shirt buttoned to the top but with no tie, had a large gold ring on one finger and smelt of cigars and eau de cologne. He spoke with a gentle Italian accent, softly, slowly.

He guided them to a large white Mercedes which he drove unhurriedly. Paul sat in front with him, Sheryl and Jack at the back. They cruised West out of Nice airport along a palm tree route towards the village of Cagnes-sur-Mer, up a small winding road, then in through some ornamental gates with the name of the house in ceramics embedded in the stone wall. 'Villa des Palmiers'.

The gates closed automatically behind them.

'Up the road, the Collettes, is the Musée Renoir, Auguste Renoir the impressionist painter lived there. You must visit it one day,' Capuela told him.

The Lidmans were clearly familiar with the villa, and were greeted by a manservant in white jacket and gold buttons as though they were regular guests.

The house was vast, on four floors, with a decorative entrance, white painted shutters at every window, stone balconies, a great mixture of Renaissance and rococco architecture covered beautifully by creepers and Bougainvillaea. The gardens were a mass of colourful flowers, and it was hot, hotter than anywhere Paul had been other than New York in August.

'I'll show you up to your room,' Capuela said, gripping his arm.

'I'm staying here?' He was surprised, he had thought he would go to a hotel.

'But of course.'

'I thought . . . '

'You are staying here as my guest, and when you have unpacked and put your things away we will have lunch, then a very long talk, for I know a great deal about you and your background, a great deal more than you know about yourself.'

He was taken up to the second floor in an elevator and shown into a quite delightful room of dark, dove grey wallpaper and yellow furnishings with a view overlooking the main gardens, a swimming pool, the town of Cagnes below and the sea beyond. By his bedside were a number of books, mainly on Italian history and Italy.

'When you have freshened up, please join us on the terrace,' Capuela said.

The manservant brought in his suitcase and he unpacked, washed his hands, his face, changed his shirt, thankful that Sheryl had been insistent on buying him more new clothes.

He went down by the marble stairs to the main hallway through an elegant drawing room to the terrace where Capuela and the Lidmans were having drinks. They then moved inside to a long dining hall, all white with chequered marble flooring and chandeliers, where they sat at a large round table to be served a pasta with seafood, the like of which he had never tasted before, followed by cold meats in various aspic jellies that melted in the mouth. The wine was another new experience and he realised how very little he knew about living, how poor his upbringing had been.

After coffee, served on the terrace, Capuela said, 'Come with me, let me show you around.'

They first started walking through the gardens which were stepped down to a wall marking the boundaries. Looking back up to the terrace, the house rose magnificently like a small palace.

'This used to belong to an actress, then it was a clinic between the wars, then a rich American business man bought it with the intention of retiring, but both his wife and daughter died and he himself lost his life in a strange accident. This man was called Michael Dartson. Does that mean anything to you?'

'No,' Paul said. 'Nothing at all.'

'You've never heard the name mentioned before in your family?'

'No,' he said, curious.

'Strange,' Capuela murmured to himself, and added, 'Perhaps she did not know.'

'Who did not know what, sir?' The 'sir' had come out quite involuntarily, but Capuela had the air of a professor who expected rather than demanded respect, and automatically got it.

'Your mother.'

'My mother? How does she come into it?'

'Before the actress sold this place, it was all fields beyond the walls, and up there on the hill you can just see the olive trees of the Renoir estate.'

They went round the swimming pool which was embellished with stone statues of nymphs and mermaids.

'You lived in the town of Syracuse, upstate New York until you were about sixteen, am I correct?'

'Yes.'

'Do you know why you lived there?'

'It was my mother's home . . . '

'Where you lived with her alone?'

'Yes.'

'Where was your father?'

'He was killed in the Vietnam war.'

'Was he indeed? When?'

'February 1965.'

'You would have been how old at the time?'

'Seven.'

'So you saw him quite often before that?'

'No. He was a salesman and not often at home.'

'Do you remember him?'

'Not really.'

'Do you recall him at all?'

'Not well,' Paul was beginning to feel uncomfortable at this personal cross-examination.

'No image of him? A man with brown hair, blond hair, brown eyes, blue eyes?'

'I don't remember.' Paul said this a little sharply. It was an area of his life he considered very private, probed only the once by Doctor Berkzic, the psychiatrist, who had concluded that he had never in fact met his father.

'So your feelings will not be hurt if I tell you something about your father, something a little disparaging?'

'No . . . '

They had reached the house now. Sheryl and Jack were still sitting having coffee, very much the tourists on holiday. They had been joined by an elegant tanned woman who waved at Capuela.

His wife? His mistress? This was a world he did not know but which promised scenes behind closed doors.

'Your father,' Capuela went on, 'was not a Vietnam war hero. He was a wealthy businessman from Syracuse who had an affair with your mother of which you were the unfortunate result. She was never married because he already was, which is why you are, if you'll excuse the expression, a bastard.'

They had gone into the house and reached a small room on the ground floor, a study lined with shelves of books with two comfortable chairs on either side of a low table.

'I call this my discussion study. It is only for two people and the books cover most reference items, so that details can be verified. Do sit down, but help yourself to anything you want. There is hot coffee, or tea if you wish. The aperitifs and liqueurs are on the trolley by the window.'

Capuela sat down, waited for Paul to sit in front of him before continuing.

'Your real father was married to a Boston lady of some means and background which forbade him from divorcing. Also they could have no children, that is to say *she* was barren which would have made matters worse if she had learnt of your existence. He was not a kind man, from all accounts, for he did not acknowledge your mother's claim that you were his son. He denied it fervently in fact to protect his reputation though your mother was his mistress for at least three years.'

Paul looked over at the display of bottles. It was very unusual for him to want a drink. Right now he felt he needed one. After hesitating he went over and helped himself to a cognac. 'Why are you telling me all this?' he asked after a silence.

'Because your real father's name was Charles Dartson and he was the brother of the man who owned this house. Michael Dartson was your uncle, though he did not know of your existence of course.'

Was he being told that he might have been a very rich young man but had somewhat missed out on an inheritance? Did the Lidmans know all this? Was it why they had been so keen for him to come down here, and behaved as though they felt sorry for him?

'Because of this link,' Capuela continued, 'you may be a fairly unique individual Paul, which is why you have been brought here. This is not my house but belongs to a Foundation known as the Dartson Psychic Research Foundation. Michael Dartson, as I mentioned before, died in strange circumstances, in this very house, and with your psychic gifts we are hoping you will clear up the mystery. But first we must carry out a few experiments to find out whether you have in fact inherited the same genes or not. What I am going to propose may not appeal to you at all, but from what I gather from Sheryl Lidman, you originally set out from America to travel?'

'Yes . . .'

'Good, so that after a few tests, which I would like to carry out, I would suggest that we journey together round the world, at my expense, to various places of great historic interest and see whether you can recall the past when in certain surroundings. Your uncle had quite unique recall.'

Paul did not know what to say. He was being told that he was important again, as Karl had already told him.

'I was put through a number of experiments in London recently by . . . '

'Mr Karl Wiser?' Capuela said with certain disdain. 'Yes, I know all about him. Did he in fact discover anything valid?'

'Unexpected sounds on tapes. I am apparently a transmitter of anxiety traces.'

'Your uncle was the same. All he had to do was pass through an anxiety trace and it would actually manifest itself visually, providing another psychic was present. This other psychic possessed certain powers which were never analysed. But tell me, do you still have recurring dreams? Recalls, visions?'

'Yes.'

'A man being castrated in Morocco? A baby being boiled alive in a medieval chapel? Yourself as a woman being raped in Spain?'

How did he know about all this? Paul obviously looked puzzled as Capuela said, 'You kept a diary, which Mrs Lidman read.'

'I see,' Paul said. She *had* taken his keys out of his jeans' pocket that night and gone to his apartment. Sheryl Lidman had been watching him all the time. How far back did it all go? 'May I ask you a few questions?'

'You may ask me anything you like at any time. It is important that you should trust me completely, it is even more important that you should feel you are free to go whenever you want and not feel you are under any obligation to comply with my requests.'

'Have I been watched by you, or by people working for you for a long time?'

'Yes.'

'How long?'

'Come with me.'

And Capuela got up, opened the door for him, ushered him through and led the way up the marble staircase.

The house was extremely bright, white, with striking modern paintings on the walls. On the first floor they went down a corridor, and Capuela opened a door and again ushered him through.

Sitting behind a large desk in the same hunched position as he had seen her seven years back was Doctor Berkzic. She stood up on seeing him, smiled genially, and came round in front of the desk to shake his hand warmly.

'Hallo Paul. You remember me?'

'Of course I remember you.'

'Well you see, one always meets an old friend again. Real friends are never lost.'

'How is it that you are here?'

Seeing her was throwing him back into adolescence, making him feel insecure, vulnerable again.

'I have been working with Signor Capuela for longer than you have been alive. It was I who first reported your psychic powers to him, and indeed it was he who suggested that we should have you write a diary.'

He felt cheated, deceived.

'But you must not feel deceived by this, Paul,' she said, as though reading his mind, a habit of hers he now remembered. 'What you must realise is that we have been protecting you because the weight you carry on your shoulders is really quite immense, which you will be made to understand over the next few weeks or so – if you choose to stay with us.'

Was he among friends? They were certainly being very gentle with him.

'There are so many things I want to ask,' he said.

'You have time. No one is pressing you to do anything but enjoy yourself.'

Capuela then interrupted.

'I have to go now, Paul, a previous appointment. Doctor Berkzic will look after you.'

Paul waited for the door to close, sat down in another comfortable chair. The room was airy, had two sets of French windows opening out on to balconies which overlooked the gardens. His room was probably just above. There were tapestries on the walls, a Persian carpet on the parquet floor. It was an aristocratic drawing room, certainly not a consulting room. Doctor Berkzic's desk was a Louis XV table, he thought, so ornate, heavy with brass mouldings. It was all beautiful.

'You'll have to give me time to come down to earth,' Paul said at last. 'It's all a bit sudden.'

'Of course.'

'Are there . . . are there other people living here? People like me?'

'There are not many other people like you in the *world*. No, six of us live in the house, four of them servants. The cook, two maids and Mario whom you've met. Secretaries come and go, guests come and go. It is an active house.'

He wanted Cathy. He desperately wanted Cathy to talk to, to help him work out what it was all about. If Sheryl Lidman, if Doctor Berkzic had motivated his life for the past six, seven years, had Cathy been involved, Karl?'

'You know of Cathy Morrow?' he asked.

'Of course.'

'Is she part of . . . your organisation?'

'Indirectly. She had no pre-knowledge of your powers until after meeting you on the boat, but she was put on the boat to watch over you.'

'A spy?' Paul said.

'A guardian angel,' Doctor Berkzic suggested.

'And did you have me watched from the moment I left Southampton?'

'You were watched once you and Cathy parted company.'

'Then your organisation is big . . . wealthy . . . '

'We are financed by the Electronic Sound Corporation of America. The importance of psychic research is not lost on big corporations, I am pleased to say. They see its potential power and eventual commercial advantages.'

'And Karl Wiser?'

'Mr Wiser is one of those persons who unfortunately does not know how to mind his own business. A dangerous amateur with a flair for drama who over-reached himself with the Vulcan bomber affair. You saw the report which the papers were going to print, but which was fortunately suppressed?'

'No . . . '

Doctor Berkzic opened a drawer and brought out a thick file. His file he presumed. From it she took a photocopy of an English newspaper cutting.

VULCAN BOMBER CRYSTAL BALL PUZZLE.

Five days before Stonehenge was laid waste by the Vulcan bomber disaster, a psychic research student foresaw the crash. Mr Paul Saralyn, an American electronics engineer working at the Karl Wiser Recording Studios, alerted the RAF that one of their aircraft would go missing. It was later officially stated that Mr Saralyn was undergoing psychiatric treatment.

'What happened to Karl?'

'We can only presume that the British authorities requested him to leave the country for a while. The experiments he carried out were completely unofficial. When he realised who you might be, that is, a relative of Michael Dartson and therefore not just a minor psychic phenomena *and* that you could warn people of danger, he decided to act on his own.'

'But his studios, did he really sell out to NPG?'

'The National Pharmaceutical Group, NPG, are a subsidiary firm of ESCA. They bought up the studios. We asked them to appoint Cathy Morrow PR so that she could again watch over you until the Lidmans could come over and bring you down here. All of course without making you suspicious of what was going on.'

'So Cathy . . . She must think me rather stupid.'

'Not at all. Why should she? She is very fond of you. Possibly a little too fond of you.'

'Will I see her again?'

'Whenever you wish. She works for us.'

'As a trained informer?'

'She worked for her father, who was heavily involved in industrial spying, which is why he got killed.'

'Cathy's father was *killed*?'

'You didn't know? Karl Wiser did not tell you? Oh yes. Mr Morrow was done away with because he knew too much about the activities of certain people – nothing to do with us.'

'How was he killed?'

'Drugs. Hallucinatory drugs which made him behave suicidally.'

Paul went over to the window and looked down into the garden. The pool was turquoise blue. It made him want to swim, but he would have wanted Cathy to be there, and then not. God! What were her feelings for him? And who was she with now? He would have to be a hell of a lot tougher than he was being if he wanted to survive this crowd.

'What you must do in the next few days Paul,' Doctor Berkzic said, not moving from her hunched position at the desk, 'is get to know your surroundings and understand that you are more than a guest in this house. You are a relative of the previous owner. You have a right to be here.' She got up, arched backwards to massage her back and joined him at the window. 'You must admit that it is a very beautiful holiday camp. We even have film shows in the evening if French television does not offer anything good. We have a tiny viewing theatre in the basement. Tonight Signor Capuela is showing one of his favourites – Fellini's *Satyricon*.'

Paul enjoyed the next few days and tried to forget Cathy. He found himself changing clothes twice a day and wearing those that Sheryl had bought him because Capuela lived in style and expected those around him to do the same.

He went for drives along the coast with the Lidmans, to Monte Carlo, to Cannes, saw for himself the places he had seen often enough in photographs, and on two consecutive mornings he talked to Doctor Berkzic.

It was comforting to be back with her, though he told her he felt it was returning to childhood and that he was afraid of relying on her again. She countered that he had self assurance now, had shed the need for a mother figure and that if he felt oppressed by her or Capuela, who was a dominant person, he should make an effort to defy them. They would understand.

They discussed at length what his feelings were about learning that his father was not a Vietnam war hero, and he admitted that, if anything, it was a relief. He had had an image of a red-neck bullying sergeant major with little sensitivity, and it had worried him. After two days of what amounted to analysis Doctor Berkzic decided that only one person seemed to be troubling him. It was not Capuela, herself or either of the Lidmans, but Cathy. They would have to do something about this because an anxious restless mind would be of little use to them.

Capuela was a meticulous man who ran the house, the Foundation, as it was known, like a headmaster. All the work scheduled for the day was put up on a board so that everyone knew what everyone else was doing. On the Monday a number of other people arrived, secretaries, an accountant, a research chemist all of whom had their separate work rooms on the third and top floor. They gave Paul a sense of security, confidence that he was not cut off from the rest of the world.

Jack Lidman went off leaving Sheryl behind, and she took on the role of constant companion, even visiting him in his bedroom one night after the private showing of *Emmanuelle*, a soft-porn movie he had heard about but never seen.

In the mornings, after a pleasant breakfast on the terrace, he regularly spent two hours with Doctor Berkzic, lying on the psychiatrist's couch and recounting all the dreams he could remember. The recurring ones of the baby in the cauldron, the castration, the suffocation in mud during a battle, the rape. Under hypnosis he recalled two other versions, one had to do with a witch burning, the other with the merciless flogging of a man on a rack, but he could never get further than describing the fear of what was about to happen, he could not re-live the experience.

Capuela joined Doctor Berkzic one morning when she tried to get him to repeat them, re-live them, but somehow Paul could not clear his mind. He was still nervous, taut, unable to relax.

Both talked to him separately and eventually came to the conclusion that he missed Cathy's company. Though Sheryl could provide him with sexual relief, it was not what was wanted. He needed the younger Cathy's love.

So Capuela put a call through to London, apparently requested Miss Morrow's presence at the Foundation for a while, and it was agreed that she would fly down within the next few days to take up employment as Mr Saralyn's personal assistant.

It was then that Paul realised how important he was, and from then on, happy at the thought of being reunited with Cathy, he was more relaxed, though he knew that he would never be able to trust her completely. Like Sheryl, she was, in the nicest way, another Suzy, and paid for her services.

That night he went to bed early to read, fell asleep but awoke feeling unbearably hot. He had a dream of himself standing unsteadily and painfully on a stack of firewood, bundles of dry twigs, with hundreds of people looking at him. They were ugly people, grinning at him with anticipation. There was smoke, an unpleasant smell and, looking to his left, he could see a human torch, like himself on a pyre, tied to a pole, the terrifying sight of this black body frying.

His mother haunting him again, the horror and fear that it might happen to him. Yet he now remembered that he had had this dream before. So perhaps it was a recall.

He had been told that if anything like this should occur he was always to tell Capuela or Doctor Berkzic immediately.

So he left his room and walked down the corridor towards Capuela's private suite. He knocked gently on the door.

'Who is it?'

'Me . . . Paul.'

'Yes Paul. Just one moment.'

Capuela opened the door.

He was wearing monogrammed burgundy silk pyjamas, the light was very low in the bedroom but enough for him to see, lying asleep in the double bed – Sheryl.

'Yes Paul?' Capuela repeated.

'I had this dream . . . I thought I'd better . . .'

'Of course. We'll record it immediately.'

They went downstairs to the recording room, a well designed studio-like laboratory with everything that was new in electronic sound equipment which Karl would have envied. When Paul sat down at the baize covered table in front of the microphone, he found he could not recall the dream, he just felt it. It was only half there.

'What's upset you? Something's upset you.'

'Yes,' Paul admitted.

'Well, what is it?'

'I didn't know you and Mrs Lidman . . .'

'Ah yes . . . I see. Well though you are an attractive young man, you cannot expect to have the monopoly of all the beautiful women in the world, Paul. Sheryl and I have been friends, should I say lovers, for a very long time. A very long time indeed.'

Paul said nothing but just felt acutely embarrassed.

'Your girl friend will be here in a day or two, so you must be patient. You must also be careful not to become spoilt. We have not yet proved that you are of psychic Dartson stock.'

The next morning Doctor Berkzic took him through the dream again, questioning him ceaselessly about the atmosphere, the fears, the smells, the colours.

After intense concentration and determination to please, he suddenly managed to cast his mind beyond the people, beyond the faces in the crowd, to the balconies, the three tired balconies of the terraced houses which formed a circle – like a bullring with no seats – and in among the crowd around the four or five funeral pyres where miscreants were to be burned alive.

Now he saw the procession coming towards him, the fearful people in white with pointed hoods over their heads, the leader holding a flaming torch.

First the screaming woman to his left, a dirge, bells, chanting, the flames sparking off deep in the pile of dry wood beneath her.

They were coming towards him, and the crowd was laughing. He was looking at his hands, his wrists; *he* was not tied, he was free and the crowd were roaring with delight for he was but a young boy placed on the pyre as a joke by his elder brother. The victim was behind him, strung tightly to the centre pole, an old man, toothless, white with fear, his eyes tightly shut.

A fraction of a second before the torch was put to the wood he touched the old man's face. It was cold. The man was already dead with fear. And to more cheers, more laughter, he jumped down, away from the sudden consuming flames, genuflecting and crossing himself before the leader of the procession whom he knew to be his father.

'What was your name?' Doctor Berkzic asked.

'Juan-Baptiste Almargo-Flores,' Paul heard himself say.

Doctor Berkzic took him by the hand and rushed him down

to the study and picked out all the travel books on Spain.

'You go through those, I'll go through these, and if there is anything, *anything* that jars your memory, let me know.'

He leafed through the three large books, all beautifully illustrated, stunning black and white photographs of Catalonia, Castile, the Levant, Andalucia, Estremadura, Madrid, then a double page spread was vividly reminiscent. Chinchon.

The village of Chinchon, some thirty miles east of Madrid, with its famous medieval bullring plaza, a circle of three storeyed balconied houses. He stared at it. This was the place, the place of excitement, the place of fear where they had burnt at the stake those who refused to bow to the demands of the Inquisition.

Excited, Doctor Berkzic rushed out to Capuela in the drawing room. 'We've found it. The first breakthrough – a memory dating back to the Inquisition in Spain. He was a young boy named Juan-Baptiste Almargo-Flores.'

'You have a date?' Capuela asked. He looked over the rim of his glasses at her, the perfectionist, the scientist unexcited by unconfirmed discoveries.

'The last burning at the stake was in Seville, 1780.'

'And you think this boy was related to Immaculada Almargo?'

'Her mother was born in 1794, we have proof of that.'

And Capuela took off his glasses and studied Paul with satisfaction.

'Come and sit down here my boy. I have a few more things to tell you about yourself.'

Paul sat down on the same sofa, turned to look at Capuela. What now?

'The name Dartson, backwards, spells Nostrad, a not overwhelming revelation, but Michael Dartson's granddaughter was called Emma, and Emma Dartson spelt backwards is – NOSTRADAMME. Do you know who Nostradamme was?'

'A 16th century French clairvoyant,' Paul said, 'who wrote his premonitions in rhyme . . . ' he added, aware that he had gone quite cold.

Is that where the strange quatrain had come from?

'He not only forecast a great number of history's major events, he also forecast your uncle's death and his relationship with another psychic whom I mentioned before. What transpires from this "vision" of yours, this "recall" is that you have the memory of one of his antecedents, which confirms our belief that you are indeed of the same lineage and therefore, presumably, have inherited the same memories and powers of premonition.'

Capuela then stood up.

'I want you to come with me now, to the top floor, which you have hitherto not visited, for a very good reason.'

Aware that something more important might be waiting for him, Paul followed Capuela to the elevator. Doctor Berkzic left them saying she would go back to double check the dates in the study.

When they reached the top floor Capuela pulled back the elevator gates and the moment they stepped out he felt a terrible oppression. It was something he had not experienced before, as though the long bright corridor with its thick blue runner was closing in on him, as though a blackness was sweeping towards him, so much so that he finished defensively, wanting to step back into the elevator, but Capuela was behind him, watching him, stopping him.

He felt his arm being gripped firmly, felt himself being led down the corridor, then Capuela stopped and turned him round.

He now saw, standing by the elevator cage, a grotesque figure, a young woman with long reddish hair, naked with a bulging pregnancy which was as translucent as the children. Within the pale milk-like transparency he could see a curled up embryo, a foetus.

The elevator gate was open and the woman was looking down the shaft, and from the depths of the well rose a scream, not the sound of a scream, but the anxiety of a scream. He could hear nothing but knew that something terrible had happened. He felt drawn towards the woman and the elevator, wanted to look down, and he felt Capuela following him, holding his arm ready to restrain him if he went too near. The woman did not sense his presence, did not turn round, and he looked down the shaft.

At the bottom, right down at the very bottom, lit by a strange bluish light, was the disjointed bloody figure of a man.

CHAPTER NINE

Paul turned away and found himself facing Capuela. He turned again to look down the well, but the vision was over, the elevator cage was back, the gate closed.

'What did you see?' Capuela asked gently.

He did not want to talk, did not want to say anything.

'You can tell me, it will help,' Capuela urged.

'I saw a red headed woman, pregnant, and a man at the bottom of the elevator shaft.'

Clearly Capuela was pleased. 'Now come in here, we call this the chart room.'

It was a bright, airy room with ceiling-to-floor panoramic windows looking out over the town and the Mediterranean. On the other three walls hung charts, family-tree charts, lists of names and maps. In the middle of the room, otherwise furnished with filing cabinets, was a large terrestrial globe.

One chart, which occupied the middle of the main wall, listed the descendants of Nostradamus. MICHEL DE NOSTREDAMME was printed at the top, and beneath were such names as Jeanne Chapelet, Michel Le Notre, Jaume Lanotte and Immaculada Almargo.

Another chart listed the descendants of Nicollo Machiavelli, one of the names at the bottom was Giacomo *Capuela*.

'History, Paul. The facts of history. If you look down here on the Nostredamme chart you will see the name of Michael Dartson. Now from him we draw a horizontal line and add the name Charles Dartson, your father, whose union with your mother, Nancy Saralyn, produces a son – Paul Saralyn. Working up through the names you then see quite simply that your cousin was Sarah Dartson, with whom you share the same grandfather, *James M. Dartson.*'

'What of Emma Dartson?' Paul asked, looking at the line down from Sarah Dartson, her offspring.

'As far as we know she died together with the mother in

childbirth, which leaves you the only survivor of the line, you see. That is why you are valuable to us.'

Paul, fascinated, moved to another chart. The descendants of Rasputin. The bottom name was Grigori Gregoriev.

'He went back to Russia,' Capuela explained. 'We worked together at one time hoping that we were as psychic as you, but though our ancestors were famous, they were not in fact clairvoyant. We have drawers full of family ascendencies.' He opened a filing cabinet. 'Very few natural psychics survive modern history. In medieval times witches and sorcerers may have been burnt at the stake, but they were respected and feared and their cabalistic knowledge handed down from generation to generation. The twentieth century does not acknowledge occult powers. But as you well know, they exist. Indeed they exist.'

Capuela moved to the centre of the room and spun the terrestrial globe.

'Have you ever been to Australia?' he asked.

'No.'

'I meant in a recall?'

'I don't think so.'

'According to some of the documents we have here, a certain Patrick O'Neil, father of the first Michael Dartson your great grandfather – therefore your great, great grandfather – was deported there, but came back.' He opened another filing cabinet and brought out a sheaf of old letters.

'We have some correspondence here, written by him, received by Sarah Field, his wife, before they were married, in which he says . . .

> " . . . I cannot tell you the horrors that we went through on the boat, the journey itself round the Cape, the discomfort and stink, so many of the crew and prisoners going down with the scurvy. Because I looked after myself and played dumb, they soon regarded me as a lunatic and left me alone, but when we reached Melbourne, there was untold horror." '

Capuela looked over the rim of his glasses. 'He had been accused, tried and found guilty of embezzlement so was himself a convict. But he apparently escaped.' He read on.

'We camp in a small village where the inhabitants were half aboriginal and half white, a strange mixture, men with the blackest of skins and the whitest of hair, penetrating eyes but gentle unless angered by insults. I spent many hours just sitting among them gazing at the sunsets and sometimes the sunrises. But all this was marred by a fearful incident. Two of the women were known as the witches and they were not unlike those I had imagined when first reading Macbeth, hideous creatures with platted hair and partly toothless. One of our troop, a dreadful man named Tomas, turned on our guards one night and there was a fight. He was a strong, powerful man and hit a guard so hard that he was sent backward flying, cracking his head against a rock. He died instantly. The penalty for killing a warder, indeed for assaulting one, was death by hanging, and the other guards hurried without trial, or indeed questions, and strung Tomas up from the branch of a tree. The knot in the rope was so badly tied, however, that it did not instantly break his neck, or throttle him, and he took a long time a-dying. We were made to sit in a semi-circle not ten feet from him to witness the hideous death. Then, as the moon rose low above the trees, the two witches appeared, breathing heavily as though in a trance, and to our astonishment brought with them a bamboo table which they placed under the swinging man. We thought, those of us who were still awake and watching, that they were going to take down the body to bury it, but no, slowly, as though it were a ritual, they shed their ragged clothes and first one, then the other, stepped up on the table and pulling down the dead man's trousers, fornicated with him as he was in a state of rigor mortis. It was so hideous a performance, so evil, that I was sick, but aware of my capabilities and knowing how close I was to the "refuge", I escaped.'

Capuela put the document back in the file and closed the drawer.

'Your cousin, Sarah Dartson, had recalls of this incident many times. She was fully aware of her ability to go back into the past. Have you had any visions of such a memory?'

'Yes,' Paul said. 'Once.'

'This particular recall is important, because in historic terms it is the most recent.'

Paul mentally counted the 'memories' which recurred most often. Certainly none were of the present day, nor any within the century.

'Doctor Berkzic and I would like to use this recall as a test. What we are interested in doing is seeing how much you can remember of your great, great grandfather's memory, how much *has* been handed down, and to do this we will give you a truth drug, and ask you beforehand not only to read, and re-read the letter I have just quoted, but also to hold the original parchment in your hand during the night. We want to *steep* you in this memory. It is also one which did not end totally unhappily for the observer. He did get away from his guards.'

The next morning he was asked to lie down on what amounted to an operating table in the middle of the electronics room and was wired up, much as Wiser had wired him up. All night he had slept with his ascendant's letter, he had read it over so many times that he could recite it. Now Doctor Berkzic gave him a painless injection, the truth drug, and he closed his eyes feeling a little drowsy. He felt Capuela take his hands and place them on his chest and thread in between his fingers the rolled up parchment letter from Australia.

The recall came to him remarkably quickly. The paper in his hands tingled, gave out a certain amount of heat and he felt himself floating, a sensation he had not experienced before.

'Can you hear me?' Capuela's voice sounded, some distance off.

'Yes . . .'

'Try and describe in words what you are experiencing, but do not force it . . .'

First he saw the gum trees white against a black sky which slowly brightened till the foliage was golden, then dark green, the sky navy blue, then turquoise, then celestial. The grass underfoot was dry, burnt. A parrot flew across his field of vision. Birds sang, hundreds of birds, he was quite alone in an unexpected paradise though ahead the rocks were threatening. He had to go to the rocks, they beckoned. He went down into a valley, across a creak; a rivulet flowed over white and brown stones. He started climbing again. The sudden elevation of the rocks now towered unexpectedly above him. It was so impressive that he was aware of a heavy silence.

' . . . There is something mysterious here, mysterious about these rocks . . . ' he said aloud.

The bright sunlight now played on the steep façade, showing up the intricate construction of the tall vertical slabs, some grooved by ice-age torrents, others smooth as honed tombstones. There were lizards asleep on the hot surfaces, a snake slithered into the shadows of a strange tropical plant, there were bright flowers he had never seen before in among the mass of ferns which reminded him of lakeside walks back home.

He climbed on.

Soon he found himself on a circular platform surrounded by boulders and a few bushes growing out of the crevices. He went on up, found another platform with much the same aspect as the lower one, ringed with boulders and loose stones.

There was a view now, a magnificent view of the plains on the other side of the rock formation. As he stood on the platform with its clumps of ferns, its carpet of dry yellow moss, he could see a ribbon of bright silver water in the mist, the rivulet he had crossed below.

He went on up.

' . . . the mystery hangs heavily about me now,' he heard himself say in a far distance. 'It is oppressive . . . '

And the atmosphere about him seemed to become heavier as he felt the physical change taking place within himself, a weightlessness he could not control, as though he would be propelled upwards by just touching the ground with the tips of his toes. As he climbed he felt himself floating above the hard hot earth, but floating strangely, and as he looked down he saw that he was not floating above but *below* the level of the rock surface. He was moving in a very straight line at the same level *through* the rock, the earth, the mounds, like a ghost towards the massive overhanging peak which dwarfed everything else around it to what seemed like an opening in the rocks, but very high up, much higher up than he had climbed. It was as though he had flown up there yet had had no sense of flying or going through the air. He was up there now, in front of this gap, a black hole, a void. And he passed through into this vacuum over this vaporous floor which was neither smoke, nor cloud, nor mist but some soft substance which neither threatened him nor aroused his curiosity. He could accept all the strange things around him, the paleness of the light everywhere and the people standing about like himself suspended in space, suspended in time *and* space. He looked at all of them and realised that they were translucent, the light was coming through them, they were like the children, they were like the obese woman transparent with the foetus inside her he had seen by the elevator shaft in the Villa des Palmiers, and he turned away and as he did so he felt himself falling, falling straight down as though through a hole in the sky, falling at incredible speed, then he opened his eyes and found himself looking up at a concerned Capuela staring at him, a curious Doctor Berkzic holding his hands which were ice cold.

'What happened?' he asked.

'You quite suddenly froze,' Doctor Berkzic said. 'Your body temperature dropped to zero, your pulse rate stopped completely, we thought you were dead. What did you experience?'

'Didn't I talk?'

'A few incoherent sentences.'

Paul told them, told them everything, every detail he could remember.

'I see no connection whatsoever with the O'Neil letters, no connection with Australia,' Capuela said to himself.

'Oh, I *was* in Australia,' Paul insisted. 'I was at a quite famous landmark near Macedon north of Melbourne.'

'How do you know?' Capuela asked.

'I just know.'

'Macedon?' Capuela asked again.

'Yes.'

'That rings a most unexpected bell . . .'

And he left the room without saying anything more.

Doctor Berkzic unclipped the various wires that were stopping Paul from sitting up, then gave him a drink of cold water. He swung his legs off the operating table and sat sipping slowly until Capuela returned holding an illustrated geographical volume open at a special page.

'Does this picture remind you of anything you have seen before?'

He held the book up.

The photograph reproduced was of the very rock he had just climbed, seen from a slightly different angle, but totally recognisable. Under the picture was the description:

THE HANGING ROCK
AT MACEDON, VICTORIA.

'Why would I have been there?' he asked.

'Because,' Capuela said throwing the book on to the table and going over to look out of the window, 'because your ascendant Patrick O'Neil went there.'

'But why would the memory of such a place be so striking as to be strong enough to be handed down?'

'At its summit, which you floated up to, you saw people hanging in space, you described the void as a black hole, you said you felt like a ghost . . .'

'Yes . . . ?'

A number of schoolgirls vanished at this Hanging Rock in 1900 and their disappearance was never satisfactorily explained. Similarly in Peru, near Machu Picchu, persons have inexplicably disappeared. Also in a Newfoundland bay in Canada, and in the Bermuda Triangle.' Capuela was not looking at him, but staring into space, thinking aloud.

Paul did not see the connection.

'The connection, dear boy,' Capuela said, 'is some sort of link with astral projection. Patrick O'Neil, Michael Dartson's great grandfather, astrally projected himself to escape his guards. You inherited that memory! This is what he meant by " . . . aware of my capabilities and knowing how close I was to the refuge, I escaped." '

Capuela turned to face both Paul and Doctor Berkzic.

'I was always curious how a man in those days could have written such a letter to his wife, a letter containing a description of witches fornicating with a corpse in the state of rigor mortis. But O'Neil and his wife were quite obviously very sophisticated people, far in advance of their time, and had somehow, *somehow* stumbled across the very secrets which we are trying to unveil. The *refuge* is a place to which people who are capable of astral projection go to when in danger, or when they wish to leave this earth and perhaps change into another time dimension. Who knows? And there are these pockets, these "refuges" in certain places for reasons obviously unknown. I believe that the Hanging Rock at Macedon is such a place. And the Triangle another. What we must now work towards is getting our young friend here to master the art of astral projection, then perhaps journey to these exotic places and see what happens!'

That afternoon Capuela drew up a formal business contract for Paul to sign. He suggested that he should find his own lawyer to verify it, but Paul said he trusted Capuela enough not to complicate things out of proportion.

They were asking him to sign his privacy away for a period of sixty months, for a sum which any middle-aged executive would have been proud to earn.

The money would be deposited in an account of a bank of his own choosing, on top of which all justifiable expenses would be paid by the Foundation.

The limitations on his life style in exchange for this was that he would not be allowed to drive any car, take any risks with his own life, that he would make himself available for experiments five days a week during normal office hours, unless it was deemed necessary to work nights or week-ends. He would be allowed to marry and to divorce, to carry on his life as he wished providing *he* was aware that at all times he might be monitored.

Paul took the draft document out into the garden and sat by the pool to study it. It was a hot day and his feelings about the proposals made him feel even hotter. It was a major decision, but only a decision that would tie him up for five years. At twenty-seven he would then be a very rich man.

He sat in a deck chair under the shade of the palm trees and read through each clause carefully, and when he looked up the children were standing there, not five feet from him, holding hands and shaking their heads. Translucent, pale, but not oppressive.

They had not killed the last time he had seen them, he had kept quiet about them; they were advising him not to sign and instead of freezing, or becoming paralysed with fear, he managed to smile at them.

'It's a lot of money . . . I don't know where you're from, but where I'm from money can do a lot for me. It can even help *you* if you need help.'

He spoke in a whisper. The idea had occurred to him right then that *they* were seeking his help perhaps, not the other way round. But they shrugged their shoulders, looked round as though seeking someone else's help, then very gently disappeared, like ghosts.

He sat there for a long time staring at the spot where they had stood. He did not have any reaction, he did not shiver or go cold or find it hard to breathe. He just sat in the deck chair and realised their appearance was beginning to be normal, something he would have to get used to. Were they guardian angels, nothing more . . . or less? He then read through the contract again and realised he needed Cathy. If possible he would wait till she arrived before signing, he would ask her advice.

And he got up and walked slowly up the steps to the terrace and into the drawing room where Capuela was sitting reading, Doctor Berkzic opposite him.

'There is nothing in this about Cathy,' he said, holding up the contract. 'I would like some assurance that she *is* coming, and will be employed as my assistant.'

He thought it a good ploy to delay.

'Cathy will be arriving this afternoon.'

'Really?' He was overjoyed.

'If you sign,' Doctor Berkzic said as a joke. 'Otherwise we'll stop her plane in mid-flight and turn it round with our specially developed kinetic ray-guns.'

Capuela did not smile. Doctor Berkzic's sense of humour, specially regarding their work, was always rather doubtful as far as he was concerned.

'Then I'll sign,' Paul said. What the hell. He was caught up with them whether he liked it or not.

Capuela handed him a gold pen, Paul got down on his knees in front of the glass coffee table and signed the document.

'You had better witness it,' Capuela said to Doctor Berkzic.

And the doctor witnessed the signature.

'Now, for a start,' Capuela said fairly severely. 'Tell us to whom you were talking down there in the garden?'

Paul felt himself blush. He felt his face growing red, a flush of fear, of all sorts of things.

'Fifty thousand dollars a year is a great deal of money for a young man, Paul. You must start earning it, and Clause 6 of the contract does state that you will not keep anything from us.'

The children had appeared at the very moment when he had been reading Clause 6.

'Who were you talking to? There was someone down there.'

'Yes,' Paul said.

'The children?' Capuela asked softly.

Capuela had never mentioned them before. Doctor Berkzic had never mentioned them before. He was astounded.

'We know they exist,' Capuela said.

It made it easier. It took the edge off the guilt of talking about them.

'You've seen them before?' Capuela went on.

'Yes.'

'In your bedroom in New York. We know that because you told Sheryl, and wrote about it. Also when your mother died. But where else?'

'In the washroom at Kennedy airport.'

'Was that the premonition that stopped you taking the flight down here?'

'Yes.'

'They warned you that the plane might crash.'

'That's what I understood.'

'Why didn't you tell us about them before?'

'Because I was frightened.'

'Of them, or us?'

'Of what might happen. I believe them to be warnings, omens of death.'

'Why?'

'Because I had only seen them when someone has died.'

'That is not strictly true. When you first saw them in your bedroom, no one died.'

'No, but they were seen by someone on board the *MS Bjornstjern* when the steward died.'

'*Did* you just see them in the garden?'

'Yes,' Paul said reluctantly. As he said it he felt incredibly disloyal. They held something over him these children, he did not know what, but they were more part of him than anything else he knew.

Capuela looked across at Doctor Berkzic who had closed her eyes in great satisfaction.

'It is surprising what money will do,' Capuela said. The remark was uncomfortably acid. 'Now you have told us you have seen them, could you describe them?'

Paul described them. The more he talked about them the more he felt guilty.

'Have you any idea who they are?' Capuela then asked.

Paul shook his head.

Capuela explained.

'The girl is the astral projection of Emma Dartson, daughter of Sarah Dartson, granddaughter of Michael Dartson. The boy is the astral projection of Adam Dartson, the *son* of Michael Dartson and Melanie Forbes, the lady you saw by the elevator the other morning, who frightened you so much.

Paul felt drained, he seemed to be caught in a web of names and relatives and ascendants and descendants.

'The younger boy is in fact the girl's step-uncle, if you care to work it out. He was born after Emma from a later union. And Melanie Forbes killed Michael Dartson, like a black-widow spider, after achieving what she had set out to do – that is, get a child from a psychic man.'

Sheryl had come quietly into the room and now sat behind Capuela on the back of the sofa. All three were staring at him.

Capuela went on.

'The children are potentially more dangerous to the world if their power falls into the wrong hands than even you would be. You are clairvoyant, can see into the past, into the future, can practise psychometry, dormant powers which do not threaten other people's lives. They, like Melanie herself however, have all these gifts *plus* the positive kinetic powers which she developed. Melanie Forbes blacked out New York, she killed your uncle by melting part of the elevator mechanism, *they* could probably burn down a city! They have now also mastered the art of astral projection so that they cannot be caught.'

Capuela sighed deeply. It was to make Paul feel like a traitor to humanity, and it certainly made him feel extremely uncomfortable.

'Fortunately, one of your potentials is to be able to see through the veil, if not astrally project yourself. You are therefore our only weapon against Melanie Forbes whom we know to be evil. We did not tell you this before because we were not sure, but now it seems that, through them, she may be trying to entice you. My own feelings are that she needs your energy to help these children get off the ground, so to speak. The human being is capable of leaving his own body, projecting himself a vast distance, and re-forming in a similar shape elsewhere. Uri Geller did it, however much one may smile and laugh at the account of his going through a plate glass window, *but* to do so he must have borrowed energy and, as we are talking of little children who have less of their own, it is possible that they need yours in particular because you are a blood relation.'

Sheryl drove him down to Nice airport to meet Cathy's plane from London. When she came through customs looking even more beautiful than he remembered her, they hugged and kissed and she hugged and kissed Sheryl and was full of wonderment at the sun and the palm trees and the atmosphere of the Côte d'Azur.

When they drove through the gates of the villa, she gasped at the splendour of it all.

They first went into the drawing room where she met Capuela who took a long critical look at her, clearly liking what he saw, causing a little pang of jealousy in Paul. He was Italian and suave enough to charm any female of any age, despite his portliness. Then they were left to themselves and he took her up to his suite of rooms – for the room next to his had been converted into a living room for their use as a place to work and relax.

'This is all ours?'

'The bedroom, the drawing room en suite and the bathroom!' he said proudly.

It was all pleasantly bright, the balcony giving out into the gardens where she kissed him lovingly.

'I've missed you, Paul, God I've really missed you, but I guess I have a lot of explaining to do before you believe and trust me.'

He shrugged his shoulders, was too pleased to see her to want to talk about the past.

'How are things?' she asked.

'I can get almost anything I want by just asking. There are a few limitations, but what job hasn't? Besides, the work we're doing is fascinating.'

'Tell me everything, but could I have a swim? The pool looks so inviting.'

Both got into their bathrobes and went down in the elevator, through the dining room and down the steps to the swimming pool.

They sat with their legs dangling in the water and he told her about the experiments they had put him through, the conversations he had had with both Capuela and Doctor Berkzic, the contract he had signed and how Sheryl had taken care of everything in New York, letting the apartment and sending over his books which would be arriving any day. He was really looking forward to that, seeing his books again, and Capuela had arranged for a carpenter to come and fix up some shelves in 'their' drawing room, specially to accommodate them. He had thought a good deal about the offer of the bookshop in the village, but then that offer had not been too genuine, nothing that Sheryl had done or said had been too genuine. Whether he liked it or not, he was somewhat caught up with the Foundation.

They dived in, swimming underwater, meeting, kissing, the young lovers, aware that they were being watched but also that they were being protected. Romeo and Juliet could do no wrong.

'Do you know how much they're paying me for being here with you in this paradise?' Cathy asked as they got out and spread themselves on the sun-mattresses.

'No.'

'Five hundred dollars a week. How about that? And I don't even know what I'm supposed to do.'

'Look after me. I am a very important but delicately

balanced creature. I can get pretty upset sometimes and then time is lost. I'll make sure that it isn't too easy for you so that you don't develop a guilt complex about not earning your keep.'

Sheryl came down to join them, swimming four healthy lengths. Then they all went up to the terrace and had lunch in their swimsuits, Capuela questioning Cathy mercilessly yet gently about her last job with NPG.

She was bright, knew all the answers, couldn't believe what fun it would all be. Then there was just one moment when Paul asked her about Wiser which caused him some surprise. She hesitated before saying anything and both Capuela and Sheryl seemed to freeze.

'Have you seen him, is he back in London?' Paul asked.

She opened her mouth to say something, there was a rapid exchange of glances between the three of them, then she too quickly answered, 'No, he's still in America,' and covered up her apparent mistake by adding, 'It's said he bummed out voluntarily on the deal he was trying to make. Rumour had it that NPG really got his business cheap and that he was unable to get what he wanted in the States. Last I heard he was in California . . .'

'I like him,' Paul said, revealing the tension. 'He's mad, but I like him.'

'He's unscientific,' Capuela said, wiping his mouth before tasting the iced white wine. 'Unscientific and therefore a danger to you, my boy.'

After coffee everyone went to their respective quarters for the traditional siesta.

Paul spread himself on the bed, he liked the feel of the silk bedspread.

'Would you go to bed with Capuela?' he asked.

'Wow yes! That man is something.'

'I don't see what's so fascinating about him.'

'His eyes, his hands. His elegance!'

'But he's fat.'

'He has a delightful middle-age spread.'

'Old-age spread.'

'Are you jealous?' Cathy asked.

'Cautious.'

And she joined him in her dry swimsuit, and they lay there

on the flat of the bed, the sun cutting through the slats of the blinds and he unclipped the top of her bikini and the pressure of her young breasts on his suntanned skin was the most sensual thing he had ever felt.

She moved on to him, gently, softly, and he eased off the bottom of her bikini as she spread her fingers between them, flat on his stomach, then moved them slowly down to grip him firmly as she kissed him passionately.

'You know what?' she said, looking at him suddenly. 'You know what ESCA do for their female staff? They fit them with contraceptives!'

He raised his eyebrows. He preferred to avoid clinical conversations when he was about to be romantic.

'They're incredible these Corporations, they really look after you. I've got this new device inside me, developed by NPG. It's much smaller than a coil, and safer than the pill. It's got a quartz thing pulsating away or something to counteract body rhythm.'

'Does it work?'

'Well, I'm not pregnant.'

'How long have you had it?'

'Couple of weeks.'

'Could you be pregnant?'

'Oh, Paulie . . . you're going to eat yourself up with jealousy with me . . . I'm faithful to the person I'm with. If I stay here five years I'll be faithful to you five years, but the occasional adventure doesn't really harm, does it?'

'I don't know.'

By then his physical desires had become so intense that the jealousy he might suffer in the future hardly mattered. He didn't want to miss her if she went away, that was all. He didn't want to be separated from her.

His passion was quick. Forty-three days of separation quick, and it was all-glorious with sensual rockets and fireworks blazing a trail through fluttering star spangled banners. He felt deliciously drained and lay there happy in his exhaustion.

'I trust that you don't imagine that I'm in any way satisfied with that performance, Mister S!' she said, still sliding over him.

'I need a breather,' he said, closing his eyes and smiling contentedly.

'I guess you men could have a pretty hard time of it hiding what you've been up to. Had you lasted a few seconds longer I would have become extremely suspicious.'

They lay there in each other's arms, striped by the sun coming through the blinds, like a pair of entangled zebras.

'What really happened to Karl?' Paul asked. 'I don't think you were able to say, you had a moment of hesitancy.'

'The hesitancy was because I went to bed with him, Paul. I'm sorry. I'd rather you knew now. That's all.'

She smiled at him.

'Before or after we got back together?'

'Before. But it still makes me feel a bit shitty. Though you should be used to my behaviour.'

She disengaged herself, knelt on the bed next to him and put a finger to her lips. She then slid off the bed quietly, crossed the room and picked up her bag from the chair, fished out a pen and a piece of paper and returned to the bed. As she scribbled something on the paper she said romantically . . .

'I think your willie's got bigger since I've been away from you. Does that Doctor Berkzic exercise it as well as your mind?' And she handed him the note.

He held it up to read.

Karl is dead – room is bugged – everyone your enemy – do not *talk – will tell you all when safe.*

'Do you think my breasts have got bigger?' she asked in the same tone of voice, then signalled *him* to say something.

'I think you're a lot more beautiful. I like your hair curly like that.'

'My hair's always been curly.'

'I meant the hair on your head.'

As they cuddled up, Cathy popping the note into her mouth and chewing it with certain disgust, the telephone rang.

It was Doctor Berkzic.

'You are ten minutes late for your session with me. If you could possibly spare me even half an hour this afternoon I would be most grateful.'

And Paul looked at Cathy, now uncertain whether they had been watched, whether the mirror on the wall was two-way, whether the paintings had peep holes, whether they were going to live a life of constant danger.

CHAPTER TEN

The session with Doctor Berkzic was uneventful, a retracing of his childhood, his school, the games he played, how he used the tarot cards to impress his friends, the way he read palms and the results.

'You're not concentrating today, Paul, I can't think why,' the doctor reprimanded him. 'Perhaps you had better go off with that young lady of yours and satisfy whatever urge it is that needs to be satisfied, because you're no good to me at all in your present state.'

He left, grinning, happy. His 'present state' however had less to do with Cathy than with his preoccupation concerning the note she had written.

His room was bugged, his conversations taped, they had the excuse to do it, even his permission, but what she did not want them to hear had nothing to do with the experiments.

After the dinner 'en famille' with Capuela and Sheryl, Doctor Berkzic and Cathy, he walked down to the pool in the dark with Cathy and was about to ask her about Karl again when she anticipated his question and squeezed his hand very tightly. So he said nothing, realising that obviously she knew a great deal more than she could convey.

They did not manage to get away from the house or the garden till the following afternoon when he just casually let Doctor Berkzic know he was taking Cathy down to the sea.

Not until they were on the rocks that jutted out from the pebble beach on the Cros de Cagnes was Cathy sure it was safe to talk.

'You have no idea what's going on, Paul, no idea what you're in. You're at the centre of a power struggle. ESCA, like all the multinational corporations, are deeply involved in politics and they are aware that by using people with psychic powers they could dominate their rivals.'

Paul looked at the sea, the crystal clear water lapping gently against the rocks, its peacock blue and green hues in the depths only a few feet away. What Cathy was saying was as remote from him as anything could be.

'ESCA, through Capuela, want to get those children.'

That was closer home.

'You know of the children?' he said, surprised.

'I know all there is to know. Melanie Forbes disappeared without trace while expecting Adam, taking Emma Dartson with her. She's trained them to practise astral projection and will then help them develop kinetic powers. These children are a danger in Melanie's hands, but under ESCA's control they could be lethal. Capuela is using you to find them.'

'Who is this Melanie exactly?'

'She's a psychic. Years ago when the Foundation was started by Capuela, he gathered together the descendants of psychically orientated historic figures – Machiavelli, his own ancestor, Rasputin, Cagliostro, Copernicus. The idea was then apparently to "mate" these families together in an attempt to produce a super-psychic being. Melanie Forbes, a descendant of an American clairvoyant family, was the only powerful female in the group. She was therefore able to choose whom she wanted to have a child by. She refused everyone within the Foundation and went out on a limb to find Michael Dartson, got pregnant by him and then killed him.'

'Why?'

'No one knows for sure. Perhaps he threatened her own life. She became a great friend of his daughter, Sarah, who gave birth to Emma, then died. One theory is that they both had plans to rebel against male domination in the psychic field. The Women's Movement was just gaining momentum then. Sarah was as gifted as you.'

'How do you know all this?'

'Daddy had photostats of Capuela's files. He was a chartered accountant working for NPG and originally employed to negotiate ESCA's financing of the Foundation.'

'And how did you come into the picture?'

'I worked for him.'

'To spy on me?'

'I suppose so, though I was unaware of it at the time. I was on that boat to keep an eye on you, but I never knew the real reason. He told me you had applied for a job with ESCA and they wanted to check you out. It didn't occur to me that Daddy might lie to me, of course.'

'So what of Karl?'

'He fell to his death from the top of the NPG building. Supposedly suicide.'

It was Karl he had seen then. It was Karl's death he had experienced back at the apartment.

'A hallucinatory drug, like your father?'

Cathy did not answer but looked out to sea.

'Karl should never have got involved,' she said after a while. 'Somehow he found out that ESCA were keeping you under surveillance, realised you were important to them and why. So he tried to make you public by telling the world of your Stonehenge premonition. He didn't reckon on their connections. ESCA suppressed the story and silenced him.'

'Why did they kill your father?'

'He knew of the children's existence and of their potential. The children are top secret. We're all being led to believe that space is the next big prize after the control and ownership of energy, Paul, but it isn't. The big prize is what is in all of us, the ability to develop our extra-sensory perceptions. ESCA knows this, so do the oil companies and everyone else who has muscle.'

Paul went on staring at the sea, the dazzling reflection of the white sun catching the wavelets on the immense blue ocean that stretched out as far as the eye could see.

There was a fisherman on another rock, sitting on a canvas stool, watching a cork somewhere on the water at the end of a long line. What did he know of ESCA, Capuela and Melanie Forbes, or the children. And why were the children haunting him?

'When they get what they want out of you, Paul, we're both going to be in danger.'

And, as though sensing something, Cathy turned round and looked at the beach road a little way behind them.

'How long has that Citroën van been there?'

Paul looked at the van, a nondescript blue vehicle with a local name on it.

'Don't know, why?'

'I've become so suspicious lately. I imagine "bugs" everywhere. I don't think my life's my own.'

'You think there's some sort of sound-beaming device in there so they can listen to us?'

'We're dead ducks if there is. Or at least I am.'

Paul stretched his hand out and took hers and squeezed it. As long as he could be with her, near her, that was all he cared about right now. He couldn't say so because she was on another level, fighting 'them'. But he was selfish. They had lulled him into a comfortable way of life where he was hidden from everyday evils, and he wanted that to go on for ever.

He looked at his watch; it was nearly dinner time and they should go.

'Have you ever thought of escaping?' Cathy asked as they made their way over the uncomfortable pebbles back to the road.

'Escaping from what?'

'From the villa, from Capuela.'

'I don't feel I'm a prisoner.'

'You're being tracked all the time, Paul. I even feel our conversation *has* been overheard.'

'Are you over-reacting, do you think?'

'Maybe. But will you just try something with me?'

'Yes.'

'When I say run up that side street, then run like mad. O.K.?'

'If you like.'

He liked the childish side of her character, the nonsense side. He loved it.

'Go!' she screamed.

They raced each other to the side street, he winning by some seven yards because she was handicapped by her sandals.

She fell into his arms panting, then pushed him against the wall behind a telegraph pole.

'Now watch.'

The nondescript van revved up to the end of the lane, braked sharply and two faces looked at them. Realising he had been duped, the driver ground his gears and drove on.

'Somehow they can listen in on us,' Cathy said. 'Right now they can hear what I'm saying. And I'm very frightened.'

She held on to Paul's arm, gripped his hand tight. Her face went pale, her lips pinched, her eyes tearful with fear.

'What do you want to do?'

'Maybe they'll allow me to talk to them before they do anything.'

'What would they do?'

'Oh, just kill me, Paul, eliminate me because I know too much.'

'If they did that I'd . . .'

And she put her hand over his mouth.

'From now on, until we know for sure it's safe, we don't talk any more.'

And bravely she started up the lane, took him through the town shopping centre to the Avenue des Collettes which led to the entrance of the Villa des Palmiers.

Capuela had guests for dinner, innocent people who had no idea what really went on in the house, but imagined that Capuela was an art historian, and Paul and Cathy two of his pupils. The talk was of Renoir, of how Cagnes had changed over the years, of how the Riviera and the Côte d'Azur had changed, of modern art, of how the paintings that hung on most of the walls by an American artist called Raulk who had met his death in a mountain storm while trying to capture on canvas just that – a mountain storm.

During the meal Paul noticed Cathy becoming concerned by something which had nothing to do with the dinner conversation. She suddenly became unsettled, even flushed.

When everyone moved to the drawing room for coffee and liqueurs she excused herself and went upstairs.

As she did not come down again after some twenty minutes, he made his own excuses and ran up to see whether she was ill. He found her in the bathroom, nude from the waist down, examining herself in the mirror.

'What's the matter?'

'We've been bugged, Paul. All this time we've been bugged. They've heard everything we've said, even when we were way out on the beach. They're listening now, I expect. But guess how. Just guess!'

He now realised she was shaking with anger, and anger which seemed to stem from some form of humiliation.

'I don't know,' he said.

She pointed between her legs.

'Their fucking contraceptive. It's a microphone.'

'How do you know?'

It vibrated during dinner. It's done it before. I never thought about it, but it's just the clever sort of device ESCA would dream up.'

She turned her back on him.

'Well, ESCA darlings,' she said through clenched teeth, 'I'm going to get the bugger out!'

She then pulled her dress over her head and went into the bedroom.

'I may need your help. Have we any long tweezers, or a crochet hook or something? God knows how I can get at it?'

'Doctor Berkzic may have some . . .'

'Paul, we can hardly ask her! She probably invented the damn contraption. Though by now it's probably general knowledge that we've cottoned on to their little invention. Our conversation's probably been taped in triplicate and sent to the U.S. of A. by satellite. God, they really stoop to conquer, these sods!'

And quite unexpectedly, she grabbed hold of his hand and squeezed it very tightly as though in a panic.

'It's getting hot. It's getting hot in there, Paul!'

And her face changed quite suddenly, she flushed, gasped, then creased with pain. She grabbed herself between the legs, doubled up and fell to her knees.

'Oh my God, Paul, it hurts!'

Her mouth stretched open, she sucked in air and, as though having an epileptic fit, jack-knifed, rolled herself on the rug, twisted, writhed, arched her back, took the weight of her body on her shoulders, on the balls of her feet, stretched her arms out, her hands and fingers extended, her nails scratching at the floor.

She rocked for a few seconds, fell heavily on her side, looking up at him with glazed, terrified eyes, trying to move her lips but paralysed.

'It destructs . . .' she whispered with great effort.

She twitched once or twice like a dismembered spider's leg, then Paul saw blood oozing down her legs.

'Cathy?'

The blood pulsated out now, a steady flow soaked up by the rug.

'Cathy!'

He turned her face towards him.

Her eyes stared straight ahead, fixedly.

She was dead.

In a frenzy Paul opened the door and screamed for help.

It was not a scream, it was a bellow, and five people came running to him from various directions, two servants, Sheryl, Capuela and Doctor Berkzic.

Losing total control Paul seized Capuela by the lapels and yelled in his face. Doctor Berkzic swung him round and slapped him hard across the face.

'The children did it!' Capuela said, recovering his composure quickly. 'The children killed her as they killed Lars on the boat. The *same way*!'

Paul felt drained.

He didn't know what to believe, at every corner, at every turning, over every hill the landscape changed, became more fearful, more entangled with things he did not understand.

'The children are being totally manipulated by Melanie Forbes, Paul. She tells them to kill, they kill. Now we believe they function in their "projected" state only because they are using her energy. She cannot go on and on giving them that energy. She must have help from another source. That other source is *you*! She is eliminating everyone who comes between you and her goal. We are all in danger now!'

While Doctor Berkzic with Sheryl and the two servants went into the bedroom to take care of Cathy, closing the door in his face, Capuela gently led Paul away down the marble staircase to the seclusion of the study.

'The children, Paul, are extremely delicate creatures, incredibly intelligent, freaks not of nature but of *supernature*. On the various occasions that you saw them, did you ever notice their height?'

Paul wasn't sure what he meant. Though he was listening, he was also aware that his emotions had been shattered, that once alone he would be very alone because Cathy was dead.

'Did you notice that every time you saw them they had grown?'

'Yes . . . ' Paul said.

'How old would you say they were? Five, six, eight, nine years old respectively?'

'About that.'

'Both were born three years ago. Physically they are still infants. Their projection is growing at three to four times the normal rate. In fourteen years time they will be older than you, and under Melanie's influence could prove a major threat to world stability. Can you imagine how the masses would react to children who can astrally project themselves across continents and appear three times their real age, then return to their true infant physical bodies but still with adult minds?'

He watched Capuela pour him out a very stiff brandy, took the glass handed to him, and tried to relax.

'Cathy's death is but the beginning, Paul. Unless you make an effort to comprehend the danger we are all in, and help us.'

He was deliberately not given time to think about Cathy. Her body was taken out of his room to a cloakroom downstairs.

Capuela called a meeting in the drawing room to discuss with Sheryl and Doctor Berkzic what the next step should be. They could go to Macedon in Australia and try a contact with the children in the refuge through Paul, though there was no reason to believe that they would be there. They could also risk a trip through the Bermuda Triangle where Capuela was sure they would find further clues to prove his theory. They could also try a new tactic and let Paul go alone, but really alone for a few days to see if the children would approach him.

Did Melanie know the plans that were made at the villa? Were they all being monitored somehow by them? It was known that Melanie could read minds. They should also be careful not to rush blindly into an obvious trap. Paul was extremely vulnerable and had no psychic armour whatsoever. He could neither judge whether an experience was past, present or future, and would certainly be no match for Melanie's kinetic powers.

'What are Melanie's kinetic powers, exactly?' Paul asked.

Sheryl replied: 'Electromagnetic manifestations characterised by heat rays aimed at a target. You do not see them, her eyes do not light up and laser rays shoot out of them. She can sit there in front of you, concentrate on, say, the refrigerator in the kitchen, and it will stop working, or overheat. She is able to cause machinery to malfunction. She would certainly be capable of wrecking the mechanism in an aircraft, thus causing it to crash, but fortunately she would have to be in the plane to be close enough to its engines to do so.'

Dr Berkzic suggested they might be pressing the panic button too soon and not giving Paul a chance to develop. 'Would it not be better to continue the experiments we have started to establish what Paul is best at, though maybe step up the activities by next taking him to Montpellier where Nostradamus studied, then Paris where he lived and died, in order to get direct visions or anxiety traces from the source of his ancestry?'

Capuela was not sure. 'Cathy Morrow is dead, killed by Melanie, I have no doubt about that. This means that she was active within our circle, within the villa. I have fears for Paul's safety, indeed I have fears for all of us.'

'Do you think, then, that it is time for us to ask for help?' Doctor Berkzic asked.

'From whom?'

'The United Nations, the United States Government, both go over the heads of ESCA.'

Paul looked quite amazed.

'Don't look so surprised, Paul,' said Capuela. 'We are not playing games here, we are at the centre of a very dangerous and escalating movement. Let me read you something . . .'

Capuela left the drawing room for a moment to go to his study and returned with a white paper. He flicked over a few pages, then said: 'This was a speech made on October 7th 1975 by Dr Eric Gairy, the Prime Minister of Grenada, at the Thirtieth Session of the General Assembly of the United Nations. "The time has come when the United Nations Organisation must seriously give thought to, and initiate the establishment of, an appropriate department or an agency devoted to *psychic research.* Man's ignorance of certain aspects of his immediate environs and, most certainly, of his esoteric or inner self, and the various inexplicable phenomena which continue to baffle even the most advanced branches of science. The Bermuda Triangle is but *one* example. The knowledge that may become available to man through psychic research could very well make him the complete master of self and circumstances, and not the subject, in some cases, the slave thereof."

'It was in November 1975 that ESCA first approached me with the proposal of injecting money into my idea of a Foundation. They were quicker than other corporations in taking Dr Gairy's speech seriously. By 1977 I had got a few key psychic people together, including Melanie Forbes. Then everyone lost interest, the world recession forced financiers to look at their balance sheets, but I soldiered on. The Foundation broke up, Grigori Gregoriev returned to Russia, and Melanie chased off after Dartson, and you know the rest.'

'What was Grigori Gregoriev's part in the researches?' Paul asked.

'He perfected astral projection. His mother claimed to be a descendant of Rasputin, thus inheriting some of his so called "magic" powers. I saw her myself, when she was an old woman, leave her body and she was seen by reliable witnesses to appear naked in a bathroom some twenty-five miles away virtually a few minutes later. Melanie Forbes claimed to have perfected astral projection to such a degree that she was able to cross the Atlantic in her astral body and ring someone up on the telephone in New York from France only minutes after leaving New York. But, and this is the unknown area which we must work very hard on, persons who astrally project cannot do so without energy. A short distance can be achieved using normal body resources, but to travel great distances, as the children are doing, there *must* be what can most simply be described as a refuelling base. I believe, with no proof, but I *believe* that on this earth there are such refuelling bases, certainly in the Triangle, possibly near Machu Picchu, in the Himalayas, and it seems at Macedon, Australia.'

Paul sat looking at them all, aware of the comfort of the sofa, the peacefulness of the room. This was how major world decisions were discussed. He had read enough historical biographies to know that nothing was ever done in a panic or on an exploding battlefield. Roosevelt, the Kennedys, Churchill had not been panicked into action; the world oil crisis was not discussed under a shower of black oil gushing dramatically out of a new well. It happened like this, coffees and brandies in hand, all in great comfort surrounded by valuable, beautiful antiques, with paintings to look at on the wall, even gentle music in the background. It was difficult to realise that what they were talking about was so important. It was even more difficult to gauge his own part in the whole business.

'I think I will try to get hold of Gregoriev tomorrow. He may well be the answer to it all,' said Capuela. 'If Paul could be taught how to astrally project, then perhaps we would have the answer. Right now I think we should all go to bed and get some sleep.'

Paul could not, of course, sleep. He was alone for the first time since Cathy had died. God, the people he was with were so incredibly insensitive! He needed Cathy, he needed her trust, her love, he needed someone to allay his fears of the whole horror of what had happened and the whole impact of what she had told him. With that monster of a woman Melanie getting closer to him, Karl murdered, Cathy's father murdered, a psychic war in its infancy, he felt totally confused. He had lost a friend, a lover before their love could be proved, he now felt anger and hate for the unknown, a sudden urge to avenge her death.

Then he became aware of a smell of burning.

He sat up.

At the foot of the bed he saw the children.

This time the boy stood a little behind the girl, while she stared at Paul intensely.

For the first time he had a good look at them. What was repulsive was that he could see beyond the translucency of their skins, which was a grey pink, and beneath it he could see the hearts and the lungs, the bowels, the veins, the muscles, shadows of bones behind the face. When they moved, their flesh trembled like a sickly white jelly. Their odour was strong, so strong that he feared others in the house would smell it.

The girl then held both her hands up and, in deaf and dumb language, started to spell out a message.

Deaf and dumb language was something he had learned at school from other kids, they had used the code in class during exams or when ganging up against one poor individual or other. It was something he remembered, like Morse and semaphore.

Half a circle formed with the thumb and index finger of the left hand – C.

Index finger of the right hand pointing at the thumb of the left – A.

Both hands forming a T.

One palm swiped across the other – H.

He understood . . . CATHY.

Then the little girl shook her head while pointing between her legs. She repeated this action several times then put her hand to her heart and twitched and cringed as Cathy had done. She then pointed at the door and down, again at the door and down, all the time keeping her eyes on him, questioning whether he understood the message.

He shrugged his shoulders, unsure.

She touched her lips and mouthed words and pointed at him.

'You want me to talk?' he whispered.

She nodded.

'I've understood Cathy. It's to do with Cathy, her death?'

The little girl nodded, then exploded her hands and fingers and, not shy, again put her finger between her legs and shook her head furiously.

'She was killed by the contraceptive device?' Paul said.

The girl nodded yes.

'Melanie did not kill her, nor you?'

The girl shook her head, the boy shook his head. Both then pointed at the door and down.

'Go and check?' Paul suggested.

Both nodded, then they pointed at the books by his bedside and insisted he should pick up one of them.

He pointed to each one in turn. They shook their heads till he reached the one they wanted. *Renaissance Florence 1464-1534.*

He pulled it out. The girl held up the fingers of both hands. TEN. Again, TWENTY. Again, THIRTY. Again, FORTY. Then THREE.

Forty-three.

'Page forty-three?'

She nodded.

He found page forty-three and read down it quickly.

It was about agriculture, about landowners and feudal relationships. It mentioned countless names. Is that what she wanted, names? Place names?

He read them out, glancing at her after each one.

'Genoa, Alberga, Savona, Cinqueterre, Moneglia, Sestri, Levante, Rapallo, Pintromelli . . . ?'

She nodded quickly.

'Pintromelli?'

She then made it clear by signals that that is where he would find them. Pintromelli, north of Florence. That is where they lived.

Hearing footsteps outside in the corridor he then switched the light off, and to his astonishment saw that the children glowed. They were phosphorescent.

Slowly they faded, very slowly, nearly flickering out like a dying candle. And as they went the smell disappeared.

The footsteps went on by. It was one of the servants, he had learnt to recognise the footfalls. A door closed. The house was in silence.

He lay back on the bed in the dark and after a long time of thinking over what he had been through came to a decision. Maybe the first major decision he had ever made.

He felt at ease with the children, he felt they were his friends. He felt he could trust them. Despite all that had been said against Melanie, the warnings that she wanted him, he felt the children had been more constant than anyone else.

He would check Cathy's death. He would find out who was telling the truth and, if the children were protecting him, which they seemed to be doing, he would then go to Pintromelli as they had asked him to.

He lay silent in the dark aware that the room was probably bugged, that somewhere in the depths of the house someone he had never met might be monitoring his every movement, his every sound, that his one-way conversation with the children was now probably taped. But maybe time was on his side for the tapes would not be heard by Capuela till the morning, and even then they would be regarded as words spoken in dreams.

Remembering some book he had read, some true-life adventure story about escaping prisoners of war, he recalled that the ones who had got away had been the ones who acted on the spur of the moment when an opportunity presented itself. The long term planners became nervous nearer their decided time of escape and failed, while those who suddenly acted, drummed up the necessary adrenalin to give them the energy and intelligence to get away with it. He would act now, while the house was asleep. He would go down and find Cathy's body and see for himself how she had died.

He got dressed and, as a precaution, slipped his passport and money in his back pocket as he had when escaping from the Bramber Hotel in London. Barefooted but carrying his moccasin shoes, he cautiously opened the door and tiptoed out into the corridor.

The night silence was broken only by Capuela snoring, which didn't mean that Doctor Berkzic or Sheryl or other servants were asleep.

He went down the main stairs thankful that they were of marble and not wood, which might have creaked. In such houses you could walk around at night for ever without waking anyone. He went quickly to the kitchen; raiding the larder would be an excuse for being out of his room. He had not eaten well and it would be understandable if he were hungry.

He waited in the dark for sounds.

Nothing.

He had got so far without raising an alarm.

He slipped his shoes on.

Cathy, he knew, had been put in the cloakroom. If he switched on lights they would shine out in the garden and be seen from upstairs. He would have to get a candle.

He went back along to the drawing room, tiptoed in, picked up one of the candlesticks from the chimney piece and a table lighter and made his way to the cloakroom. In the dark he knew she was there because of the smell of surgical spirit.

He set up the candlestick on the edge of a washbasin and lit the candle.

His eyes, accustomed to the dark, found the flame very bright.

Cathy had been laid out on three trestle tables and covered with a sheet.

He drew it back.

Her face was quite beautiful, at rest now, a slight tightness round the mouth, but nothing as horrific as he had expected. He pulled the sheet slowly off her.

She had been stripped, cleaned, her arms had been crossed over her breasts; over her lower abdomen a complication of bandages had been taped. He took hold of a corner and slowly ripped the bandages off. An incision had been made which was still bloody. If any device had been in there it could have been removed. If she had died from supernatural causes, like Lars, he would not know. He was no surgeon. The question remained unanswered.

Then he was startled by the metallic click of a door opening. He wasn't sure where. He blew out the candle, had the presence of mind to pick up the candlestick and the table lighter and slipped into the lavatory.

He was aware of the candle smoke, the give away, but he held his breath and the lights went on outside in the hallway.

'It's in here.'

Sheryl talking, to one person or two?

The door opened. More lights on.

'Someone been in here! My God!'

Hurried footsteps, sharp heels on the marble in the hallway.

Paul eased the lavatory door open and looked. There was no one there. Sheryl's companion, whoever it was, had followed her.

He darted across the cloakroom into the hallway, felt the fresh draught from the open door to his immediate right leading out to the side of the house, the tradesman's entrance. He did not hesitate, ran out into the night and saw the Citröen van in the courtyard, the back open.

He did not pause to think. Everything was in his favour. They had come to take Cathy's body away, the gates would probably be open. He would risk it.

He got into the driver's seat, felt around in the dark, along the dashboard for the ignition keys, found them under the steering wheel. He switched on. The dashboard lights lit up.

He turned the key further; the engine hummed into life, loudly. He pressed the clutch down, put it in gear, let the clutch out gently and moved forward.

He put his foot down a little further on the accelerator and he was away, through the arch on to the front drive, the gravel crunching loudly, but the engine purring obediently. He accelerated, saw the gate ahead in the darkness, felt around for the light switch, inadvertently pressed the windscreen wipers, the traffic indicators, now the headlamps blazed and he put his foot down further.

He was away. Left, out of the gates, down the winding narrow lane, round the hairpin bend and again taking the second bend a little too fast. At the crossroad, he turned left, now the main road, then he realised the back doors were flapping open. He would be stopped by the police. It was too suspicious. He couldn't risk it.

He pulled up, leapt out, slammed the back shut and looked up the hill at the house. It was ablaze with lights. They would not be long in giving chase now. He got back in, feeling safer, and drove on, fast. The road was easy, deserted, only an occasional car coming the other way.

He took the Nice road; he would head for Italy. He would get as near to the border as possible then abandon the van and walk across the frontier.

He roared along, nothing threatening in his rear view mirror. They would phone the police, claim their vehicle had been stolen. He was vulnerable, could easily be recognised. Then ahead he saw the turning off to the airport. He took it, swinging the van wildly down the underpass.

People now, officials, cars, movement, noise. He was in the middle of bustling civilisation where a van would not be noticed. He pulled up outside ARRIVALS. There was an airport official there, or was it a porter? It was a porter who glanced at him with little interest.

Paul pulled the keys out of the ignition, left the sidelights on, got out and walked into the terminal building so as not to arouse suspicion.

It was quiet, a few people were drinking at the bar, several travellers waiting for a flight. He went round the closed boutiques, the bookshop, the various booths, then left by the

DEPARTURE doors, glancing to see if the porter was looking his way. The porter had gone.

He wanted to run, but he walked, slowly, hands in his pockets. Thank God for the heat of the night, for the fact that casual wear was normal.

He followed the road round the cluster of palm trees, the spotlit flower borders. He crossed the roadway to keep in the shadows, went through a pedestrian tunnel, up some steps but found himself in an enclosed car-park. It was higher, a vantage point. He could see the whole terminal building, the van parked there with no one taking any notice. Then he saw the line of taxis parked not far behind.

Could he risk that?

He retraced his steps, back through the tunnel, across the road. He went over to the first taxi.

'Monte Carlo, s'il vous plait.'

'Oui monsieur.'

The man leaned backwards over his seat to open the door for him. Paul slipped into the comfort and safety of the warm leather, slipped down and waited for distance to be put between himself and the villa and everyone in it whom he no longer trusted.

On the way out of the airport they passed two cars. Neither of them were Sheryl or anyone he recognised. Down the underpass and up on to the highway, east along the coast road to Nice, the Promenade des Anglais, up and above the sea, Villefranche, Cap Ferat. The meter was ticking, he had exactly two hundred francs, it might well cost him that.

Along a high road with overhanging pine trees, the moonlit sea wall below on the right, magnificent villas behind stone walls and hedges. How many of those hid psychic foundations, he wondered. They went up a steep hill when the taxi's head-lamps blinked and went out and the engine stalled.

The driver was surprised, cursed, put on the brake. He tried the starter, the electrical system was dead. He couldn't believe it.

From the glove compartment he brought out a torch, got out, opened up the bonnet and looked.

Paul did not move. Engines were not his strong point.

'Je m'excuse, Monsieur, mais . . . . une faute electrique . . . que je ne comprend pas . . . '

Paul wasn't sure he comprehended either.

The driver returned to the depths of the engine, fiddled about, and Paul closed his eyes, relaxed, trusting the man's ability to put it right.

Then he heard the woman's voice.

'Puis-je aider, Monsieur?'

He looked up. She was young, very feminine, her features delicate, her skin extremely pale with reddish hair. All this he sensed rather than saw because it was dark.

It was Melanie Forbes.

CHAPTER ELEVEN

He was fascinated enough by her presence to sit up, then he opened the door and got out.

'Hallo Paul,' she said in a quiet, penetrating voice.

It was the woman he had seen by the elevator shaft at the villa, but slim now, even beautiful.

Instinctively he reached out to touch her.

'Oh I'm real, Paul. This is the real me. My car's up the road, I hope you'll trust me enough to let me help you.' She smiled winningly, then turned her attention to the taxi's engine.

'Je pense que c'est ceci . . . ' she said and touched the fuse box. The lights went on immediately.

'Ca alors!' And the driver got into his vehicle and started up the engine.

'Ca c'est vraiment bizarre. Merci, hein, Mademoiselle, ca . . . c'est drole . . .'

She smiled some more and suggested to Paul that he should pay the man off. The driver accepted a token fare, and Melanie put her arm round Paul's shoulder and led him to a small Renault parked further down.

'Where are you taking me?' he asked.

'You know that already. If you think a little you know a great deal without asking. Just accept the fact that your first intuitions, the ones which need little concentration are probably always right. You suspected Capuela and Sheryl Lidman and you were right to do so. You suspected that they were responsible for Cathy's death and you were right. We're going to Pintromelli, which is where you were heading.'

'Are the children there?'

'Of course.'

'How did you know I'd be on the road? This road?'

'It's the only likely one you'd take for the frontier.'

'How did you know I'd be on it tonight?'

'I didn't. I've been waiting for more than twelve hours.'

They reached the Renault, she got in, unlocked the passenger door, and he sat beside her.

'Did you stop the taxi? Did you cause the electrical fault?'

'Yes.'

'How did you know I was in it?'

'I guessed, Paul. If you want to know I stopped seven cars along this road today by mistake. I'm not perfect.'

She careered on to the road, sitting bolt upright in her seat with arms fully stretched, her hands gripping the wheel.

He liked her.

And he was very thankful he liked her.

'Have you been to Italy before?' she asked.

'Don't you know?' he asked humorously. He felt he could tease her, already.

'No. Where you have been is of no great importance. All I know about you is that you are Charles Dartson's bastard son, that you look a little like Michael, and that Capuela thought you important enough to get ESCA behind his interest in you.'

Ahead he saw a beautiful bay lit up by the tight conglomoration of high rise buildings and realised they had already reached Monte Carlo. They drove through its empty night streets. He recognised two or three of the roads he had seen in films of the Rally. He watched her drive, steadily, occasionally glancing in the rear view mirror. They went up the hill and out towards Menton, and on a straight piece of road when he expected her to accelerate, she quite suddenly turned left, cutting right across to drive a few hundred yards down a dirt track.

She stopped the car in a clearing, next to a small rusty grey Fiat.

'That's my car,' she said, getting out. 'I only borrowed this one so that we could not be traced. Now you must take off all those lovely clothes and your watch and your beautiful shoes and put on these I've brought you. If they can bug poor Cathy's vagina, they can bug your buttons and anything else.'

She opened the door of the Fiat, brought out a plastic bag and handed it to him. It contained a pair of jeans, a T-shirt and some sandals.

'Not quite what you've been accustomed to of late, but your standard of living is going to somewhat slip. So get used to it now. Have you had any fillings lately, false teeth, false eyes, anything shoved up you?'

'No,' Paul said.

'Then I only hope they haven't bugged the shampoo you use or your aftershave. ESCA will stoop to anything.'

He changed into the older clothes quickly, thankful that it was still dark.

'What shall I do with these?'

'Leave them in the car. It won't make any difference whether they find them or not.'

He got in next to her again. She started up the little old buggy, reversed it like a dodgem, and shot on to the main road.

Paul looked back, they were alone, no one was following them.

'In answer to your earlier question of where we are going, we're not going to Pintromelli. That was a decoy name in case you were bugged and our conversation was being heard. We're not going too far from there, still north of Florence, but a very remote place, so remote that no one has lived there for a hundred years.'

It was about four in the morning now and Melanie drove at a steady pace. Perhaps her foot was flat down and it was as fast as they could go.

'Did you check on Cathy?'

'How she died, you mean? I couldn't tell, she was all bandaged up.'

'They're pretty ruthless.'

'They said you had killed her and that you killed the steward on the boat.'

'*You* killed the steward on the boat.'

He felt himself going numb.

'I didn't know . . . ' he said eventually.

'But you willed it. You concentrated hard enough. That's what you wanted, that's what you achieved.'

'I had no control.'

'Control has nothing to do with kinetic powers. That's why it's so dangerous. I'm surprised Capuela didn't lecture you on that.'

Paul fell silent. Went over the episode of his jealousy, his hate for Lars in his mind.

He had killed without knowing.

'Could I do it again?'

'I expect so. With a little help from your friends.'

'I don't understand.'

'The children were there.'

'You mean I couldn't have done it without them?'

'I mean that they obeyed your command. They were the weapon.'

'But I didn't even know of their presence.'

'It was a long distance experiment, Paul, don't worry about it. Just a little something to prove to you that we were a team.'

'Capuela has a theory about the Bermuda Triangle. We were in the Atlantic, some way north, but was there any connection?'

'That is a mystery which will be revealed to you when you are fully initiated. I must leave you some incentive, a goal to work towards, or you might get bored.'

She let go of the wheel with her right hand and gently patted his knee. They were through Menton and ahead was Ventimiglia, with its brightly lit customs post, the French police and the Italian standing about smoking the night away.

A uniformed man asked Melanie something. She waved her passport in his face and he signalled them on.

'No problems with the EEC now, it's all one big happy family feeding on itself.'

'How long have you been living in Italy?'

'Since last year, when your uncle died.'

'I was told you killed him,' he said bravely.

'I did.'

A shiver ran down his back.

'What you must understand Paul is that there is a continual power struggle going on in the world. You have, on the one hand, as I'm sure you know, the so-called world powers, then behind them the financial world which has the true control. When they master the psychic powers in key individuals, then the struggle will be another ball game altogether. The ones who get there first will of course make bloody sure that no one else does or finds out how. And I've got there first.'

Dawn was breaking, the colours were beautiful. They were travelling along the Italian coast now towards Savona and Genoa.

'Which is why,' Melanie said after a while, 'you are so important to Capuela and his Foundation.'

'Why couldn't he work on himself?' Paul asked.

'He's basically lazy. He loves the role of master of the villa, of the important executive and possible politician. If he could he'd become President of Europe, that's where he sees himself – which is not surprising considering he is a descendant of Machiavelli. But he also wanted you as a weapon against me. What I have to do is convince you that my ideas are right. I failed to do that with Michael, which is why he tried to kill me and his then unborn son. His death was self-defence on my part, Paul. That you must believe.'

'How old are Emma and Adam?'

'They were born in 1977.'

'You're not answering my question.' It was strange how familiar he could be with her. He felt he knew her better than Cathy, as well as his mother.

'No one knows this, Paul. Spiritually they grow at the rate of three times their natural age, but their natural age is already three times what is expected. They should be infants but spiritually Emma is nine, Adam eight. She is very bright, understands problems extremely quickly. Adam is quite strange. He has tremendous energy resources and incredible recall. Sometimes I'm a little frightened of him.'

She slowed the car down on seeing a café-bar ahead.

'Are you hungry?'

'Yes, very,' he said.

'Then we'll stop here,' and she drove the Fiat off the road, jamming on the brakes.

'Is it safe?' Paul asked.

'Not really, but they will be confused for a while, then eventually they'll trace you, because ESCA has informants everywhere and Capuela will have to take orders from them once they learn of your escape. I'm just banking on him not telling them that too soon.'

They had a strong coffee and very rich cakes, standing at the bar.

'How fond were you of Cathy?' Melanie asked.

It was the first time he had seen her in a bright light; she looked very young, and really quite attractive.

'Very fond,' he said.

'In love or infatuated?'

'I thought I was in love.'

'She's not lost Paul. She left something behind. Memories. It's up to you to use them or discard them. We'd best get on.'

He felt better after eating. They got back into the small car and drove on.

'The man at the bar next to us, did you notice him?' Melanie asked.

Paul had not.

'No friend he.'

'How do you know?'

'I know who all my enemies are. Their vibrations stick out a mile. It's called first impressions. They can save you a great deal of trouble. I've worked hard on mine. You should do the same. Take note of them, be aware of them, gauge your feelings about people the second you set eyes on them. A minute after it's too late. Their smile, their studied charm erases intuition. You liked me the moment you heard my voice. I liked you when I saw your silhouette in the back of the taxi. That was all I needed.'

After a while Paul asked, 'What exactly do you want me for?'

'The children need a second parent, and they will need more protection than I can give them. Capuela is not a danger to their lives, he will want to preserve them, develop them, control them, but the others, the ESCAs, the CIAs and the Cougars of the world – they'll kill them because they'll be afraid of what they don't understand. And what they don't understand, or rather refuse to understand, is that the children can put us on a level footing with other intelligences in the universe.'

'Is there life elsewhere in the universe?'

She slowed the car down and leaned forward to look up at the sky through the windscreen. Though it was getting light a few stars and the moon were still shining.

'Do you honestly imagine that we are the only form of life in among all that? The conceit of man astounds me. We're developing slowly, very slowly, but eventually there will be fewer of us and we will be more intelligent and we will travel, not by vehicles like this, but in our minds, and we'll visit the other planets as I'm sure we're being visited now. Not by spaceships or spacemen or anything we can imagine, but by some psychic means.'

'What happens when we're dead?' Paul asked.

'You know the answer to that as well as I do.'

'We go on?'

'We *can* go on. We *have* the choice. It's a question of work. You've read enough to know that every philosopher gets near to the truth when they work. Many go in the wrong direction, but that doesn't matter. What is important is not to be negative. There's a positive and negative side to everything. And everything is so much simpler than the academics and scientists will allow. There is a positive and negative side to instinct. You either develop it and work towards the future, or you suppress it, become negative and die. Instinct is vital.'

By now they had gone inland and reached a much lusher countryside, hills and trees and a river. They drove through an old village which seemed deserted, the tiled roofs and heavy stonework were medieval; it was like moving into the past. He liked it, wanted to stop, but she drove on through, then branched off along a very bumpy dirt track.

'There's three miles of this, so you'd better get used to it.'

The car dipped and jumped, got caught in ruts, the bottom scraped on boulders. Melanie took no notice but kept on, her foot flat down regardless.

'Was that Pintromelli, the town we passed through?'

'No, a little place called Sieta. Pintromelli is some sixty miles due west of here.'

He looked at the countryside. The colours had a pinkish hue about them, the greenery more yellow than he was used to. It was comfortable, homely, he liked it. Then in the far distance on a small hillock he saw a picturesque building, larger than a church, a monastery perhaps, and he just blurted out without thinking, 'Is that it?'

'Yes,' Melanie said, smiling. 'You see, you know automatically. Just accept the fact that you are right first time, nine times out of ten.'

She changed gear to go up an incline, then down again into a valley so that everything was lost from view.

'It's an old monastery which you bought,' he said, then

corrected himself. 'It's a disused monastery which you are occupying, and no one knows you're there.'

'A few locals do. They think I'm an eccentric American artist. I have quite a number of paintings in fact to prove my identity. No one can understand how I can live in such a place alone. There's no running water or electricity, but there is a fresh water well.'

They were up out of the valley now and much nearer home. The place had a surrounding wall and a bell tower and reminded him of illustrations from an edition he had of Cellini's *Autobiography*.

She stopped the car in front of the huge old wooden double doors, 'Could you open them, and close them again when I've driven through?'

He got out. As he pushed the doors open he had a momentary feeling that she might run him over.

Why the fear?

Why the suspicion?

If everything she had said was right and he should trust his instincts, they were now telling him she was dangerous.

As she drove through she stopped and looked out of the car window at him, smiling.

'*If* I wanted to kill you Paul, I wouldn't run you over with a small car.'

She bumped through into the cobblestones courtyard and got out.

'What you have to do, I realise, is also eliminate all the negative intuitions you have cluttering up your mind.'

She helped him close the doors.

It was eight in the morning, a warm sun was well up in the pale blue Tuscan sky. He was in a country rich with Renaissance history, the Medicis, the Sforzas, the Borgias. He breathed in the fresh country air and sighed out loud.

He was happy to be here.

He was really happy.

The old monastery consisted of a main building with outer buildings off it, and an overgrown ruined chapel. From the outside it certainly looked uninhabited.

Melanie led the way to a side door which was so low that Paul had to bend double to go through. Once inside they walked along a dark stone passage, then turned into a vast hall.

'This was the refectory, where we live. There's a beautiful fresco on the wall, I learned, by Masaccio; it was painted over in 1769 by a mad monk who thought it lewd. The children are asleep at the moment, so it's best not to disturb them.' He walked into the large dining hall. It had a vaulted ceiling. The white walls were yellow with age, there were benches and oak tables, and at the far end on a raised stone floor in front of a massive fireplace were two iron bedsteads with old mattresses; in one of them he could see the shape of the sleeping children under a blanket.

It was poor. Washing hung from a line stretched across a corner, a pile of clothes was on a table, plates, mugs, fresh fruit and vegetables in bowls, a ham hanging from a hook in the wall. In the fireplace, an iron pan; under it, the hot ashes of a log fire.

He approached the children's bed with a certain amount of trepidation. Then he saw them. They were not at all like the children he knew. They were infants, hardly more than babies. The girl, with curly blonde hair, pale pink complexion. The boy, straight dark hair, frowning in his sleep and sucking his thumb. Neither of them a threat.

'They look quite normal, don't they?' Melanie said.

'I don't understand.'

'A maturity is reached in astral projection. You leave your physical body and enter the one which is in your head. When you are young you project yourself forward, when you are old, you can become young.'

'But the astral body. What is it made of?'

'Thought transference. When you are day-dreaming you are going through the very early stages of astral projection. You are projecting your mind to somewhere else, visiting your friends in another country, living through an imaginary sequence. It's a development of that. As I said, everything is much simpler than everyone tries to make out. We *had* all these faculties in the past, but lost them with negative knowledge, with the idea that we needed to believe in something greater than ourselves, needed to worship images. The Egyptian gods, the Greek gods, did a great deal of harm, Christianity even more. We should not need to rely on a God. It is only because we have become weak that we seek to have an image take care of our responsibilities.'

Off the refectory was the kitchen, an outhouse with stone sinks and a brick oven which Melanie had put to good use. Draped over an open window was some muslin to stop the flies coming in, and across the opening which had been the door, a cane wattle. She lifted this aside and led him into what she called her garden, the walled ruins of the chapel which had been gutted by fire. Overgrown and wild, she had cleared a patch where she grew vegetables, pointed to apple and pear trees, a peach sapling growing in a corner, and grape-vines covering a network of old copper pipes. There were lettuces in a row, artichokes, aubergines, onions, potatoes, even an avocado.

She looked healthy.

'All I buy is milk, fish and meat. I bake my own bread, we eat mainly soups. I seldom go beyond the boundaries. The locals have accepted me. I came with two babies and, as Mediterranean people love children and understand parenthood, they soon saw that I could cope, wanted to, so no one asked me any questions. In America and in England I'm sure I would have been visited by countless authorities not minding their own business.'

'Do you speak Italian?'

'Enough to get by. Besides, I mind-read so can usually answer them before they ask their questions,' she said lightly.

'Can you always mind-read what I'm thinking then?' Paul asked.

'When I want to.'

'How disconcerting.'

'Most people can mind-read if they only stopped to think about it. It's all in facial expressions, the eyes, a movement of the lips, a twitch of the nose, perhaps.'

'What am I thinking now?' he asked as they made their way with big strides through the undergrowth towards the chapel tower at the far end of the garden. On the left she had grown a large quantity of tomatoes.

'You're thinking that it would be very romantic if we were holding hands.'

The thought had crossed his mind. It had been one of those

quiet thoughts that had hardly registered with him, but he had thought it.

'And that I'm younger and more attractive than you imagined. So you're worried about tonight.'

'Tonight?'

'Yes. You're worried about where you're going to sleep.'

'I'll sleep anywhere.' He was on the defensive.

'But you'd rather sleep with me.'

She turned to face him, staring into his eyes.

'There are only two beds. The children sleep in one, and you'll have to sleep with me in the other. Besides, we have to get to know each other for the purpose of the work.'

He felt dumb again.

'I'm going to teach you astral projection, Paul, and one of the first things you have to know about it is that you must be totally uninhibited about your body. The orgasm creates the energy which enables one to leave one's physical casing.'

'Is that why . . . '

'The children copulate? Yes.'

'But surely they're too young to have . . . orgasms?'

He was pleased that he had been able to say it, without blushing. She couldn't have picked a more inhibited individual if she had tried.

'No. Their bodies actually experience the pleasure of an orgasm, otherwise they wouldn't do it. Come this way.'

They entered the tower.

'I have a perfect lookout post here to watch for the oncoming enemy.'

They climbed up the spiral stone stairs and reached the top. The brickwork was crumbling, but it was safe enough. The view was quite magnificent over the Tuscan landscape, the vineyards, the river, the village beyond. It was beautiful.

'You've really found nirvana here.'

'There's a better nirvana than this, which you'll be visiting in due course.'

'Mummy!' A small voice shouted from far away.

'Coming!' Melanie shouted back. 'They're awake. Come and meet them.'

The two little infants in tiny T-shirts were sitting on their bed, Emma with her little legs dangling over the side, Adam still sucking his thumb. Now he recognised them. It was so strange to see these two little people with the features of the older children he had seen before.

'This is Paul,' Melanie said, introducing him.

'Hallo, Paul,' said Emma. 'We met in your bedroom in New York.'

'Hallo, Paul,' Adam said, and just stared at him.

Emma had incredibly mauve eyes, he had never seen eyes quite like them. Adam, more like his mother, had green cat's eyes, but the blackest of hair.

'Get dressed, kids, and we'll have breakfast.'

Paul followed Melanie into the kitchen area.

'Emma is only half psychic, Adam is totally. Which is extremely rare. I chose his father. Capuela and Gregoriev wanted to father the superchild, but I decided the Nostradamme line was by far the most powerful available. So I went after it.'

She looked at him for a long time and smiled.

'We could have a child, and it would be equally psychic.'

Melanie made some coffee, warmed some bread, poured out two pottery mugs of milk.

'That's for them. Can you take it through?'

They all sat at one refectory table. There was such a potent historic atmosphere about the place that Paul felt a great wave of peace. There were no anxiety traces in this place, peaceful traces, humorous traces perhaps. He could imagine the young monks in their simple way, playing pranks on each other, flicking breadballs at each other when the Father Superior was not looking.

'Are we going to have lessons today?' Emma asked.

'No, not today. We're going to go for a lovely walk and enjoy nature. Then tonight, maybe, we'll have a lesson.'

After breakfast they went down to the river where Emma and Adam paddled in the water as though they were ordinary children. They screamed and yelled and splashed each other and splashed Paul and he splashed them, then he gave piggyback rides to each of them in turn and enjoyed the warmth of their friendship, the family feeling, the older brother, young father position he was in.

At one moment Emma stopped what she was doing and said, 'There's someone coming.' Adam, not looking in any direction but into the depths of the water where he was hoping to see a fish, said simply, 'It's all right, it's old Luigi.'

Melanie explained that Luigi was a local peasant with psychic tendencies which is why they could home in on him. He was totally unaware of this but like many country people his very simplicity opened him up to original instincts. He had helped her in the beginning, finding materials to make the place homely, the iron bedsteads, the old mattresses, the plastic sheeting over the tomato plants when the winter had got cold.

That night they ate by candlelight. They drank red wine from pewter goblets Melanie had found buried in the garden. The children went to bed. The moment now came when they would go to bed too.

Melanie undressed in front of the fire on which she cooked, and stood there quite nude, lit by the flickering flames. Paul started to undress but as he did so, shyly, nervously, Emma stirred and he hesitated.

'You'll have to get used to the children looking at you, at us. You'll just have to get used to it.'

They got into the single bed, under the one rough blanket. The mattress was lumpy, it was not what he had been used to at the villa, as she had quite rightly said. But at the villa he had not felt her extremely sensuous body either.

A trace of guilt went through his mind, a thought of Cathy, but it quickly passed, he did not dwell on it.

They kissed and fondled, then he became aware that they were being watched. Looking up he saw Emma and Adam at the foot of the bed watching.

'You'll have to get used to it,' Melanie said, unperturbed. 'They've never seen me with a man before.'

And suddenly, violently, she got hold of him, swung herself from under him to straddle him and was very nearly brutal in the way she took him.

He kept his eyes closed, not daring to look up, but it didn't work.

'I'm sorry. I just can't. Not with them looking.'

'I don't see why not. They were watching you when you were with Cathy on the boat.'

The reminder of Cathy did not help either.

'You want romance? Come on then!' And Melanie got off him, took his hand and led him out into the kitchen.

'Both of you go to sleep,' she said to Emma and Adam. 'We won't be having a lesson tonight.'

And she took Paul out into the garden and, in the moonlight between the ruined chapel walls on a hard flat surface which might well have been an altar, she slipped herself on him and he felt his very lifeblood being drained deliciously from him. He thought of Patty, of the girl whose name he could not remember who had insisted on trying it in the back of the car where it had worked but had given him no pleasure, he thought of Sheryl, of Cathy, but this was something else. It was something . . . else.

Then both heard the air being cut far above them by the rotating blades of a helicopter, and seconds later the children came out screaming.

'They must have trained someone else. They must have trained someone to home in on you!'

Heedless of pain, Melanie tore back to the refectory, leaping over bushes, through the vegetable patch, ducking under the sharp branches of the trees. Picking his way more carefully, Paul followed her, aware now that the helicopter was hovering directly above and that a powerful beam of light was shining vertically down, searching the terrain.

He moved faster across the stone kitchen floor and into the hall itself. To his surprise Melanie was already out of the other door, having picked up both children, one under each arm. He followed her down the passage where she put Emma and Adam down.

'You'll have to help me, it's very heavy,' she said.

She was pulling at a large iron ring in one of the flagstones. He got a good grip on it, pulled and lifted it.

Below it smelt musty; a gush of warm air came up.

'O.K. kids. Down! This is it! The day of reckoning.'

The children disappeared into the dark, Emma first, little Adam afterwards.

'There's a ladder, you'll feel it with your feet, just go down as far as you can and wait at the bottom.'

Paul went down.

The ladder had thick wooden rungs, he had no difficulty except when he stepped on a small hand and Adam yelped.

'Shut up!' Melanie whispered.

Then Paul heard a dull thud as she lowered the slab on top of them and let it fall into place.

He felt her just above him on the ladder, got to the bottom, some good twelve feet down, waited, embarrassed by the fact that both Emma and Adam had now grabbed his legs for security. He was naked, they were naked, their sensuous little bodies rubbing against his.

Melanie felt around in the dark, then found the torch she was looking for.

'It's been poverty line up above, but down here is where the money's been spent – luxury plus!'

She shone the torch on to a door, pushed it open and found a switch. A dim light went on in a room comfortably carpeted and covered with thick cushions everywhere.

Both children immediately ran across to hurl themselves joyfully into the pile of cushions. Melanie closed the door. On the inside were three bolts and a large lock.

'It'll take them a while to find us down here, and that might give us enough time to help Emma and Adam escape. But you'll have to provide all the energy.'

'How?'

'It's not a frightening experience, it's an exhilarating one. I'm sorry we couldn't have rehearsed, but we have to work very fast.' She closed her eyes.

She knelt down on one of the cushions. She breathed in deeply two or three times and, once composed, calm, serene, she opened her eyes and looked at him.

'On the ship, and with Wiser, you were able to detect and transmit sounds from some distance away on to tape?'

'Yes.'

'Those sounds must have come through you, therefore you are a receiver and you must be able to hear them yourself if you concentrate hard enough. Now what you must do is to beam your mind on to what is happening above us, and think *only* of what you are hearing. The sounds that come into your mind, the impressions, that is all we need to know. Do not analyse, do not form opinions, just tell me what you are getting. Clear your mind and receive. And lie down flat with your head well back, breathe two or three times very slowly.'

Paul lay down flat on the carpet, Melanie and the children looking at him. He breathed deeply, was aware of the earthy musty odour, closed his eyes, cleared his head of all thoughts as Doctor Berkzic had taught him by counting backwards from five and expecting a void at zero. Then he heard, quite distinctly, the swipe of the helicopter's rotating blades cutting the air some distance away, but slowing down, slowing right down, then stopping. Loudly, as though they were right above him, he heard footfalls, people running, three people. And then he saw her quite clearly in her safari suit, hair pinned back, the efficient, determined look on her face.

'Sheryl,' he whispered.

'Fuck!' Melanie swore under her breath. 'Why didn't I think of it before. She's been tracking you all this time, she's the one who can home in on you. Who else is up there?'

'Capuela,' Paul said. He could see him clearly in his mind's eye. 'He's wearing one of those black combat uniforms.'

'Drama queen!' Melanie said with contempt. 'Who else?'

'A man . . .'

'The doctor?'

'No.'

'O.K. Sit up, break the circuit, think of something different.'

Paul sat up. He couldn't break the image, he could see Sheryl and Capuela with the man running round the outer wall of the monastery, the helicopter in the field down by the river. There was someone else in the helicopter with a searchlight scanning the area, and there were cars coming up the road, the policia . . .

'Break!' Melanie shouted, then she unexpectedly lunged out at him and grabbed hold of his penis and yanked it hard. The shock was instantaneous, he doubled up to protect himself; the children laughed. She smiled. 'If you think about them she'll be able to pinpoint you more easily. You're into thought-warfare now. Make your mind a blank. She squeezed him harder, he tried to stop her but she went on. He was aware of the children watching, was embarrassed and this was exactly what Melanie wanted. While reacting to direct environment he couldn't concentrate on what was happening above.

'This is what we do now. *You*'re going to give all your energy to the children so that they can project out. I'll tell you exactly what to do. While you're doing that I'll hold the fort, so to speak. I'm going to use all *my* energy to keep them out of here and if I have to, destroy them.'

She was still holding him, squeezing him hard, and he was feeling an intense heat from her hand. It did not hurt, but it was frightening, then he saw her eyes glowing. There was no particular colour in them, they were still the same penetrating blue, but they were vibrant with an inexplicable energy, and her whole body was becoming taut, the muscles seemed to stand out white, the veins purple now, and the heat from her hand was working deep inside him.

'The carpet,' she said to the children.

Emma and Adam went to the far end of the room and started rolling back the carpet. Melanie let go of Paul, got up, he got up and they stood aside as the children went on rolling.

Under the carpet was a thick sheet of glass the size of a double bed inlaid into the floor. Some five feet below the glass was a mirror. It was a rectangular pit of glass and mirrors and very brightly lit.

'Lie down, Paul, lie down on the glass as comfortably as you can.'

He got down on the glass which was cold. She got down beside him, grabbing him again. He was erect and she was using his penis like a handle, like a lever to control him; his whole being was radiating towards that area and, as he looked down, he could see himself, his body flattened against the glass, her body. He wanted to laugh at the ridiculous position she had him in, the way she was using him, but he was paralysed by her grip.

With her other hand she reached out for Emma, pulled her on to the glass by the arm and made her hold him. Then she reached out for Adam, pulled his hand towards Emma's and he felt the small fingers encircle him, then she let go.

'Now embrace him with all your energy, my darlings, and remember everything I've taught you, *everything*. Don't relax, don't let your minds wander, until you are totally safe.'

Paul wanted to look up, sit up, he wanted to move, see what

was happening, but he felt himself engulfed in a motion of liquid currents. He looked down, saw the reflection of himself and the children, a tangle of bodies, but his eyes were failing him, the brightness was so dazzling that he was blinded and now could only see pulsating, woolly spots, multiplying so that he could see nothing at all, and he felt as though he had fallen into a vat of thick unguent. It was not frightening, it was not painful, but it was draining him, from every pore he could feel his body fluids leaving him. Then came sharp stabs, unbearable jabs against his knees, against his stomach, in the small of his back, in his chest; all over, the sharp stabs multiplied, and he felt his mouth being forced open, and felt the little girl's tongue, like a red hot rivet darting down his throat and behind his neck another red hot tongue licking him. The stabbing eased to an all burning sensation as though he had been stung by nettles, and his whole being was filled with an incredible ecstasy, all his emotions now centred back to the children's hands which fluttered on him with overwhelming frenzy.

The agony of holding back was too much.

He abandoned the inhibitions he had held on to for so long, ignored who they were, how old they were, what they were, and then caught his breath as their limbs clamped on to him, arms, legs gripped him like tentacles and started to squeeze, and as the pressure tightened, the cold set in, ice cold, hard cold bars of steel slowly contracted till he could no longer breathe. He screamed in agony, twitched, buckled, jack-knifed, then suddenly it was over – he was released, sprung loose.

Bruised, every part of his body aching, he lay quite still for a while, tensely waiting for something else to happen. He opened his eyes. On either side of him were sickly jelly-like forms of the children, opaque white, yellow, blue, inhuman colours, and he looked at his own body which was the same, a tortured expression on his face, the hair as fine and grey as cobwebs, the body ashen, the veins bilious brown. And he was aware now that he was not looking down at his reflection in the pit-mirror, but looking down from above his real self, and now he saw the children in the corner holding hands as he had always seen them. He stretched out and saw his own hand in more natural colours, fleshy, though somehow bloodless, and he pushed down and with the tips of his toes he felt himself floating. He ducked to avoid the low ceiling, but passed through it. A blackness enveloped him, a thickness as if he were going through a warm air duct. He was *in* the earth, projecting himself. Afraid of the blackness he again pushed with his toes and went on up and found himself emerging like a ghost into the open. He was outside the monastery walls, and he was still rising, he was above the monastery now gathering speed. Then a wind took him, he doubled up, curled up into a ball and then suffered unbearable pain again. A shower of hailstones peppered him mercilessly; he twisted and turned, propelled by a force he could not control. He was frightened now, knew that he was travelling at immense speed like a meteor through space. He saw a blackness ahead coming towards him, a massive wall; he tensed up for the impact and hit it with his back. His head snapped forward, blood came into his mouth; he choked, stopped breathing.

Then he felt himself falling into a gentle, welcome void.

He knew exactly where he was when he opened his eyes.

He was aware, alive, his eyes were not blurred, his senses wide awake.

On his right was Doctor Berkzic, on his left, looking much older, more tired, Capuela.

He was lying on his own bed at the Villa des Palmiers, wired up so that his pulse, his heartbeat, his breathing, his blood pressure could all be monitored.

What he did not know was how long he had been gone.

'What day is it?' he asked.

'September four,' Doctor Berkzic said.

He had been unconscious for nearly a month.

He looked up and around. The room had become an intensive care unit; he had been fed intravenously, there were oxygen cylinders next to a diabolical looking machine by the door.

He moved his head, instantly felt dizzy, and realised that though his mind was functioning normally, his body was weak. Very weak.

He looked at Capuela.

The man had lost his elegance. He was sitting forward on a chair breathing hard, with difficulty, as though he had pains in his stomach. His hair was thinner, uncombed, his face drawn. He had been through an experience which would mark him for the rest of his life.

Doctor Berkzic had not changed; if anything she was brighter, more in her element now, dressed in a clinical white coat, a thermometer in her pocket, a stethoscope hanging round her neck.

'What happened to Melanie?' he asked.

'You should not talk,' Doctor Berkzic said.

'We don't know,' Capuela breathed out heavily.

'And the children?'

'The children are in the next room. At least their bodies are.'

'They're dead?' A terrible depression fell on him.

'No. Their bodies are alive. Their minds are not there, but the bodies are alive.'

So Capuela had not totally won. He had the children's bodies but not their projected minds, and Melanie had escaped, or perished?

'Am I allowed to eat?' Paul asked.

'You may drink fluids.'

'I would like something,' he said.

Doctor Berkzic rang a bell and shortly after a nurse came in, uniformed, efficient.

'The protein milk for Mr Saralyn, slightly warm.'

The nurse left.

'We will have to feed you like a baby for a while, until you are stronger. But you will live.'

'I know.'

Capuela tried a smile, got up, exhausted, and went over to the window.

'Sheryl Lidman is dead,' he said, looking through the slats of the blinds into the garden. 'She was murdered by your friend, Melanie.'

So it had been decided that he had taken sides, was being accused of treason. He had been disloyal, which of course was true. Hadn't he stolen the van and escaped them, and broken every clause in his contract.

'How was she murdered?' Paul asked.

'You should not excite him,' Doctor Berkzic warned Capuela.

'I don't think Sheryl's death will particularly excite him. He is a reasonably civilised young man, unlike his female friend.'

It was going to be bitter sarcasm from now on.

'You killed Cathy,' Paul said.

'ESCA killed Cathy, not us. We have never killed anybody.' Capuela let go of the blinds but did not move, he stood with his back to the room staring at the blind, or maybe had his eyes closed. 'Melanie Forbes ran off out of the monastery and Sheryl, who saw her, decided to give chase.' Capuela paused, breathed heavily again. 'I tried to warn her, I shouted, but it was too late. Melanie lured her into an open space where she was brutally torn apart by an inexplicable force. What ESCA did to Cathy was nothing in comparison to what that witch did to Sheryl.' He breathed heavily again, then turned to face Paul. 'After that we all gave up. I had not fully realised till then what we were up against. Miss Melanie Forbes is an ugly power to be reckoned with.'

He crossed the room towards the door.

'I am glad you are alive, Paul, and that you will recover. I am under orders to keep you here until there is an official investigation. The world, you will understand, is now interested in you, and by "the world" I do not mean the innocent masses who are ignorant of what is going on, I mean those very powers I was trying to combat.'

Capuela opened the door and left.

Doctor Berkzic said nothing for a while, then herself got up and walked to the window.

'He was badly burnt trying to save Mrs Lidman. His chest mainly, and the front of his legs. Acid burns he suffered when he tried to pick up her remains. He was much fonder of her than anyone realised, then even *he* realised.'

The nurse came in with the beverage in a special cup from which he could sip without sitting up.

'You will be hospitalised like this for several weeks. Certainly you will have to convalesce. After that I am not sure what will happen to you.'

'Will I be allowed to see the children?'

'In due course.'

'Will Signor Capuela allow it?'

'Signor Capuela no longer makes the decisions. The Foundation is now being run by a committee.'

The disdain with which she said this told him all.

ESCA had taken over.

Melanie had been right.

It would now be a minority group against 'them'.

If the children were still alive there was hope. If Melanie was still alive she would not desert them. Emma and Adam would be in limbo, in the refuge; they would wait there till someone could help them back. Melanie would bide her time, would watch, and he would help.

He would certainly help.

When he had finished drinking the fluid and the nurse left and Doctor Berkzic closed the shutters and left the room as well, he concentrated hard on Melanie.

He travelled back in time to the monastery, went through the gates, across the cobblestoned yard, in through the low door, down the passage and into the refectory. He stood by the squeaky beds, the lumpy mattresses, then he went out into the garden, lit by moonlight. She held his hand, both were naked. He was back there now in the warm night air, with the coldness of the slab beneath them. He managed to recall the ecstasy he had experienced; he held on to this, then an image came into his mind quite slowly.

First a range of mountains in the distance, the far distance, and an awareness of a vast expanse of desert all around him, a wasteland, heat, dust, cracked stony earth, then a figure, a young woman walking towards him holding a bundle in her arms, rocking the bundle gently, smiling at him.

It was Melanie with a baby, a new born, *their* new born.

She would have his child then.

She would hide in this far off place until she had had the baby, she would protect it, protect herself, until it was safe for her to join him and the children.

All he had to do was make sure those two little bodies in the next room were kept alive.

He would pretend behaviour, pretend loyalty to Capuela, to ESCA, become the perfect corporate man, until the three children could be looked after together by Melanie and himself.

A supernatural trinity.

Then as he felt himself slipping gently into sleep, he saw a clear vision of the children, Emma and Adam, Emma holding the newborn, Adam looking on proudly, so proudly.

But it was a father's pride.

And Paul then instinctively knew that this baby was not his, was not the one that Melanie would give birth to, but the children's own.

It was an unnatural child, born of unnatural children.

And it was fearful.

THE END

PAUL SARALYN ASCENDANCY CHART

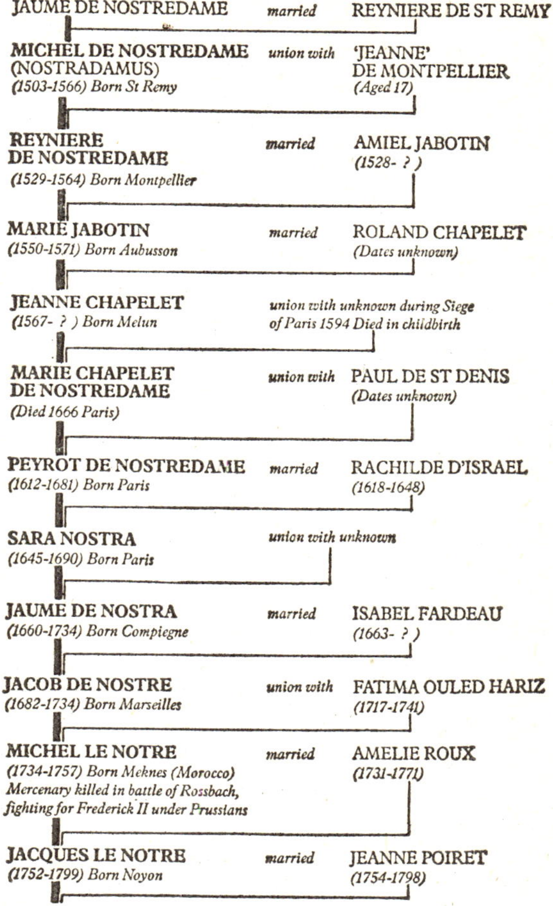

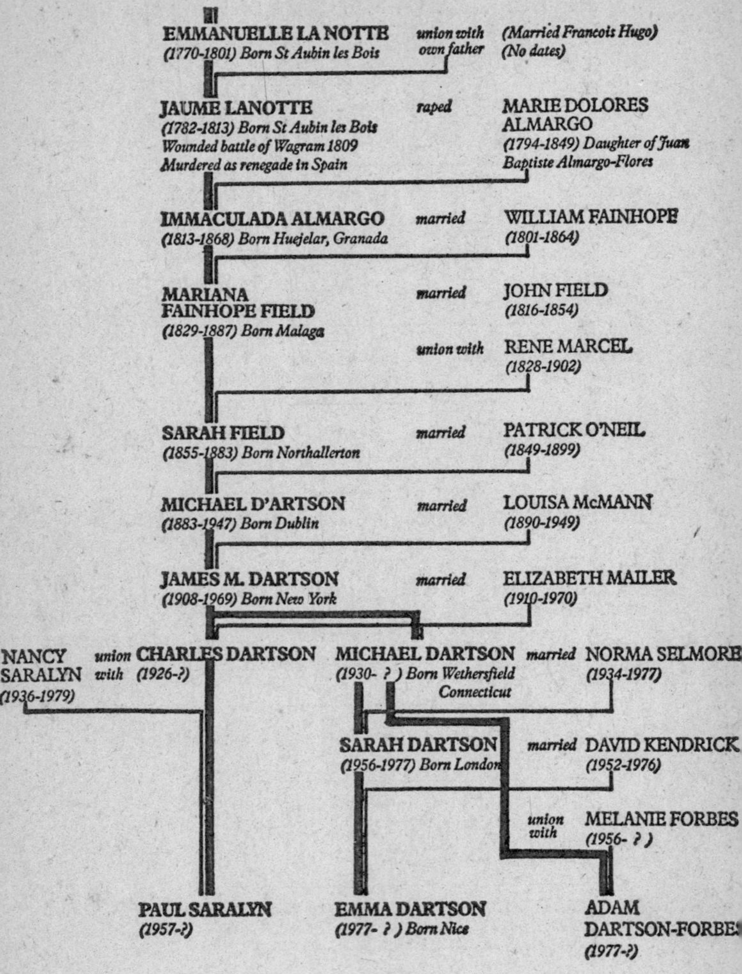

EMMANUELLE LA NOTTE
(1770-1801) Born St Aubin les Bois
union with own father
(Married Francois Hugo) (No dates)
JAUME LANOTTE
(1782-1813) Born St Aubin les Bois
Wounded battle of Wagram 1809
Murdered as renegade in Spain
raped
MARIE DOLORES ALMARGO
(1794-1849) Daughter of Juan Baptiste Almargo-Flores
IMMACULADA ALMARGO
(1813-1868) Born Huejelar, Granada
married
WILLIAM FAINHOPE
(1801-1864)
MARIANA FAINHOPE FIELD
(1829-1887) Born Malaga
married
JOHN FIELD
(1816-1854)
union with
RENE MARCEL
(1828-1902)
SARAH FIELD
(1855-1883) Born Northallerton
married
PATRICK O'NEIL
(1849-1899)
MICHAEL D'ARTSON
(1883-1947) Born Dublin
married
LOUISA McMANN
(1890-1949)
JAMES M. DARTSON
(1908-1969) Born New York
married
ELIZABETH MAILER
(1910-1970)
NANCY SARALYN
(1936-1979)
union with
CHARLES DARTSON
(1926-?)
MICHAEL DARTSON
(1930- ?) Born Wethersfield Connecticut
married
NORMA SELMORE
(1934-1977)
SARAH DARTSON
(1956-1977) Born London
married
DAVID KENDRICK
(1952-1976)
union with
MELANIE FORBES
(1956- ?)
PAUL SARALYN
(1957-?)
EMMA DARTSON
(1977- ?) Born Nice
ADAM DARTSON-FORBES
(1977-?)